Addison was vaguely aware of Carter's presence just over her shoulder as she maneuvered her way through the crowded bar.

But then the strangest thing happened as she slid onto the supple leather seat of the banquette—Carter slid in place directly opposite her, flanking Colette on the other side.

Addison gaped at him. *What are you doing?* He just winked at her, as if this was all some hilarious joke.

Apparently, the joke was on Addison.

"Addison, you look lovely." Colette leaned over to give her a kiss on each cheek. Bisous, as the French called it. "I'm so glad you could join me for a little tête-à-tête before the Cartier party. We have much to discuss about the future of *Veil*. But first, I need to introduce you to someone who's going to play a big part in that future."

Colette turned smiling eyes on Carter.

No.

Addison's stomach plummeted. This couldn't be happening.

No, no, no.

"This is my nephew, Carter Payne." Colette beamed at him. Addison wasn't sure who seemed more enamored with the man—her boss or Sabrina the Cavalier.

"You two will be working very closely together."

Dear Reader,

Welcome back to New York City and the sparkly world of *Veil* magazine! *Marry & Bright* is the third book in the Love, Unveiled series, which follows the romantic adventures of a group of family members and friends who make up the editorial staff of Manhattan's premier bridal fashion magazine.

Marry & Bright tells the story of *Veil*'s deputy editor, Addison England, and her rivalry with the maddening Carter Payne, who swoops into NYC on a Learjet, determined to steal Addison's big promotion right out from under her. For years, Addison has been working under her ultra-challenging boss (major Miranda Priestly vibes), waiting for the day when she'll take over as editor-in-chief. Colette has all but promised the position to Addison, but right before the Christmas holidays, the notoriously mercurial editor announces that her nephew Carter is also in the running to take over the helm of *Veil*. Their competition gets off to a mortifyingly rocky start, but against the snowy backdrop of Christmas in New York, they begin to realize that being pitted against each other just might end up being the greatest gift of all.

If you missed the first two books in the Love, Unveiled series, you can still pick them up at any online retailer. Look for more from the glittering world of *Veil* in 2024!

Have a very merry Christmas,

Teri

Marry & Bright

TERI WILSON

HARLEQUIN
SPECIAL
EDITION

HARLEQUIN®
SPECIAL
EDITION™

Recycling programs
for this product may
not exist in your area.

ISBN-13: 978-1-335-59440-2

Marry & Bright

Copyright © 2023 by Teri Wilson

For questions and comments about the quality of this book,
please contact us at CustomerService@Harlequin.com.

Harlequin Enterprises ULC
22 Adelaide St. West, 41st Floor
Toronto, Ontario M5H 4E3, Canada
www.Harlequin.com

Printed in U.S.A.

USA TODAY bestselling author **Teri Wilson** writes heartwarming romance for Harlequin Special Edition. Three of Teri's books have been adapted into Hallmark Channel Original Movies, most notably *Unleashing Mr. Darcy*. She is also a recipient of the prestigious RITA® Award for excellence in romantic fiction and a recent inductee into the San Antonio Women's Hall of Fame.

Teri has a special fondness for cute dogs and pretty dresses, and she loves following the British royal family. Visit her at www.teriwilson.net.

Books by Teri Wilson

Harlequin Special Edition

Lovestruck, Vermont

Baby Lessons
A Firehouse Christmas Baby
The Trouble with Picket Fences

Furever Yours

How to Rescue a Family
A Double Dose of Happiness

Montana Mavericks: Six Brides for Six Brothers

The Maverick's Secret Baby

Love, Unveiled

Her Man of Honor
Faking a Fairy Tale

Visit the Author Profile page
at Harlequin.com for more titles.

For all the good dogs and amazing people
in my pet therapy volunteer group, Paws for Service,
in San Antonio, Texas.

Charm and I are so happy to be part of this
special organization. xoxo

Chapter One

Addison England was seeing double.

She brushed a pink crepe-paper streamer away from her face and narrowed her gaze at her sister, Everly—the guest of honor at the modest surprise party Addison had thrown together this morning with the help of the third member of their girl squad, Daphne. Everly looked lovely, as always, with her dark hair pulled back into a high ponytail that was exceptionally bouncy and shiny for a woman who'd given birth to twins a few short months ago. It wasn't the twins that were throwing Addison for a loop, though. They weren't even there. This being the new mom's first day back to work at *Veil*—the high-fashion bridal magazine where Everly, Addison and Daphne worked—the babies were back home with their dad for the day.

The dogs, however, were very much in attendance.

Two of them, flanking Everly on either side like a pair of canine bookends.

"Everly?" Daphne tilted her head. Clearly Addison wasn't the only one confused by the sight of an extra party guest. "Why do you have *two* Cavalier King Charles spaniels with you right now? Oh my gosh, did you get Holly *cloned*? You did, didn't you?"

"What? No, of course not." Everly laughed, as if cloning her beloved Cavalier was something she'd never even consider.

Addison wasn't buying the nonchalant act for a second. Everly worshipped that dog. Holly had her own iPad and a subscription to DogTV. From where Addison was standing, cloning seemed like it was definitely on the table.

"This is Holly." Everly nodded at the dog to her right, who was staring up at Everly as if she'd hung the moon. Then she turned her attention to the other spaniel, who had the same chestnut-and-white coloring as Holly. Same melting brown eyes. Same merrily wagging tail. "And this is Sabrina. She's a foster dog from Manhattan Pet Rescue."

Oh, boy.

Addison braced herself for whatever was coming next. Her sister had a tender heart, and Addison loved her for it. But did any brand-new mom to not just one, but *two* infants need to adopt a second dog?

Daphne frowned. "Isn't Manhattan Pet Rescue the place where you adopted Holly?"

And then there was *that*. Everly didn't exactly have a great history with Manhattan Pet Rescue. As far as Addison knew, Everly's last contact with the organization had been the time she'd basically pet-napped the bride during a dog wedding she'd been covering for the magazine.

"Come inside. We can't have this conversation in the office hallway, you guys." Addison grabbed Everly by the hand and dragged her sister fully inside the luxurious confines of the *Veil* fashion closet.

The space was more than just a closet, really. It was more like an exquisite bridal fashion warehouse, lined with rolling racks of couture gowns and shelves upon shelves of beaded shoes and bespoke wedding veils. The closet housed all the designer clothing that had either been loaned or gifted to *Veil* for magazine photo shoots or in-person events, as well as couture pieces from their advertisers. It also happened to be the place where Addison, Everly and Daphne converged whenever one of them needed a little moral support.

Not today, though. Today, Addison had sent a fashion closet 911 text to the other members of the *Veil* trio so they could welcome Everly back to the office in celebratory style. She'd hung streamers from the ceiling in shades of pink ranging from blush to Barbie. Daphne had stopped at Magnolia Bakery for cupcakes topped with tiny plastic baby bottles. Addison had even thrown caution to the wind and brought the fixings for mimosas—heavy on the OJ since they still had work to do today. Still…

Addison knew how excited Everly was to be back in the office, even if only part-time since she was planning on working half days for a while so she could be home with the twins. Henry, Everly's husband, worked as the travel editor for *Veil*, and they'd arranged a short-term tag team schedule with the babies while she adjusted to being back. The closet had seemed awfully quiet these past few months without Addison's sister in the office. If wedding gowns could talk, they probably would've asked where everyone had gone. Addison couldn't remember the last time the *Veil* crew had gathered on the white silk damask ottoman situated in the center of the glamorous space. It was crazy how much had changed recently. Two weddings, two babies, two promotions. Everly and Daphne were living their dreams.

Addison seemed to be the only one stuck standing still.

Not for long. She pasted on a smile. Colette Winter, their boss and editor-in-chief of the magazine, had bought a Peloton a while back and told Daphne she was preparing for a six-month bicycle tour through Europe. And that could only mean one thing: Addison was going to be promoted to head of the magazine. *Finally.*

So long as Colette didn't lose it when she realized the office had been overrun with dogs. A definite possibility, considering Colette had one stylishly clad foot in the Miranda Priestly camp of employer-employee relations. As it turned out, the devil didn't necessarily wear Prada. Sometimes the devil wore Vera Wang.

"This is really sweet, girls." Everly pressed a hand to her heart as she took in the cupcakes, the mimosas and the crepe paper draped from the clothing racks to the glittering chandelier that hung over their faithful ottoman. "I didn't expect a party."

"Clearly not. From the looks of things, you expected a doggy day care instead." Addison's gaze flicked toward the new dog. Sabrina.

Was it just a coincidence the pup was named after Addison's favorite Audrey Hepburn movie? Everly had named Holly after the legendary heroine Holly Golightly from *Breakfast at Tiffany's*. Everly had adored that movie ever since their mother introduced them to Audrey Hepburn's filmography when they were little girls.

Addison had always preferred *Sabrina*. Once upon a time, she'd even dreamed of *being* Audrey Hepburn's character from that film, running away to Paris and starting a whole new life there. She'd dreamed of learning French, walking along the Seine and eating buttery croissants dunked in warm, milky coffee. Maybe she'd even have gotten a poodle.

But that was ages ago. Addison hadn't watched the movie in years—not since her post-college gap year in Paris had been abruptly canceled and she'd taken a job at *Veil* as Colette's lowly assistant. It had been horribly painful at the time, but now here she was, deputy editor of the entire magazine. Just one step away from the top job.

"Everly, hon." Daphne reached for a cupcake as she twirled one of her blond curls around her finger. A single pearl dotted each of her fingernails, right in its center. She'd recently given up her job as *Veil*'s beauty editor to pen a brand-new fiction series for the magazine, but Daphne Ballantyne King could still rock a bedazzled mani with the best of them. "You're the best doggy mom I know, but don't you think fostering a dog when you have four-month-old twins at home might be taking on a bit more than necessary?"

"That's the thing." Daphne blinked wide, innocent

eyes. *Too* innocent, now that Addison thought about it. She'd seen this look on her little sister's face before, and it usually meant trouble. Specifically, trouble for Addison. "The rescue group contacted me because they knew how…*ardent*…I'd felt about adopting Holly."

Understatement of the century.

Addison arched an eyebrow at her sister. That little episode had nearly cost Everly her job. Thanks to her now-husband Henry, she'd walked away unscathed, eventually working her way up to features editor.

"Anyhoo." Everly cleared her throat. "The rescue folks told me they'd recently taken in a Cavalier with a teensy separation anxiety problem, and they just knew I was the right person to foster the little sweetheart. How could I say no?"

Addison shrugged. "Easy. It goes like this—'Sorry, I can't. I just gave birth to twin human infants.'"

"Sometimes you sound so much like Colette it's uncanny." Daphne shuddered and then flashed Addison a smile. "I mean that in the nicest way possible."

"Gee, thanks," Addison said flatly.

If her *Veil* crew wanted to compare her to Colette, then so be it. Colette was a legend in the fashion industry, and one day, Addison would be one too. Maybe with a tad bit more warmth, that's all.

"You're absolutely right, Addie." Everly smiled. The dogs wagged their tails in perfect unison, like furry little Rockettes, as if this entire conversation had been choreographed ahead of time. Addison was beginning to realize it had. Everly never called her Addie unless she needed a favor. "Which is why I'm not the one fostering her. I was thinking that maybe you could do it."

And there it was.

"Absolutely not." Addison shook her head. Hard. "This the worst possible time to ask me a favor like this."

"Come on, Addie. She's a total sweetheart." Everly picked up the dog and made a big show of oohing and aahing as Sabrina nuzzled the side of her neck. At Everly's feet, Holly let out an annoyed whine.

Addison shot Everly's dog a sympathetic glance. *I'm with you, Holly.*

"She does seem sweet." Daphne reached out a hand and let the dog in question lick a dab of cupcake icing from her fingertips. Sabrina's tail beat a happy rhythm against Everly's hip. "And weren't you saying recently that you needed to develop some interests outside of work, Addison?"

Everly nodded. "I remember that conversation. Work isn't everything. Remember to actually live your life and all that."

Addison glanced back and forth between them. Were they legitimately being serious right now? "I never said those things. *You* did."

They'd stood in this very spot, right here in the fashion closet on the day that the Peloton showed up in Colette's office, and basically told Addison she needed to get a life.

Addison never agreed with that statement. Why would she? She had a life, thank you very much. And soon, that life would include a new job title, a new office and every professional perk she'd ever wanted. What it would not include was a needy little rescue dog.

Even if that dog was named after her very favorite movie…

And even if the canine in question was currently looking at Addison with the biggest, saddest puppy-dog eyes she'd ever seen.

"The answer is no." Addison straightened her head-band—a nervous habit she sometimes resorted to when she was trying to project a perfectly composed girl-boss aura in the face of opposition.

Today's headband was black velvet with a knotted bow on top. Very retro. Very *Sabrina*. Now that Addison thought about it, the headband would've matched per-fectly with the little black Givenchy dress that Audrey Hepburn wore in the movie—the one with the bateau neckline and bows on the shoulders.

Addison averted her gaze and sipped her mimosa, but she could *feel* the dog staring at her, waiting for her to melt like Daphne and Everly.

Not going to happen.

Her heart gave a tiny, almost imperceptible twinge. Why, oh why, did the Cavalier have to have that name?

"Perhaps you two are forgetting that the Cartier holi-day party is tonight?" Addison huffed. The dog cocked its head, ratcheting up its cuteness factor by a large mar-gin. "Colette and I are both invited. Colette asked me to meet her for drinks first at the Carlyle. Tonight is *it*. I can feel it. Her big European bicycle trip starts just after the first of the year. She's going to tell me about the promotion over cocktails. Think about it—Colette never invites me out for drinks. I'm going to walk into the Carlyle as the deputy editor and walk out of there as the future editor-in-chief."

Everly shrugged one shoulder. "The Carlyle is dog friendly, you know."

"She's right." Daphne nodded. "They're kind of famous for it. Have you seen their Instagram page? So cute. Glamorous dogs everywhere. Sabrina would fit right in."

Addison glanced back and forth between them, tossing in a glare at the Cavalier for good measure. "Your takeaway from everything I just told you is that the Carlyle is dog friendly?"

Unbelievable.

Everly thrust Sabrina toward her, and the Cavalier's tail wagged like crazy as she settled into Addison's arms with a satisfied sigh. Clearly the dog had yet to learn the meaning of the word *no*—much like Addison's sister.

If Addison had her own special form of kryptonite though, it was Everly. Since the sudden death of their father in a car accident during Everly's freshman year at Columbia, Addison had felt responsible for her younger sister. They'd always been close, but tragedy had taken their sisterly bond and transformed it into something else. Something sacred. Addison had promptly canceled her plans to attend graduate school in Paris so she could stay in New York and be there for Everly and her mom. Their poor mother had been reeling, hardly able to take care of herself, much less comfort her daughters. So Addison had stepped up and become the head of the England household. She'd gotten the job as Colette's assistant at *Veil* and never looked back. Not even once.

"Colette loves Holly, and you know it," Everly said as the Cavalier snuggled into Addison's arms.

True. For some unknown reason, Colette's stone-cold heart had melted when Holly Golightly came on the scene. In a move that made zero sense to Addison or the legions of other tortured assistants who'd come before her, the notoriously difficult editor-in-chief even let Everly bring the dog to work every day.

"Colette will probably adore Sabrina too, you know. They're practically identical twins." Daphne reached for another cupcake. "Just take her for one night and see how it goes."

Everly nodded, eyes dancing. "Yes! Just one night. If it doesn't work out, I promise I'll take her back to Manhattan Pet Rescue first thing tomorrow."

Addison sighed. It *wouldn't* work out. She was sure of it. She didn't want a dog—not even temporarily. Hopefully, tonight was going to be the most important night of her career. The very last thing she needed was a furry little interloper ruining things.

"Please?" Everly pressed a hand to her heart, and her eyes went shiny. Were those actual *tears*?

Addison told herself that her sister's emotional display had to be postpartum hormones or something, but it was no use. When Everly looked at her like that, all Addison could see was her baby sister as a young freshman girl who'd just lost her dad.

"Fine," she said and instantly regretted it. Tonight was supposed to be perfect, and spontaneity wasn't Addison's strong suit. Things worked out best when they were carefully planned out with no room for surprises.

A random newcomer definitely qualified as a surprise.

Sabrina licked the side of Addison's face with a gentle swipe of her dainty tongue.

Dramatic much? It's a dog, not a professional saboteur.

Addison held up a single, determined finger. "But for one night only."

What had she been thinking?

Addison planted her hands on her hips and gave Sabrina the sternest look she could muster. "I'm leaving now. There's no reason at all to be this upset. You and I don't even really know each other."

She was going to strangle her sister. Every time Addison slipped out of view, the poor dog panicked. It hadn't been much of a problem during her workday, given the fact that Addison spent so much time at her desk. On the few occasions when she'd gotten up and Sabrina followed suit, prancing alongside her, it had even been sort of cute.

But *this*—the way the Cavalier had turned into a shivering, drooling mess the instant Addison had tried to leave her apartment for her meeting with Colette at the Carlyle—was not cute. Honestly, it was alarming.

"Look." Addison crouched down to peer straight into the dog's sad puppy-dog eyes. Not an easy task in a strapless evening gown crafted from yards upon yards of fine pink satin with a train covered in hand-sewn rosettes, but desperate times and all that. "You've got a doggy bed, toys, blankets, treats…everything. What more could you possibly want?"

Everly had dropped off a ridiculous amount of pet supplies in Addison's office before she'd gone home, despite Addison's fervent reminder that Sabrina's stay would be temporary. The Cavalier came with more baggage than Everly's twins. It was ludicrous.

Even more ludicrous: Sabrina wasn't the least bit interested in any of it. All she seemed to care about was not being left alone.

Addison stood. If she didn't leave soon, she was going to be late and that could *not* happen.

"We're going to try this one more time. Be strong," she said, and she wasn't altogether sure if she was talking to herself or the dog.

The second she shut the apartment door, Addison could hear the poor thing panting and whining on the other side. She felt like the world's biggest monster... or sort of like Colette that time she'd fired an intern for wearing tie-dye to the office.

I can't do this.

"Fine, you win," she said as she flung the door open. "You're coming with me."

Her tenure as a doggy foster mom was going to be the longest twenty-four hours of Addison's life, wasn't it?

Fortunately, Everly and Daphne had been right about the Carlyle being pet friendly. The doorman didn't bat an eye at Addison when she stepped beneath the famous black-and-gold portico with Sabrina nestled in her arms. The hotel was all decked out for Christmas, with twinkle lights and garland strung over the awnings and a massive, flocked tree in the lobby. The snowy evergreen almost caught Addison off guard. With her big promotion on the horizon, she'd hardly given a thought to the holidays. But there would be time to celebrate Christmas once she was editor-in-chief.

Listen to you. Now you really do sound like Colette... with a dash of Ebenezer Scrooge for good measure.

Wrong. Ebenezer would've rather died and joined his gang of chain-wielding ghosts than bring a dog to a work function.

Addison's stilettos clicked on the smooth marble floor as she headed toward the hotel's piano bar, famous for its charming murals by Ludwig Bemelmans, the artist and writer best known for the *Madeline* picture books. Addison adored those books as a young girl. She'd always imagined herself as Madeline going on all sorts of wild adventures around Paris in her chic little school uniform. By the time her mother had shown her *Sabrina* for the first time, Addison was already familiar with places like Notre Dame and Sacré Coeur from the Madeline stories. It made perfect sense to her that Audrey Hepburn would go off to Paris and come back a few years later completely transformed.

But why was she thinking about Paris again when she was mere minutes away from being promoted? Addison had given up on that dream years ago. Everything she wanted was right here in New York.

"Nice dog."

Addison tore her gaze away from Bemelmans' murals and found a man standing beside her near the entrance to the bar. How she'd failed to notice him before that moment was a mystery, because he had piercing blue eyes and dark hair. Such a striking combination. He grinned and a dimple creased his right cheek, almost like a wink amid the dark layer of stubble that lined his finely sculpted jawline.

You didn't notice the man because you were worried about work, as per usual.

Ugh. It was like her *Veil* girls were sitting on her shoulder, whispering straight into her ear.

She cleared her throat. "Pardon?"

The man smoothed down his tie—ice-blue silk, which made those eyes of his sparkle like new-fallen snow. "I was just admiring your dog."

"Oh, I don't have a dog." She had a 401K, access to the *Veil* fashion closet and regularly ate wedding cake samples for lunch. What more could she possibly want?

The man's eyes danced as he cast a pointed glance at Sabrina wiggling with glee in Addison's arms. He arched an eyebrow. "My mistake."

Addison's face went warm. "No, you're right. She's a dog. She's just not mine."

He looked Addison up and down, gaze lingering on her couture gown, courtesy of the aforementioned closet. "You've got to be the most glamorous dog walker I've ever seen."

Cute. And was that a slight French accent she detected?

Maybe Addison wasn't as dead inside as her loved-up friends seemed to think. Of course she wasn't. She had priorities, that's all.

She squared her shoulders and refocused her attention on the bar, searching for Colette's signature swingy bob. Addison didn't see her boss, but that didn't necessarily mean Colette hadn't arrived yet. Half the tables were obscured by the grand piano in the center of the room.

"I'm not a dog walker. I'm actually here for a very important meeting with my boss and somehow, I ended up with a rescue dog for the night. I tried leaving her at home and that didn't go over well at all," Addison said.

"So you brought her along to your important meeting?" The man's lips quirked into a crooked grin. "That's very kind of you."

"Or very stupid. It's a toss-up at this point." Addison blew out a breath.

"Oh, come on. Who could resist this face?" He reached to give Sabrina a scratch under her chin. The dog responded by squirming out of Addison's grasp and launching herself at the handsome stranger.

Addison sort of understood why, although she never would've admitted as much to Everly and Daphne.

"You clearly haven't met my boss." Addison let out a shaky breath.

The man regarded her while Sabrina attempted to climb his neck like a tree. He gently wrestled the Cavalier under control and cradled the dog in a way that reminded Addison of the hot-groomsmen-with-puppies feature pictorial they'd done for *Veil* last year.

He shrugged. "I could always watch her for you."

What? No. Everly would murder her if she ever found out she'd left Sabrina in the care of a perfect stranger. *Emphasis on perfect.*

She looked away. Just because the man was handsome and charming didn't mean he was a proper dog sitter.

"I couldn't possibly let you do that." Could she?

"I'm having a quick drink here with my aunt. I'm sure she won't mind a surprise guest. She's got a weak spot for cute puppies. Go figure." He glanced at the sleek silver watch on his wrist. "I've got a Christmas party to attend in about an hour, but I'm happy to help out until then."

Sabrina nuzzled her little head into the crook of his neck. Clearly the dog had no problem with this bonkers plan.

"I don't even know your name," Addison said.

"It's Carter." He extended a hand while maintaining a comforting grip on Sabrina with the other. "Carter Payne. I honestly don't mind. I love dogs, too. Where I'm from, they hold a special place in society. In Paris, dogs are welcome in five-star restaurants."

So Addison hadn't been imagining things. He did indeed have a hint of a French accent…another ding in Addison's armor.

"We'll be seated in the same bar. You'll know if I try and abscond with this dog that doesn't belong to you." He gave her another crooked smile.

Carter had a point. Sabrina wasn't hers, and he seemed to know far more about dogs than she did. Maybe he'd even consider adopting her, and she'd be rid of the Cavalier problem once and for all.

"I need you to know that I'd never let you do this if I wasn't completely desperate," she said.

His dimple flashed again. "That's certainly flattering."

"I didn't mean it like that. I'm just saying that I'm normally a very responsible person. This meeting with my boss is just really, really important. I'm pretty sure she's about to retire, and she's going to tell me she wants me to take over her position," Addison said.

"That does sound important." Carter nodded, and his forehead creased ever so slightly.

"I've been working for this for a long time." Addison took a deep breath and then, before she could stop herself, she launched into a detailed monologue about her tenure at *Veil*—the highs, the lows and everything in between.

She might have even told Carter Payne about those awful first years as Colette's assistant when she'd wanted to resign at least five times a day. She definitely told him about the time she'd had to cancel a long-planned trip to the Hamptons because Colette had broken an ankle after donning a particularly tall pair of stilettos at Bridal Fashion Week and she'd expected Addison to *move into the servant's quarters* of her penthouse for the duration of her recovery. The poor guy looked like he wanted to interject a few times, but she wouldn't let him get a word in edgewise.

It wasn't like Addison to babble on like this. She never complained about her job. *Ever.* It was just so nice to talk to someone who wouldn't judge her for her unfailing devotion to her career, even though the road to the top of the masthead had been rocky at times. Someone who knew nothing whatsoever about *Veil* or Colette Winter.

Just as Addison was about to tell him how it had all been worth it now that the brass ring was within reach, she caught a glimpse of Colette in her periphery. A server in a festive bow tie was showing her to a seat in one of the booths that backed up to Bemelmans' fabulous murals.

"Oh, she's here." Addison grabbed Carter Payne's forearm. "I've got to go. Thank you. I love you for this."

His brow arched again.

She swallowed. "You know what I mean. I just really, really appreciate the help."

Then before he could respond, she swished past him, bustling toward Colette's booth as fast as her pink satin gown would allow.

Addison was vaguely aware of Carter's presence just over her shoulder as she maneuvered her way through the crowded bar. He was apparently making good on his promise to stay close enough for her to keep an eye on Sabrina. She thanked her lucky stars that he'd come to her rescue, just in the nick of time. The man was a bona fide Christmas miracle.

But then the strangest thing happened as she slid onto the supple leather seat of the banquette—Carter slid in place directly opposite her, flanking Colette on the other side.

Addison gaped at him. *What are you doing?* He just winked at her, as if this was all some hilarious joke.

Apparently, the joke was on Addison.

"Addison, you look lovely." Colette leaned over to give her a kiss on each cheek. *Bisous*, as the French called it. "I'm so glad you could join me for a little *tête-à-tête* before the Cartier party. We have much to discuss about the future of *Veil*. But first, I need to introduce you to someone who's going to play a big part in that future."

Colette turned smiling eyes on Carter.

No.

Addison's stomach plummeted. This couldn't be happening.

No, no, no.

"This is my nephew, Carter Payne." Colette beamed

at him. Addison wasn't sure who seemed more enamored with the man—her boss or Sabrina the Cavalier. "You two will be working very closely together."

Chapter Two

Carter almost felt sorry for Addison England as she gaped at him from across the table and tried to form a coherent sentence.

"I...um..." She blinked and then shook her head a little. Carter had the feeling she was trying to convince herself this was all a bad dream and if she woke herself up, it would all be over and she'd find herself back in bed at home in her pajamas with her cute little dog snuggled beside her.

Scratch that—it wasn't her dog. She'd made that much clear.

"It's a pleasure to make your acquaintance," Addison finally managed to say in a small, panicky voice.

So this is how she wanted to play it? By pretending they hadn't just met and she'd never spilled her guts and shared all of those deeply uncomplimentary stories about his aunt?

A bold move, but Carter could play along.

"The pleasure is all mine." He flashed her a smile as her cheeks went a lovely shade of pink that perfectly matched the satin fabric of her gown.

The dress was a knockout. So was the beautiful, if slightly unhinged, woman wearing it. Carter really had no business feeling sorry for her, though. None of this awkwardness was his fault. She was the one who'd thought it appropriate to vent her obviously pent-up feelings about her boss to a complete and total stranger.

Once Carter realized who she was, he'd tried to interrupt and give her a gentle heads-up. It had seemed like the honorable thing to do, but Carter hadn't been able to get a single word in among the constant flow of babble coming from Addison's mouth. Then, after a few futile attempts, her monologue had simply become too entertaining to put a halt to it.

Carter had heard a few things about his aunt's management style. The publishing world was an intimate one. People talked, even in Paris. But Addison had let loose with some real doozies.

"Carter?" Colette's lips pursed as her gaze homed in on the Cavalier pup in his lap. "Is that the dog Addison had at the office today? How on earth did you end up with it?"

"It's not her dog," Carter said blithely.

At the same time, Addison let out a strangled laugh. "That's kind of a funny story, actually."

Colette glanced back and forth between them. "I'm confused. Addison, is that your dog or not?"

Carter tilted his head and shot Addison a questioning look. The rules for this simple social interaction were changing so fast he couldn't keep up with them.

"Yes, and if you don't mind, Carter—" she pinned him in place with a smile that was mostly just gritted teeth "—I'll take her back now."

She crossed over to his side of the booth just long enough to pluck Sabrina from his arms, leaving a sweet-smelling cloud in her wake. Carter had noticed the scent earlier when they'd been standing at the entrance to the bar. He couldn't quite put his finger on it, but it was vaguely familiar, like whipped meringue, strawberry créme or some other sweet treat he might find in a French patisserie. For a dizzying moment, a wave of homesickness had washed over him.

Which was patently ridiculous. New York was home, not Paris. The past ten years in Europe had all been in preparation for this very moment. He just wasn't altogether sure why Colette had invited her deputy editor along when she made things official. It seemed as if meeting the rest of the staff could've waited until tomorrow at the office.

"Now that the matter of the dog is settled, is everyone ready to proceed?" Colette asked as a server delivered a trio of crystal champagne coupes to their table filled to the brim with fizzy liquid.

"Absolutely." Addison lit up like a Christmas tree at the sight of the celebratory cocktails.

And that's when Carter remembered something she'd said among all of that endless chatter earlier…something that made him pause as he reached for his glass.

This meeting with my boss is just really, really im-

portant. I'm pretty sure she's about to retire, and she's going to tell me she wants me to take over her position.

Addison England was certainly in for an unpleasant surprise, wasn't she?

"Carter."

He tore his gaze from Addison's heart-shaped face and big brown doeeyes, as innocent and pure as Bambi's, and aimed a tight smile at his aunt. "Sorry, my mind got away from me for a minute there. Must be the jet lag."

He took hold of the last remaining champagne coupe. The cocktail was topped with a sprig of rosemary and a few floating cranberries in a nod to the holiday season, which only added to his gnawing sense of unease.

Carter had assumed the staff had already been briefed about the upcoming change to the top of the masthead. He hadn't realized he'd signed on to witness the deputy editor getting her dreams crushed...

While hugging a homeless puppy...

At Christmas, no less.

If this were one of those schmaltzy, made-for-television holiday movies, he would definitely be the villain. The big-city workaholic with the expensive ties and impeccably cut suits who eventually got dumped for some loser in flannel.

Well. Carter held his glass aloft. *If the Armani fits.*

This was business. Addison had clearly worked for his aunt long enough to develop a thick skin. She was a big girl and moreover, none of this was his fault. He was simply here to do the job he'd been promised nearly a decade ago.

It wasn't as if Carter hadn't earned it. He hadn't been yacht-hopping around the Riviera for the past nine years. He'd been working his way up the mast-head at *L'homme*, the most widely read men's magazine in Europe. He'd interviewed scores of famous figures, including the president of France. Being Colette Winter's nephew, he knew there'd be whispers of nepotism once he took over the helm of *Veil*. It was inevitable. But those whispers didn't have to be true, and Carter had worked himself into the ground to make damn sure they wouldn't be.

Colette raised her glass but stopped short of clinking it with Carter and Addison's. She took a deep breath, and if Carter hadn't known better, he might have thought he spied a flicker of hesitation in her gaze.

Colette had never been one to doubt herself, though. His aunt had a backbone made of pure steel.

"I know you've both come here with certain...*expectations*...this evening," she said, and all of a sudden, she couldn't seem to meet either of their gazes.

A prickle of unease made its way up Carter's spine. Something was wrong. He could feel it, like tiny pricks of a needle along the back of his neck. He ventured a glance at Addison and spied a momentary flash of panic in her big brown eyes. The champagne glass in her hand trembled ever so slightly just as Sabrina let out a tiny, high-pitched whine.

Well, of course. Addison had reason to be nervous. Carter, on the other hand, did not. He cleared his throat and refocused his attention back to Colette.

"After thirty years as editor-in-chief at *Veil*, the time has come to pass the torch. Without the two of you, I'd never be able to walk away. I know without a doubt that the magazine will be left in capable hands. You, my darlings, are the future of *Veil*," Colette said, still holding her champagne coupe aloft.

This was turning into the longest toast in the history of fashion journalism. Again, odd. Colette was rather famous for cutting straight to the chase.

Carter felt Addison's gaze on him, and when he flicked his eyes toward her, he found her beaming again. Clearly she'd missed the part where Colette had just spoken in the plural.

Carter sure hadn't.

What was going on? Surely he hadn't just resigned from *L'homme*, packed up all his possessions and traveled clear across the world for an editor-in-chief job that his aunt expected him to *share*. Oh, hell no. He shuddered at the thought.

She wouldn't, he told himself. No freaking way.

"I'm sure you're both wondering why the three of us are here together, so I'm just going to come straight out and tell you," Colette said. *Finally.* "Both of you are perfectly capable of running the magazine, so I've decided to do something rather unconventional."

Here it comes, Carter thought. His aunt was about to split the job in two and attach Addison to him for the foreseeable future—the professional version of a ball-and-chain. This was a nightmare.

But, no. It wasn't a nightmare. It was worse.

"For the time being, you'll both be involved in the day-to-day running of the magazine. You'll work together to edit the next issue, while I watch closely and make my decision."

"Your decision," Addison echoed, forehead crinkling.

"About who will take over as editor-in-chief after the

first of the year. I can sense your confusion and disappointment, Addison. There's nothing at all to be upset
about, though. You're perfect for the job, but so is my
nephew. You might end up learning a few things from
each other during this trial period. I, for one, can't wait
to see how things pan out," Colette said, grinning like
the Grinch who'd just stolen the roast beast.

That's when Carter realized that Addison hadn't been
exaggerating earlier. The crazy stories about his aunt
were true, and he'd just walked away from a perfectly
sane life in Paris to become a pawn in some weird publishing version of the Hunger Games.

"I'll announce my decision at the *Veil* holiday party
on Christmas Eve." The clink of Colette's champagne
glass tapping against his and Addison's signaled a clear
end to the conversation. Like it or not, she'd made up
her mind.

Carter's head throbbed. He only had twenty-four days
to convince his aunt to give him the job she'd promised
him years ago. And if she chose Addison? Then what?

He shot an appraising glance at the deputy editor sitting across from him. She couldn't possibly be up for
this. Being forced to compete with the boss's nephew
for a job she'd clearly assumed was already in the bag
had to be the final straw. The ultimate indignity. With
any luck, she'd gather the pink satin train of her gown
and the cute dog that supposedly didn't belong to her
and flounce off in a huff, never to be seen again.

"May the best editor win," Colette said. Then she
merrily sipped her cocktail like this madness was all
just a harmless party game at a holiday open house instead of real life.

Ho, ho, ho.

Carter took a long swallow of his drink. The shock of the cold bubbles on his tongue made his eyes water. He blinked hard and when he opened his eyes again, Addison England was staring daggers at him from across the banquette. Carter got the message loud and clear: it would take nothing short of a Christmas miracle for her to give up her hard-earned seat at the table. If he'd thought he could waltz into town and claim the top spot at *Veil* without a fight, he'd been dead wrong.

Merry Christmas.

Moments later, Addison sat beside Carter in the back of Colette's sleek black limo with Sabrina perched in her lap. They did, after all, still have a party to attend. Never mind the fact that Addison felt like the entire world had just slipped right off its axis. The luxury jeweler Cartier was one of *Veil*'s biggest advertisers. There was no possible way she could bail.

Especially not now that she was being forced to compete for the top job with Colette's own flesh and blood.

Addison couldn't believe it. She felt like she was trapped in a bad dream or one of those Christmas movies where the main character suddenly found herself living in an alternate universe. But no matter how many times she pinched herself, she couldn't seem to wake up.

This is happening. The truth settled in the pit of her stomach like a lead weight as she snuck another glance at the very real, very good-looking man beside her. Handsome or not, she loathed his very existence—from the top of his stylishly coiffed head (because of course he had a perfectly tousled Parisian haircut) to the tips of his patent leather tuxedo shoes.

"You tricked me," she whispered through gritted teeth.

Colette was sitting farther up in the spacious limousine, flipping through a mock-up of the latest version of *Veil*'s current issue-in-progress as they crawled their way through Manhattan traffic. The editor-in-chief was responsible for reviewing the ever-evolving mock-up on a nightly basis until the magazine went to press. Addison wondered if Carter Payne was aware of that significant fact.

Doubtful. How could he possibly know? He'd basically just dropped out of the sky in a cloud of chic, French aftershave and been dumped into Addison's lap out of nowhere. In all her years at *Veil*, she'd never seen him darken the door of the magazine's office. If she had, maybe she wouldn't have stuck her foot so spectacularly in her mouth before she'd realized who he was.

Carter cast a wary glance at his aunt before responding in a deliciously low voice that tickled Addison's insides. Goose bumps broke out over every square inch of her skin. She blamed the mortifying reaction on the fact that most of her coworkers were women. Carter was a novelty, that's all—a chiseled, masculine, annoying novelty who wanted to steal her job. "Are you sure you want to discuss that here and now?" He arched a single, knowing eyebrow, and then he had the nerve to wink at her. "Just trying to save you from yourself…again."

Addison could not roll her eyes hard enough. "Where was that sense of gallantry an hour ago?"

She couldn't believe all the things she'd said to him

when she'd mistaken him for a random dog-loving stranger. What on earth had gotten into her? Her *Veil* girls weren't going to believe it.

Carter straightened his tie, as cool as an unwelcome cucumber. "Don't blame me for your indiscretion. Once I realized who you were, I tried to stop you."

"Not hard enough," Addison hissed.

As much as she hated to admit it, Carter was right. They couldn't have this conversation with Colette anywhere nearby. Addison would simply have to hold in her fury until they were alone.

It was shockingly difficult. Under normal circumstances, Addison was a master at controlling her emotions. She never would've survived as Colette's assistant as long as she did if she wasn't self-disciplined. Weren't Everly and Daphne always accusing her of being professional to a fault?

Not so anymore, apparently. First, she'd allowed the dam on her self-restraint to completely crumble, and now she wanted to wring Carter's neck in full view of her boss. She just couldn't help it. It was as if she'd been up against a ticking clock all those years she'd tried so hard to be the perfect *Veil* girl, like Cinderella cutting it so dangerously close to midnight. Except Addison hadn't dashed out of the ballroom in time. Her charmed life had turned straight back into a pumpkin in full view of Colette Winter's nephew, and now he wanted to stomp all over that pumpkin and turn it into pie.

She'd been *so* close to having everything she'd ever wanted. So. Frustratingly. Close.

Sabrina craned her dainty neck and licked Addison's cheek, tail thumping against the skirt of the pink satin gown. For some crazy reason, the sweet gesture brought tears to Addison's eyes. What was *happening* to her?

"Look, if it makes you feel any better, I had no idea this is what Colette had in mind when she told me it was time to come home and start working at *Veil*," Carter murmured.

"It doesn't." Addison fixed her gaze out the limo window. The massive Christmas tree at Rockefeller Center glittered in the distance.

She sniffed and blinked away the tears gathering in her eyes. *The most wonderful time of the year, my foot.*

As always, the Cartier flagship store on Fifth Avenue was wrapped with an enormous ribbon for the holidays and tied with its signature red bow. The building itself was a gilded age mansion, impressive on any given day. But in December, the famous jewelry store really pulled out all the stops.

It had been a while since Carter had spent Christmas in Manhattan. The high-end shops along the Avenue Montaigne in Paris always shimmered a little brighter during the holiday season, but nothing compared to Christmas in New York. Despite the current abysmal circumstances, his heart swelled as he stepped out of the limo. The air was perfumed with the scent of roasted chestnuts, and the surrounding twinkle lights cast a golden glow over the city skyline. For a second, he felt like he'd really come home.

And then he made the mistake of glancing at the furiously beautiful woman beside him.

He'd been on the verge on placing his hand on the small of Addison's back as they walked toward the building. It seemed like the polite thing to do. A gentlemanly reflex.

But Addison wasn't his date. They weren't even friendly business associates, apparently. She was Carter's newly minted rival, thanks to his aunt's questionable management style.

He busied himself with buttoning his tuxedo jacket to give his hands something to do as he followed Addison through the glittering doors of the jewelry store. Colette had swept inside several paces ahead of them and was already making the rounds with another glass of champagne in her hand. As far as Carter was concerned, there weren't enough cocktails in the world to make this awkward encounter feel like an actual party.

"Where shall we start?" he said as he joined Addison near a display case filled with luminous pearls.

She tore her gaze from a triple-strand necklace to gaze impassively at him. "We? Have you got a mouse in your pocket?"

Carter cast a pointed glance at the Cavalier in her arms. "Says the woman who brought a stray dog to the Cartier Christmas party. Did I miss a memo about animal plus-ones or something?"

"You're hilarious," she deadpanned. "And if there was a memo, of course you would've missed it, seeing as until five minutes ago, you'd never worked at *Veil* and yet somehow you're now in the running for editor-in-chief."

"You think I'm unqualified," Carter said. It was a fact, not a question. Addison had clearly already made up her mind about him, despite not knowing a thing about his work history.

"I didn't say that."

"You didn't have to." Carter shrugged one shoulder. "Go ahead and underestimate me. We'll see how that works out for you."

Addison's big brown eyes went dark. Dangerous. Angry? Or aroused. Carter honestly couldn't tell.

Definitely the former. This isn't attraction swirling between us. It's competition.

Funny, Carter couldn't remember feeling this twitchy around any of his opponents on the tennis court back when he'd been state champion in college.

"And to think, an hour ago I thought you were charming." Her lips pursed, drawing Carter's attention straight to them. For a nonsensical moment, visions of mistletoe danced in his head.

"I've tried being polite. I explained that this situation was as much a surprise to me as it was to you, and just now, I was hoping we could mingle together. Present a united front to one of the magazine's most important advertisers. But clearly you'd prefer to do this the hard way," he said and then promptly looked away, because he still couldn't seem to stop staring at her mouth.

If there was a flirtatious undertone to this back-and-forth, she'd been the one to start it. She'd called him charming...sort of.

"I just need to know one thing." Addison squared her shoulders and peered up at him through the thick fringe of her eyelashes. The dog glanced back and forth between them with a worried crease in her furry little brow. "Are you going to tell Colette what I said about her before I knew who you were?"

So that's how highly she thought of him? She expected him to go running to his aunt so he could tattle on her instead of fighting fairly?

Nice.

Carter opened his mouth to assure her that he wasn't the type of guy to play dirty. The last thing he wanted… or needed…was a job he hadn't earned, fair and square. He could go back to Paris tomorrow and find another position in a heartbeat. Duty was what had brought him back to New York, not desperation. He'd made his aunt a promise, and he'd intended to keep it. He just hadn't anticipated Colette would change her mind.

But why should he tell Addison England that when she'd already slotted him neatly onto Santa's naughty list?

"I haven't decided," he lied.

She blinked and then started to say something but couldn't seem to find the words.

Carter flashed her a wink. "Cat got your tongue, Cruella?"

"Cruella?" Addison gasped and tried her best to cover Sabrina's ears. "You can't call me that. That is *not* a thing."

Oh, but it was now. At last, this shindig was beginning to feel like a party.

"You were all too happy to pawn that poor creature off on me earlier. All you could think about was your meeting with Colette." Carter made air quotes and parroted Addison's own words back to her. "'I don't have a dog.' Sound familiar?"

He was baiting her now, and he knew it. But she'd asked for it. If she wanted a fight, then a fight was what she'd get.

"That's hardly the same thing as wanting to make a

coat out of her." She shifted the dog in her arms. Addison looked wounded, as if he'd touched a nerve. Carter's chest gave a little twinge, which he promptly chalked up to jet lag and the five-hour time difference between Paris and New York. "Besides, that was before I knew you."

"We've only just met. I've got news for you, Cruella. You might think you know me, but you don't," Carter said with more bite to his tone than he'd intended.

He was done with this conversation, and anyway, he was supposed to be mingling. This was a party, not a playground fight. So, he turned to leave without another word. If Addison didn't want to present a united front for *Veil*, he'd handle it on his own. They'd see how Colette felt about that come morning.

"That nickname still isn't a thing," Addison called after him.

Carter didn't respond. He didn't so much as flinch. Why bother?

And yet…despite himself—and despite the asinine situation he now found himself in—he felt the corner of his mouth twitch into a grin as he walked away.

Chapter Three

Fashion closet. Fifteen minutes!

Addison banged out the text message to the other *Veil* girls the second she arrived at the office the following morning, breezing past the empty receptionist desk, straight toward the fancy espresso machine in the break room.

For as long as she could remember, Addison had usually been the first person on the entire staff to report to work in the mornings. She liked to get a jump on things before the hallways of *Veil* descended into chiffon, bridal white chaos, as they were wont to do on occasion. Plus she lived by Colette Winter's oft-proclaimed personal motto: "if you're not early, you're late."

Addison loved being the first to arrive at *Veil*. She loved flipping on the lights in the hallway as she made her way to her office. She loved the clean antiseptic smell that the meticulous folks on the cleaning crew left behind after the night shift. Addison found comfort in those things, as silly and insignificant as they seemed. She felt at peace on those quiet mornings. Completely in control of her own little world.

Unfortunately, today was *not* one of those mornings.

The lights in the lobby area were on, illuminating the lush bouquet of white roses that always sat atop the receptionist's desk. But that was normal. Colette wanted the magazine to present a chic, welcoming presence at all hours of the night and day.

But when Addison rounded the corner and reached for the hallway light switch, as if by rote, it was already flipped to the on position. The cubicle area was already aglow in fluorescent light. Even the *Veil* Christmas tree—a snowy, flocked spruce laden with white-and-silver mercury glass ornaments, thin silver icicles and wrapped in a white tulle cloud—glittered with twinkle lights.

Addison stumbled to a halt on her stilettos, and Sabrina glanced up at her from the end of her leash, reluctant to stray more than a foot away from Addison's side.

"Your guess is as good as mine," Addison muttered to the dog.

She'd been doing that a lot lately—talking to Sabrina as if the little Cavalier was actually listening with a sympathetic ear. The past twelve hours had been a complete and total disaster. Addison had to talk to *someone*.

She hadn't been ready to face the *Veil* crew until now. She'd needed to wrap her head around the fact that she wasn't getting promoted before she gave Everly and Daphne a rundown of the latest mortifying developments. If she'd called an emergency fashion closet meeting late last night after the Cartier party, Addison would've burst into tears the minute she set eyes on her best friends. Everything had been too fresh. Too achingly raw. At least now she'd had a chance to get her bearings before telling them the messy truth about everything that had gone down.

Yeah...because you are just chock-full of bearings right now.

Ready or not, Addison would have to face the *Veil* girls in approximately fourteen and a half minutes. An emergency summons to the fashion closet was serious business. Everly and Daphne were probably tripping over themselves to get there.

Or maybe one of them was already in the office...

Doubtful, but a girl could dream. More likely, Colette had been the one to beat Addison to work. Sometimes she came in early to ride her Peloton.

But then, the rich scent of freshly ground coffee beans filled Addison's senses. Whoever opened up shop at *Veil* this morning had also fired up Addison's beloved European espresso machine. That *never* happened. Colette drank nauseating-looking green juices in the mornings—which proved without a doubt that Addison was *not* a mini version of her boss. Because yuck.

Hardly anyone else on staff even used the espresso machine this time of day. The coffee truck around the corner from the office did a brisk business, whipping up frothy lattes that tasted more like sugary baked goods than anything resembling actual coffee. Addison preferred her espresso dark. *Like my soul*, she sometimes joked.

For some reason, that didn't seem remotely funny this morning.

Cat got your tongue, Cruella?

Addison's face went hot as Carter's words from last night seemed to burn themselves onto her heart.

Cruella? Was he serious?

Addison was no villain. She was a *delight*, thank you very much. Everyone in the office thought so.

Maybe if you hadn't tried to pawn Sabrina off on a total stranger and dragged your boss through the mud in the process, Carter might think so too.

Whatever. Carter Payne's days at *Veil* were numbered. Last night, she'd been caught off guard. Now that she'd had time to absorb the fact that she was going to have to fight for the editor-in-chief job, she was ready for battle. This was going to be an all-out *war*. Carter wasn't going to know what hit him. Addison didn't care a bit about his deeply flawed opinion of her.

What she *did* care about, however, was the fact that he'd just strolled into view from the confines of her office and was currently lounging in the doorway, sipping espresso from her favorite demitasse cup. Last night, he'd invaded her life. Now, like a hunky Goldilocks, he'd invaded her personal space as well as her special quiet time.

Addison gazed longingly at the cup and saucer in his hands. They were bone china, white with whimsical Tiffany blue detailing. Everly had given the matching set to Addison for Christmas last year, and now here they were, balanced in Carter Payne's masculine hands.

"Morning," he said, glancing pointedly at the watch strapped around his wrist. At first glance, Addison recognized it as one of the magazine's advertisers—Chopard. A French luxury brand, because of course. "Or should I say 'afternoon'?"

Addison glared at him. "It's seven a.m."

"I realize that, but you know what people say…" He flashed her a wink. *Don't say it, you job-stealing jerk. Do. Not. Say. It.* "If you're not early, you're late."

People didn't say that. *Colette* did, and Carter knew good and well that Addison would recognize the sentiment as coming from his aunt. He was toying with her. Their cat-and-mouse game was getting exhausting, and Addison had only known of the man's existence for less than a day.

To add insult to injury, Sabrina strained at the end of her leash and her entire body wiggled, enamored at the sight of Addison's worst nightmare.

Carter's gaze dropped to the dog. "Hey there, cutie. How's Cruella treating you this morning?"

Addison bent to scoop the Cavalier into the crook of her elbow while somehow maintaining a grip on her phone and her Louis Vuitton tote. Thank goodness for barre classes and a modicum of grace under pressure.

"She's as happy as a clam," Addison said, pretending to ignore the Cruella barb. Maybe if she didn't react, he'd finally stop saying it. "You seem to be lost, though. That's my office."

He shot a glance over his shoulder, toward her neatly organized desk. A rose-gold laptop sat on the smooth white surface just behind a nameplate that read *Addison England, Deputy Editor*.

"I'll cut you some slack since you clearly don't know your way around the *Veil* offices," she said. *Seeing as you've never set foot here before.* "Feel free to set up elsewhere. I'm sure we've got an extra cubicle around here someplace."

Someplace far, far away. Preferably in the building's mailroom, down in the basement.

Carter's left eyebrow inched upward toward his hairline. "I see you haven't logged into your email yet. Check your inbox, Cruella. This office belongs to both of us now."

Then he turned to stroll casually back inside Addison's workspace.

Sabrina whined the instant he was out of sight. Did the dog have to like him so much? It rankled Addison to no end. Yet another reason why she wasn't in a hurry to call the rescue organization and fill out adoption papers. The Cavalier clearly had terrible taste in men.

He had to be lying. Why in the world would they share an office? He was just trying to get under her skin again.

Not going to happen.

Addison pasted on another smile and marched toward her desk. The second she crossed the threshold into her office, her shin collided with hard wood. She teetered on her high heels and nearly dropped poor Sabrina.

"Easy, there." Carter reached to steady her with a gentle grip on her shoulders. Addison dropped her phone and clutched a fistful of his Oxford shirt in her hand in order to avoid colliding directly with his chest.

"Sorry," she said, shaking her head.

Carter nodded toward a desk sitting directly opposite hers, in the exact spot where her elegant, blush-pink velvet love seat used to be. "The maintenance staff did a little redecorating overnight. Again, if you would've checked your email…"

So this was real? They were *officemates* now?

This must have been what Alice felt like when she tumbled down the rabbit hole. Up was down, down was up. Nothing made sense anymore.

For a second, Addison gave up the fight and dropped her head onto Carter's chest. She just wanted to burrow right there and have a good cry. He was so warm, so solid. And the crook of his neck smelled amazing—rich and woodsy, with just a touch of French lavender. It made Addison want to bite into a buttery croissant.

She closed her eyes, took a deep inhale, and for a brief, nonsensical moment, she tightened her grip on the fine Oxford cloth fabric curled in her fingertips. Then Sabrina's tail began to wag into overdrive, beating softly against Addison's side. She opened her eyes, mortified to her very core, just as Sabrina reached up to lick the side of Carter's neck.

Addison sprang backward, almost colliding with the strange new desk again. She gripped the edge of the hard wood, righting herself before Carter could touch her.

"For the record, that was not me who licked you just now," she blurted.

Carter's brows rose. "Pardon?"

"It was Sabrina." Addison tipped her head toward the dog, still vibrating with glee in her arms. "I didn't lick you."

"Duly noted." Carter's mouth twitched as if it were taking superhuman effort for him not to laugh.

Addison wanted to die on the spot.

"I've got to go." She dumped her Louis next to her laptop, and that's when she noticed the careful positioning of the two desks.

They faced directly at each other. Addison was going to spend the entire month of December staring right into Carter's dreamy blue eyes. She might actually throw up.

Quel nightmare.

"I have a meeting," she said, even though he hadn't asked where she was off to this early in the workday. "It's urgent."

Then, before he could utter a word, she turned tail and ran to the only place in the *Veil* headquarters that Carter Payne hadn't managed to infiltrate.

Yet.

"Surprise!"

The fashion closet door had barely clicked shut behind Addison when Everly and Daphne jumped up from behind a rack of wedding gowns, making jazz hands and blowing into noisemakers.

Addison blinked. What was going on? She'd been the one to call this emergency meeting. Why would she be surprised to find the rest of the *Veil* crew here? Then Everly pointed overhead, and Addison lifted her gaze to a banner slung from one end of the ceiling to the other.

Congratulations, it screamed. Addison was pretty sure she recognized both the banner and the noisemakers from a photo shoot they'd done for a feature on bachelorette parties, but the handmade poster propped on the ottoman was definitely Daphne's handiwork. Its message was spelled out in multicolored glitter.

Addison England, Editor-in-Chief!

Addison's chest grew tight as she took it all in—the banner, the poster, the telltale orange label on a bottle of Veuve Clicquot she spied peeking out of the top of a silver ice bucket. They'd sprung for the good stuff. After all, their trio had been waiting for this day for a long, long time. Or so Daphne and Everly thought...

Addison shook her head. She couldn't bring herself to say it. When she tried to force the words out, her knees buckled, and she felt like she might hyperventilate.

Daphne and Everly exchanged a confused glance.

"Addison, what's wrong?" Daphne asked, wide-eyed.

"I didn't..." Addison took in a gulp of air. "He..." She pointed in the direction of her office, and then she gave up trying to explain as she burst into tears.

"Oh, no. This is bad. This is really, really bad," Everly said. Addison was vaguely aware of her sister turning toward Daphne to whisper, "Addison doesn't cry. Like, ever. I don't even remember her shedding a tear at our dad's funeral."

Of course Addison hadn't cried that day. She'd needed to keep it together for her mom and her baby sister. Everly and Mom had barely been able to function, going through the motions in a dumbstruck daze. Someone needed to be strong during that dark time, so Addison had taken it upon herself to greet the mourners who'd turned up at the brownstone after the service. She'd taken over paying the household bills when she'd realized her grieving mom had started letting them pile up, just like she kept tabs on Everly after she drove her back to school at Columbia.

So no, she hadn't shed a tear back then.

And she wasn't going to start now. No way was she going to be reduced to a blubbering mess from the likes of Carter.

Addison sniffed, blinking furiously. "Sorry. Low point. I'm over it now, though. There's no crying around wedding dresses." She waved her free hand at the nearest rack of frothy designer gowns. "And these are couture, for crying out loud."

"Um. Literally everyone cries around wedding gowns. Brides cry 24/7. I'm pretty sure that's why waterproof mascara was invented," Daphne said with an authority that only a former beauty editor could muster.

"Sis, it's okay to cry. Bawl your eyes out if you need to, but please tell us what's going on." Everly bit her lip and looked up at Addison with the same soulful eyes that had always made her want to move heaven and earth to make sure her baby sister was happy.

Everly *was* happy, though—the happiest Addison had ever seen her. She had Henry, the twins and Holly Golightly. She was a grown-up woman with a family of her own. Addison didn't need to worry about her anymore.

Maybe that's what had her feeling so unsettled. She'd spent so many years holding everything together and now that she had a little breathing room, she was coming apart at the seams. Why else would she have let herself be so vulnerable with the first handsome man with a French accent who crossed her path?

"I didn't get the promotion," Addison said, wincing as her gaze darted to the poster again.

Daphne immediately grabbed it and shoved it out of sight behind a voluminous ball gown. "Oh, hon. I'm so sorry."

Everly shook her head. "I don't understand."

That makes two of us.

Addison set Sabrina down gently on the floor and collapsed onto the ottoman with her head in her hands. Then, while the dog explored the closet, she spilled the beans on everything that had transpired since the last time they'd all seen each other. It felt like a lifetime ago. Had it really been less than twenty-four hours?

"This is exactly what we've been afraid of," Everly said once Addison had managed to spill the whole ugly truth.

Addison felt herself frown. "You were afraid Colette's hot nephew would turn up out of nowhere to try and steal my promotion right out from under me?"

"Wait a minute." Daphne held up a finger. Today, her nails were tipped with hot-pink glitter. "You failed to mention that he was hot earlier."

"He's not." Addison shook her head. "I mean, maybe he is...objectively speaking and all. But his hotness is completely irrelevant. He's a total jerk."

"A jerk who volunteered to puppy sit for you while you had drinks with your boss." Everly's lips twisted. "Got it."

"I know what you're thinking, and you're wrong. I'm *not* attracted to Carter Payne," Addison said.

Daphne bit back a smile. "Obviously not. You were

quite adamant about the fact that you didn't lick his neck."

"Both of you are completely missing the point," Addison said, straightening her headband. Their plan to take over *Veil* was in serious jeopardy, whether Addison wanted to admit it or not.

"This is what happens when you make work the only thing in your life. Eventually, you crack. We tried to warn you." Everly scooped Sabrina off the floor and pressed a kiss to the top of the little dog's head. "You're going to win, Addison. I know you will. And Daphne and I will obviously do everything in our power to help you. Whatever you need…all you have to do is ask. But maybe this is just the tiny wake-up call you needed."

Daphne nodded. "Sort of like Scrooge."

Everly kicked her with the pointy toe of her ballerina flat. "Not like Scrooge…not exactly, anyway. I'm just saying try and think of this whole ordeal as a reminder to appreciate all the other wonderful things in your life. More than anything, I want you to be happy, even if *Veil* somehow vanished overnight."

Addison's hand flew to her throat. "Why would *Veil* vanish overnight?"

Quel horror. The very idea was inconceivable.

"Never mind." Everly sighed. "But I'm glad to see that you and Sabrina seem to be bonding."

"We're not bonding," she said, even as Sabrina jumped out of Everly's arms, scurried over to Addison and pawed at her shins, begging to be picked up.

"So you want me to give her back to Manhattan Pet

Rescue, then? I'll just give them a quick call…" Everly started digging through her handbag for her cell phone.

"Don't," Addison said just a little too quickly. "I'll keep fostering her. *Temporarily.* Just until after the holidays."

Or until Carter packed up and went back to Paris so she wouldn't have to hear him call her Cruella. Whichever came first.

Everly's face split into a wide grin. "Whatever you say, sis."

"Meanwhile, we should probably get out of here." Daphne held up her phone. A message from her husband, who worked as a senior features writer for *Veil*, lit up the tiny screen. "Jack just texted to say that Colette has called a mandatory staff meeting this morning. I'll bet it's got something to do with her evil-but-hot nephew."

"Emphasis on evil," Addison muttered.

Everly plucked the bottle of Veuve from the ice bucket and tucked it away in the fashion closet's mini fridge. This morning had been a complete waste of premium champagne. They hadn't even bothered to open it. "What time is the meeting?"

Daphne glanced at the text message again. "Eight o'clock."

"It's already seven forty-five," Addison said as she adjusted her headband again, readying herself for the battle ahead. "You know what that means."

The *Veil* girls exchanged knowing glances. They were still on the same page, Scrooge comments forgotten. Addison had nothing but love for Everly and Daphne. With the *Veil* crew on her side, there was no way Carter was going to walk away as editor-in-chief. He might as well go ahead and pack his bespoke suits and fancy French cologne and give up.

"We're already late," they all said unison.

All for one, and one for all. They were the *Veil* girls. Together, they were unstoppable.

Chapter Four

Unlike Addison, Carter had seen Colette's 4:00 a.m. email about the shared office arrangement the second it landed in his inbox. There'd been zero chance of missing it because he'd been up for hours already, hitting refresh on his email app more often than he cared to admit—and not because he was eager to know where Colette wanted to put his desk.

As much as Carter loved his aunt, this entire arrangement felt like a bad idea. It wasn't at all what he'd expected when he'd resigned at *L'homme* and headed back to the States. Nor was it what Colette had proposed all those years ago when she'd told him that she wanted him to take over the helm of *Veil* someday. He'd worked hard for the editor-in-chief job—just as hard as Addison England had. His path had been different, that's all. It wasn't unusual in the slightest for a magazine to bring in a top-level executive from another publication instead of hiring from within. In fact, coveted EOC positions were more often than not filled from recruiting and hiring from outside the company. It was Business 101.

Carter had been prepared to prove his worth once he was on American soil. He'd even been prepared for naysayers once the staff found out he and Colette were related. But he most definitely hadn't been prepared to participate in a competition for the top job that felt like a plot from a bad reality television show.

No, thank you. Or, as the French said, *non, merci.*

He jammed a hand through his hair at his new desk and refreshed his email again. Still no word from his former editor at *L'homme*. That didn't bode well. Unlike in Manhattan, office hours in Paris typically didn't start until midmorning. But it was already lunchtime in France. Odds were his former boss had read the message Carter sent late last night hours ago.

He hadn't outright asked if he could step back into his old position as deputy editor at *L'homme*, but he'd hinted strongly at it. As far as Carter knew, they hadn't replaced him quite yet. Still, he didn't want to look desperate. Maybe he could somehow parlay his return into a promotion or a pay increase.

Either way, Carter couldn't stay here. That much was clear.

His gaze shifted toward Addison's desk, situated directly across from his. Her workspace was pristine, decorated in soothing shades of white and blush pink. Even her laptop was pink, and there wasn't so much as a paper clip out of place…except for Carter, of course. He'd never been more out of place in his life.

Carter was about as welcome as a cockroach in this

girly candy dish she called an office. Her reaction to finding him there, desk and all, had come as no surprise whatsoever, save for the part where she'd accidentally ended up in his arms. That had definitely caught him off guard.

Had it been his imagination, or had she lingered there with her face buried in the crook of his neck, almost as if she'd enjoyed it? Carter honestly didn't know, because time had slowed to a stop the instant she'd curled her fists around his shirt. In that hot, heady moment, he'd forgotten all about the email he was still waiting on. He'd forgotten about his aunt and *Veil* and pretty much anything other than the way his blood suddenly felt like warm honey flowing through his veins. Deliciously sweet.

Addison was wound so tightly, it was no wonder she'd come unglued at the Carlyle before she'd realized who he was. She'd been the most beautiful mess he'd ever set eyes on, and then she'd flipped a switch and turned into someone else entirely. Someone who could probably run *Veil* with her eyes closed and one graceful hand tied behind her back. But it was moments like that sudden meltdown at the hotel and the one earlier in their office—moments when she let her guard down and the real Addison came out to play—that rendered Carter spellbound.

Instinct told him it didn't happen often. Or maybe it wasn't instinct at all. Maybe it was the fact that she'd repeatedly told him that her job was her *life* during her little freakout at the Carlyle, along with the litany of indignities she willingly suffered while she'd been working her way up the career ladder at *Veil*. She'd recounted more than a few of them in vivid detail. Either way, bearing witness to those rare moments of vulnerability felt sacred somehow...

Like he'd caught lightning in a bottle. It was almost enough to make Carter want to stay. But that was ridiculous—and yet another reason why he longed to get on the first plane out of the country.

His gaze drifted to the bulletin board hanging on the wall above Addison's desk. Page layouts from the latest issue of *Veil* were pinned to the corkboard, so straight and evenly spaced that it looked like she'd used a ruler to align everything. But tucked into the bottom corner, she'd pinned a haphazard collection of Polaroids that all featured the same group of women—a trio of stylish girlfriends in a variety of poses and locations. Those snapshots were the only visible sign that his new rival had any semblance of a personal life, other than the dog bed tucked beneath her desk. But they both knew that wasn't a permanent fixture.

Carter's phone pinged with an incoming email, and he dragged his gaze away from Addison's pictures. *Finally.*

The message wasn't from his editor at *L'homme*, though. It was Colette. Again. Funny how she kept popping up in his inbox when she seemed to be avoiding meeting with him in person for a one-on-one discussion. He wanted answers, and she knew it. So far, he'd had zero luck pinning her down. And now his presence was requested at a mandatory staff meeting scheduled to start in five minutes.

This was it, wasn't it? If he took a seat at the head of that conference table and let his aunt introduce him to the rest of staff, he was stuck here for the long haul. It would be too late to back out.

Speak now, or forever hold your peace.

Carter sighed. He was already thinking in terms of wedding metaphors. Maybe he really did belong here, after all, regardless of Addison England's opinion on the matter.

He stood, fastened the button of his suit jacket and picked up his espresso before heading to the conference room. Then, at the last second, he turned back to grab his cell phone, still opened to his email app…

Just in case.

Addison managed to get to the conference room before her nemesis, which seemed like a small victory until he strolled into the room still carrying her demitasse cup.

She shot a meaningful glance at Everly and Daphne, who were sitting at the far end of the table with the other junior editors and department heads. Addison's eyebrow lift was meant to send a very clear message.

See, I told you he was a monster.

Everly just squinted and shook her head a little, clearly missing the point while Daphne batted the eyelash extensions she still rocked since her days as the beauty editor and mouthed a single, annoying word as she took in the sight of Carter's tailored suit and piercing blue eyes.

Hot.

Addison rolled her eyes, even as her face burned with the heat of a thousand fire emojis.

"Where's your dog?" Carter murmured as he took the

seat beside her and glanced at the empty space around her chair.

"She not my…" Addison began, then caught herself. She was *not* going to keep playing this dumb game with him. "Sabrina is in the fashion closet, perfectly happy with a peanut-butter-stuffed Kong toy, if you must know."

Never mind the fact that Addison had never heard of a Kong until Everly had pulled it out of her purse, as if designer handbags were meant to be receptacles for that sort of thing. Coco Chanel was probably rolling in her grave.

The dog was fine. Addison was no Cruella de Vil. He needed to worry about running the magazine, not whether or not Addison could properly care for a Cavalier King Charles spaniel with a mild case of separation anxiety. How hard could that be?

Carter placed his iPhone face-up on the table in front of him, further evidence that he had no idea how things worked around here. Rude, much? Colette wanted the staff's undivided attention during these meetings.

"You might want to put that away," Addison said.

Carter shook his head. "Can't."

"Fine. Don't say I didn't warn you," Addison whispered as Colette strode into the room. With any luck, Carter would remember she'd tried to save him the next time he was tempted to tattle on her for bad-mouthing Colette behind her back at the Carlyle. She was already beyond exhausted from waiting for that shoe to drop.

"Good morning, everyone. Thank you for getting here so promptly." Colette took her place at the head of the table. As usual, her sleek bob looked extra-glossy beneath the fluorescent lighting of the conference room. Addison could practically see her reflection in it.

Concentrate, she told herself. Now wasn't the time to get distracted. Like her *Veil* girls, the rest of the staff had probably assumed that Addison would be promoted to editor-in-chief before the end of the year. The news of Carter's arrival was going to be a shock to everyone, not just to her. She needed to paste a gracious smile on her face and pretend to be completely unfazed just like the celebrities who clapped politely when they lost an Oscar.

Hold your head high. You haven't lost anything. Addison swallowed. *Yet.*

"I've called you all here for a special announcement," Colette said in her trademark calm and deceptively soft voice.

No sooner had the words left her mouth than Carter's cell phone vibrated. In the hush of the conference room, the abrupt buzzing noise sounded as loud as an entire hive of bees.

Addison's knee-jerk reaction was to kick Carter's shin underneath the table. She didn't even think. She just did it, and judging by the *oof* he emitted, it surprised Carter as much as it did herself.

Her heart pounded while she waited for him to glance at her so she could send him silent *put that thing away* vibes. Addison really shouldn't have cared. Let him make a fool of himself. She'd only look better by comparison in Colette's eyes.

But weren't they a team, of sorts? They were sharing an office, and Colette had made that whole speech last night about how she wanted them to work closely together, to *learn* from each other. As nauseating as that sounded, if they were partners in any capacity, Addison wasn't going to let Carter drag her down. The December digital issue was going to be the best in *Veil* history.

His gaze shot toward hers and when their eyes met, a dimple flashed in his left cheek. The unexpected sight of it made Addison feel all fizzy and light inside. Laughter bubbled up her throat and she choked down a giggle. What was it about this man that always seemed to make her behave like a child instead of the confident girl boss that she was supposed to be? It was beyond unsettling.

Then Carter's gaze flitted toward his phone on the surface of the conference table, still illuminated as bright as Clark Griswold's house on Christmas Eve. Addison spied a notification for an incoming email, but he snatched the device off the table before she could make out the name of the sender.

Surely he wasn't going to sit there and read the message in the middle of the staff meeting that was supposed to be his grand introduction to the magazine he supposedly wanted to run?

Addison could only look on in horror as he did exactly that. His eyes scanned the tiny screen, and for the life of her, she couldn't imagine what could be so vitally important. Colette couldn't either, apparently.

"Carter," their boss said, with an unmistakable edge to her tone. "Do you need to excuse yourself, or shall we proceed?"

Carter's eyes swiveled toward Addison for a beat. Something about the look on his face made her go a little breathless, despite her best efforts to keep her composure. Then he quietly slipped the phone into the inside pocket of his suit jacket, out of sight. "My apologies. Please continue."

Colette went on to introduce him to the staff, and Addison tried her best to pay attention. What had that buzzing phone been about? An urgent new apartment lease? Medical test results? Crazy ex-girlfriend?

More importantly, why did she care?

"Does anyone have any questions?" Colette asked, dragging Addison back to the present. She'd completely zoned out during the recitation of Carter's bio and his list of qualifications.

Fine. That's what Google was for.

"I do." Eli Cross, the staff writer responsible for *Veil*'s *Everyday Groom* column raised his hand.

Colette's eyebrows arched ever so slightly. "Yes?"

"You mentioned that Mr. Payne is going to be working closely with Addison. Does this mean there are two deputy editors now?"

Every head in the conference room swiveled in Addison's direction. She wanted to crawl under the table with a pint of Ben & Jerry's and disappear.

"For the time being, yes." Colette nodded, and then her red lips curved into a knowing smile. "The staff can expect an important update at the company Christmas party. Until then, the junior editors will report to both Addison and Carter. Understood?"

No! Addison wanted to scream. She didn't understand. Not at all.

An awkward silence fell over the room, and suddenly, no one could seem to meet her gaze, other than her *Veil* girls. But the sympathy in their eyes was too much to take. Addison thought she might be sick.

She'd just been effectively demoted in front of the entire magazine. Outside, Manhattan rang with the sounds of Christmas cheer. Or maybe Addison was mistaken and the bells she heard were actually the death knell of her career.

Chapter Five

At the close of the staff meeting, Carter was swarmed with warm wishes from the *Veil* staff. It was such a startling contrast to the way he'd been welcomed by his co-deputy editor that he wasn't altogether sure how to react. So he spent the next few minutes shaking hands, making small talk and doing his best to remember everyone's names and job titles.

Among the last to introduce themselves were two women he instantly recognized from the photos on Addison's bulletin board. Carter learned their names were Daphne Ballantyne King and Everly England Astor— the serialized fiction column writer and features editor, respectively.

"England?" Carter angled his head toward Everly as she shook his hand. "Any relation to Addison?"

Everly nodded. "She's my sister."

Ah, so it was worse than he thought. These women

weren't simply his nemesis's work acquaintances. They were family. Then again, Colette was his aunt. Turnaround was fair play, he supposed.

"Welcome to *Veil*," Daphne said brightly. Her bubbly demeanor matched the sparkles that glittered in her hair...until she glanced around the conference room to make sure no one was listening. Then she lowered her voice to a barely audible whisper and added, "Just so you know, we're hashtag #TeamAddison."

Colette hadn't breathed a word in the meeting about the future editor-in-chief job, but obviously Addison had confided in hashtag #TeamAddison. Whatever the heck that meant.

"Noted," Carter said. These women were a force. He wondered if anyone had ever been impaled by the heel of a stiletto before.

"It's nice to meet you, though," Everly said, giving him a quick once-over. "Everything seems much more clear now."

"Right?" Daphne nodded, and the rhinestones twinkling in her blond waves nearly blinded him.

Everly's gaze snagged on the knot in Carter's Hermés tie. "It's got to be the French thing."

Carter's interest was officially piqued. *The French thing?*

"Excusez-moi?" he asked with a wink.

Daphne and Everly exchanged a knowing glance.

"Definitely the French thing," Daphne said with a snort.

"Don't worry. We mean that as a compliment, I promise," Everly said.

The last of the stragglers exited the conference room,

leaving Carter alone with Addison's friends. Addison, however, was nowhere to be seen. She'd bolted from the room as soon as the meeting adjourned.

Carter didn't like the way her absence left a hollow feeling in his chest. Not one iota. "You realize I'm actually American, don't you?"

"Yes, we listened to your bio just now. But you've been in Paris for almost a decade, and believe me, it shows." Everly's eyes darted toward the cut of his suit. Slim and sleek, bordering on tight-fitting, because that's the way they wore them in Europe. Especially at a men's magazine like *L'homme.*

"Kind of like a Cronut," Daphne said.

Were they always like this? Carter was the one who'd just crossed five time zones to get here, but it felt like these *Veil* women were the ones speaking a foreign language.

He felt his gaze narrow. "What, may I ask, is a Cronut?"

Daphne's eyes lit up. "You've never had one? Oh, my gosh. *So* good. Not as yummy as a cupcake, but close. A Cronut is a pastry that's basically a marriage between a donut and a croissant."

More wedding metaphors. Carter had worked at *Veil* for a grand total of an hour, and he already felt like if someone cut him, his veins would bleed bridal white.

He didn't exactly hate it. It was just…different. No one at *L'homme* had ever compared him to a baked good. "Just to be clear, I'm the Cronut in this scenario?"

"Obviously," Daphne said.

"So…not as good as a cupcake, but still yummy." A smile tugged at Carter's lips. "Understood."

Everly held up a hand. "I promise that wasn't supposed to sound like an HR violation. Daphne just has a tendency to think in terms of sugar and buttercream frosting. Her sweet tooth is legendary around here."

"Again, noted." He flashed them both a smile as he headed toward the door. Best to leave now before things got even weirder. Besides, he was beginning to suspect that Addison was up to no good in their shared office. The way things were going, he fully expected to find a whoopee cushion on his chair or a canned snake in one of his desk drawers.

When he got back to the office he shared with Addison, he found it empty. Not even a trace of her lovely strawberries-and-cream scent remained.

Good, Carter told himself. He had work to do, and as much as he didn't want to admit it, Addison was a distraction. A beguiling distraction, to be sure, but a distraction, nonetheless.

Two hours later, however, Addison's absence started to grate on his nerves. He stared across the small room at her empty desk. Where could she be? Her pink laptop was still there, snapped closed to protect whatever secrets Addison wanted to keep from him. Even the dog bed still sat empty. There wasn't a trace of Sabrina in sight.

Then Carter remembered what Addison had said about the little dog just as the staff meeting started. *Sabrina is in the fashion closet, perfectly happy with a peanut-butter-stuffed Kong toy, if you must know.* He sat for a moment, tapping his pen on his desk. He hadn't set eyes on the *Veil* fashion closet yet, but perhaps it was time to go find it.

Carter pushed back from his desk and stalked toward the hallway. He wasn't sure why he was so bothered by the fact that Addison seemed to be avoiding him, except how were they supposed to put an entire digital issue together in just a few weeks' time when they couldn't even seem to hold a simple conversation?

"You." Carter pointed to the first person he saw in the hallway—a member of the staff he recognized as the reporter who'd asked Colette to clarify whether or not Carter and Addison were both co-deputy editors now. "What's your name, again?"

"Eli Cross. I write the *Everyday Bachelor* column." The other man offered his hand. "Welcome to *Veil*."

"Thank you, Eli. I'm trying to find the fashion closet. Can you point me in the right direction?"

Eli looked at him askance. "The fashion closet?"

Carter nodded. "Yes, do you know where it is?"

"I do, and I'd be happy to take you there." Eli jammed a hand in his hair and glanced around as if worried someone might overhear their conversation. He cleared his throat. "I guess I just never realized guys are allowed in the fashion closet. Rumor has it that some of the more senior editors have secret meetings in there."

"Would those senior editors happen to be Addison, Everly and Daphne?"

Eli's head drew back. "Yeah. How did you—"

Carter held up a hand. "Never mind how I knew. Let's just go see what they're up to."

"Ah, sure," Eli said, not looking sure at all. In fact, he looked as if he were longing to return to his desk.

Carter charged ahead before Eli could change his mind. "Let's go."

"It's actually this direction." Eli hooked a thumb toward the opposite side of the building.

Carter spun on his heel. At least they were getting somewhere now.

Eli led him down the corridor before stopping in front of a plain white door and shifting from one foot to the other. "This is it."

Carter's gaze narrowed. Maybe if he looked at the door hard enough, he'd be able to discern whatever was happening on its other side. "Do you think we should knock?"

"Probably." Eli nodded, still focused on the door. Neither of them could seem to tear their gaze from it. They both just stood there with their hands in their trouser pockets, gazes locked on the closet. "From what I hear, there are a lot of gowns in there. Like, *a lot*. It's possible someone could be getting dressed. To be honest, I haven't the first clue what actually goes on in there."

"Well, Eli." Carter's gaze slid toward his colleague. "I think it's high time we found out."

He knocked hard three times. A yip immediately sounded from inside the closet, followed by a few muffled thuds.

Carter and Eli exchanged frowns.

"That didn't sound good," Eli muttered.

No, it hadn't. Carter leaned closer to the door. "Addison, are you in there?"

"Um, yes." Her voice sounded nearer than he'd expected, like she was positioned just inches away, whispering into the crack between the door and the frame.

"Is everything okay? You've been gone a while and you sound…" *Guilty.* Whatever was going on inside the fluffy, bedazzled interior of that closet, Addison wanted to keep it a secret. Which naturally made Carter more determined than ever to get inside. "…odd. You sound odd, Addison. I'm going to need you to open the door, so we know you're all right."

"*We?* Who else is out there? It's not Colette, is it?" The door flew open just a few inches, and Addison stuck her head out to glance around, wide-eyed. She sagged in relief when she spotted Carter's partner in crime. "Oh hi, Eli."

Eli held up a hand. "Hi, Addison."

She straightened, and Carter could see her future-editor-in-chief mask slip back into place along with the upward tilt of her chin. "What are you two doing here?"

"We're coming in, that's what we're doing," Carter said.

"Please don't." Addison winced, and then she bit her bottom lip, drawing every ounce of Carter's focus to her shimmery pink mouth.

The woman was downright kissable. She was maddening beyond belief, but for some insane reason, Carter hadn't felt such a fierce desire to kiss a woman in a long, long time. Maybe ever.

An ache wound its way through him as he gazed at her perfect, bow-shaped lips. What was wrong with him? He couldn't go there, obviously. They weren't just coworkers. They were competing for the same job. Carter could only guess that the forbidden nature of his attraction toward her was adding to his current angst. That had to be it, because the pull he felt toward her at times made no logical sense.

"Hey, man," Eli said under his breath as he jabbed an

elbow into Carter's side. "What happened to 'it's high time we found out'?"

Carter gave himself a shake.

Focus. This is war, remember?

"Addison." He leveled his gaze at her.

She swallowed. "Yes?"

"Open the door."

Addison glared at him for a beat and finally huffed, "Fine. Get in here."

She grabbed him by the elbow and hauled him inside. Eli stumbled in after him, and Carter was vaguely aware of Addison slamming the door closed behind them. It was kind of hard to think straight because an unmistakable jolt of pleasure shot through him at the unexpected contact. It didn't feel at all like war. Far from it, in fact.

But then he was so stunned at the sight before him that all he could do was stop and stare.

"Whoa." A bark of laughter escaped Eli. "This is…"

"Bad. I know." Addison groaned. "Really, really bad. Would you believe it was even worse an hour ago?"

It looked like a bomb had gone off in the fashion closet—a tulle explosion. The floor was covered in mounds of airy fabric in various shades of white and ivory. The clothing racks stood empty with hangers dangling from the rods in all directions, while wedding gowns were *everywhere*, littering every possible surface.

"How could it possibly have been worse?" Carter heard himself say.

Then, before he could say another word or ask what in the world had happened, Sabrina came flying out of a nearby puff of fabric with a bridal veil clasped in her teeth. She tore past him in a whirl of chestnut-and-white fur, making a frenetic loop around the three humans in the room—unless there were more people in here, buried among the fluff. It was a real possibility.

"That tiny dog did—" Eli gestured to the surrounding mounds of tulle, piled up around them like snowdrifts *"—all this?"*

Addison crossed her arms and nodded. She seemed to be doing her best to look anywhere and everywhere except at Carter.

"Something tells me that peanut-butter-stuffed Kong didn't exactly do the trick earlier," he said quietly.

"Not exactly." Addison made a valiant attempt at a smile, but then her bottom lip began to quiver, and her eyes went shiny.

Sabrina came to an abrupt stop in front of her and dropped into a play bow. The pup had abandoned the veil somewhere and now a rhinestone tiara hung cock-eyed around her neck. Carter bit back a smile.

Addison, however, was not amused. A tear slipped down her cheek, and Carter's gut churned as she sniffed and wiped it away with the back of her hand.

"You have to admit she's kind of cute." Eli squatted and held a hand out to Sabrina, who bounded toward him with a full-body wiggle. "A nightmare, obviously. But cute."

"Eli." Carter caught the other man's gaze and jerked his head toward the door. "Thanks for your help, but I think I've got it now."

"Oh, sure. I should probably get back to work, anyway." Eli stood, while Sabrina wandered off to collapse into a heap on top of a Vera Wang gown and Addison covered her face with her hands.

"Do me a favor and keep this between us, okay?" Carter said as he walked Eli to the door.

"No problem." Eli gave him an odd look, no doubt wondering why Carter would want to protect Addison.

Carter was beginning to wonder the same thing himself. Addison England didn't need his help. She'd gotten herself to the second-in-command position at *Veil* all on her own, which was no small feat. She was perfectly capable of cleaning up her own messes.

It had been a rough couple of days, though. Carter was well aware that his presence had a lot to do with the vulnerability that he could see shining back at him from her eyes. And he liked this woman, damn it. He didn't want to, but he did. If he hadn't, the sight of that little quiver in her bottom lip wouldn't have hit him like a ton of bricks.

He liked Addison's ambition. He liked the way she challenged him. Most of all, he liked how she seemed fiery and tenderhearted at the same time. Case in point: the mess in which they currently stood. She had no idea how to care for this dog but still hadn't managed to let the little creature go.

And if Carter wasn't mistaken, Addison liked him too. She could try and hide it all she wanted, but he was no fool. He'd yet to have a woman who truly despised him nestle her face into the crook of his neck and cling to him like a barnacle. *Busted, Cruella.*

Carter cleared his throat and redirected his gaze back at Eli. "Thanks, man."

Eli held up a hand as he disappeared down the hall.

Carter shut the door and locked it behind him. Without a word, he bent and picked up the closest handful of organza and fished around until he found the bodice of a gown. He grabbed a padded satin hanger and hung the dress neatly on one of the garment racks, smoothing down the front of the gown's skirt until it looked as pristine as if hadn't just been piled on the floor.

Then he bent and grabbed another puddle of fabric at his feet and did it all over again. And again, one gown at a time.

"What are you doing?" Addison asked with a sniff.

Carter stole a glance at her and breathed a little easier when he saw that she was no longer on the verge of tears. "I'm helping you clean up this disaster. What does it look like?"

She looked at him for a long moment until, at last, her lips curved into a slow smile. Then she went to work alongside him, knee-deep in wedding gowns and a strange sort of mutual affection that they both pretended not to notice.

An hour and a half later, Addison could finally breathe easier. With Carter's help, the fashion closet had been restored to its former glory and once again resembled the comforting, safe space she knew and loved—with the added bonus of an exhausted rescue dog snoring away with her naughty little head perched on a satin ring pillow.

Did she enjoy being indebted to Carter Payne? Not in the slightest.

Was she also so full of gratitude that she sort of wanted

to kiss him silly right now? Absolutely, one thousand percent yes.

"You didn't have to do this, you know," she said as she reached inside the mini fridge for the bottle of champagne that she and her *Veil* crew had abandoned earlier this morning. The man deserved a proper thank-you, and since kissing him was clearly out of the question, a sparkling glass would have to do.

Carter cocked an eyebrow at the bottle in her hands. "If the tables had been turned, you would've done the same."

"No, I wouldn't," she said as she began to peel the foil label from the champagne.

"Here, let me do that while you get us some glasses. I now know where literally everything in this closet belongs except champagne flutes." He took the bottle from her, fingertips brushing against hers in the process, forcing Addison to suppress a ridiculous and highly inappropriate shiver. "And yes, if my dog had caused a scene like this, you would've been the first person to swoop in here and help me fix everything."

I told you…she's not my dog.

The thought flitted through Addison's head, but she couldn't bring herself to say it out loud. Sabrina had just had a meltdown of epic proportions, all because Addison had left her alone for ninety minutes. The poor dog had been in a state of panic when Addison had returned from the staff meeting. Her separation anxiety was far more troubling than the mess she'd caused in her distress, which was really saying something.

In any event, Addison couldn't imagine what would

happen if she dropped the Cavalier off at the shelter. At this rate, neither of them would survive it.

Still, she couldn't keep her. Not after this.

Addison's heart gave a pang as she glanced at Sabrina's little paws twitching in her sleep. How could one tiny dog completely upend her life and career overnight?

News flash: It wasn't just the dog.

Addison's gaze shifted back to her bigger, more vexing problem. Unfortunately, he'd just rolled up his shirtsleeves, exposing a rather nice and commanding set of muscular forearms.

She swallowed. Hard. "Trust me, if the tables had been turned, I would've been more than happy to let you fall on your face."

As grateful as she was, Addison needed Carter to know that this changed nothing. They were rivals, not friends.

"Says the woman who bent over backward earlier— *twice*—to try and get me to put my phone away so I wouldn't get in trouble at the staff meeting." Carter shot her a cocky grin, which negated the appeal of his forearms by only a minuscule margin. "Face it, Cruella. I've got your number."

Addison smiled into the glass of champagne he'd just handed her, relieved that he'd gone back to calling her by that dreaded nickname. This type of banter, she could handle. The rules were cut and dried—she was on one side, and he was on the other. Unlike earlier, when he'd been so gentle and so kind that the margins had gone blurry for a bit.

"Do elaborate," she said, injecting a hint of challenge

in her voice. She'd been off her game ever since she'd set eyes on him. He had no idea what she was really like.

"Just admit it. You don't hate me nearly as much as you pretend to." Cater held his glass aloft, clinking the flute against hers. "Cheers."

"Cheers, and thank you for your help today. I truly appreciate it." She took a sip, and bubbles danced on her tongue. Everly and Daphne were going to murder her when they found out she'd cracked this bottle open without them. Addison made a mental note to replace it. "I do still hate you, though."

"A little bit less now, though." Carter gave her a lop-sided smile. "Don't worry. I'm not going to make you say it."

"You're impossible." Addison rolled her eyes and looked away so he wouldn't see the dumb grin that she couldn't seem to stop from rising to her lips.

"I'm also curious." He studied her as if she were a science experiment. "Why were you in here all by yourself earlier? Where was your chick clique in your time of need?"

Addison nearly choked on her champagne. "My chick clique?"

Carter shrugged. "You know, your babe bunch. Your leading ladies. Your—"

Addison held up a hand. "Please stop before you say something even more gross and condescending."

He grinned as he reached for the bottle to top off their glasses. Clearly he was doing his best to get a rise out of her, and she was falling for it, hook, line and sinker.

Carter smirked. "More condescending than your glossy posse calling me a Cronut?"

What? Addison blinked. "They didn't."

"Oh, but they did. Apparently, it's a combination of a croissant and a donut. In Daphne's words, 'not as good as a cupcake, but still yummy.'"

She'd really missed a lot while she'd been stuck in this closet, hadn't she?

Addison pulled a face. "I'm suddenly willing to forget I ever heard you utter the phrase 'chick clique.'"

Carter laughed, and the sound floated through her like a whisper. No doubt, the champagne was to blame. Addison set down her glass. Being cordial was one thing, but actually letting herself enjoy Carter's company was another entirely.

"The three of you are obviously close. Everly and Daphne told me they were on your side in no uncertain terms. I get the feeling they would've dropped everything to come help you," Carter said.

"You're absolutely right." No one was as loyal as her *Veil* girls. They'd seen each other through thick and thin.

"Then why didn't you let them?" Carter took a step closer—close enough for Addison to lose herself in those dreamy blue eyes of his. "Blue Christmas" began to play in her head on a soulful, continuous loop.

She took a tiny, nearly imperceptible step backward and bumped into a shelf lined with white satin stilettos with rhinestone accents. Still, she had to tilt her face upward in order to meet Carter's gaze. "I'll answer that question as soon as you tell me who sent you such a vitally important email during the staff meeting that you stopped what you were doing and read it on the spot."

His eyes glittered with surprise, and Addison arched a triumphant eyebrow. *Still think you've got my number?*

"Okay, I'll accept those terms." His gaze narrowed ever so slightly. "The email was from the editor-in-chief of *L'homme*, my former employer."

Addison tried—and failed—to hide her surprise. Surely he wasn't planning to go running back to Paris. The prospect sent an irrational stab of disappointment square to her heart.

How much champagne had she actually consumed? It hadn't seemed like too much at the time.

"What did the email say?" she asked, doing her best to feign casual interest.

Carter wagged his pointer finger back and forth. "Nope. That wasn't part of our deal. I answered your question, and now it's time for you to answer mine."

She crossed her arms, feeling vulnerable all of a sudden. They had a deal, though, and what was the harm in telling him the truth when he'd already witnessed her at her worst…a couple of times already.

"I didn't ask the *Veil* girls for help because that's not how things work with Everly and Daphne. I take care of them, not the other way around," she said, voice breaking ever so slightly. When had they started putting truth serum in Veuve Clicquot?

"That must get lonely sometimes," he said, and his smile went sad around the edges, as if Carter Payne knew a fair bit about loneliness himself.

It does. Addison bit down hard on her tongue. She'd said too much already, and it was long past time to get back to her office.

"It's fine," she said after a beat. Because it was. *Everything* in her life had been perfectly fine up until twenty-four hours ago.

Carter's eyes glittered. "Why don't I believe you?"

She shot back with the only thing she knew would effectively end the conversation. "Why won't *you* tell me what was in that email?"

"Well played, Cruella," he said with a quiet laugh. Then he set down his champagne flute and started unrolling his shirtsleeves. *Quel pity.* "What do you say? Shall we take up arms again and get back to work?"

Back to the battlefield.

Relief tipped the edges of Addison's lips into a smile. Out there, she knew exactly what their roles were. She knew who she was and what she wanted. More to the point, she knew that this man was her rival, not her friend. Everything was clearly defined and tied with a neat little bow, unlike these messy moments that somehow kept happening between them.

She gave her headband a tiny adjustment, anchoring it more firmly in place. "I thought you'd never ask."

Chapter Six

Four days later, when Thursday evening finally rolled around, Addison nearly wept with relief when the bartender at Bloom placed a frothy wedding cake martini on the high-top table in front of her.

"This has been the longest week of all time," she said, reaching for her glass and taking a generous gulp.

"I see we're skipping the cheers, then?" Daphne frowned as she held her wedding cake martini aloft.

Everly aimed a reproachful look at Addison and clinked her glass against Daphne's. "Cheers."

Addison winced. "Sorry. We've just really been looking forward to this."

Daphne's gaze flitted to Sabrina, merrily perched in Addison's lap with red satin bows on her ears—a special holiday treat from the pet spa. "You and this dog are officially a *we* now?"

Everly did a little dance on her barstool. "I knew it."

"Don't get so excited." Addison shook her head and covered Sabrina's furry ears so she wouldn't overhear. "I'm only keeping her for the holidays, remember?"

"Sure you are," Everly said, grinning from ear to ear.

"She's right." Daphne tapped her glass against Everly's again to punctuate their point. "I don't see you giving Sabrina up anytime soon. You and that dog are practically joined at the hip."

"That's by necessity. She doesn't like to be left alone." Addison twirled the stem of her martini glass. She still hadn't told the *Veil* girls about the fashion closet incident. For now, it remained a secret. "I had to send her out to the doggy spa today just so Carter and I could take one of the advertisers out to lunch."

Everly tucked a dark lock of hair back into her Audrey Hepburn *Breakfast at Tiffany's* updo. "You make the perfect pair. That's all I'm saying."

"Hardly." Addison rolled her eyes. "We barely speak, even though we work three feet from each other all day, every day."

Once they'd exited the fashion closet, things had gone back to normal. It was almost as though their brief truce had never happened. Carter continued stealing her coffee cup when she wasn't looking, and Addison did her level best to ignore his existence altogether. Not an easy task, given that he and his glorious forearms were always *right there*. But at least he'd started calling her Cruella again. As much as she loathed that nickname, it was far easier to take than unexpected kindness.

Everly bit back a smile. "Um, sis. I was talking about you and Sabrina. Not you and Carter."

"Oh." Addison took another gulp of her drink.

Thursday nights at Bloom, a cozy bar tucked around the corner from the magazine's office, was a weekly tradition for the *Veil* crew. They'd been regulars ever since Bloom's owner had concocted a signature drink just for them. The wedding cake martini was a mysterious blend of whipped cream vodka, pineapple juice and vanilla vodka that somehow combined to taste exactly like a slice of white wedding cake piled high with frosting. It was as much of a dessert as it was a cocktail, and it was exactly what Addison needed right now. Not just because of the sugar and the alcohol, but because now that Carter had breached the perimeter of the fashion closet, Bloom was now officially her only safe space.

"How are things going with your work husband anyway? We've hardly seen you all week, and we're dying for details." Daphne waggled her perfectly groomed eyebrows.

"Ew. Do *not* call him that ever again." The back of Addison's neck went warm all of a sudden. "And please don't call him a Cronut either."

"He told you about that, huh? All I meant was that he's like an American and a Frenchman all rolled into one. I mean, that accent of his…" Daphne sighed.

Oui, Addison's subconscious screamed. *That accent.*

She squared her shoulders. "Trust me, he's no pastry. He's a workaholic of the highest order."

For the entire week, they'd been in an unspoken competition to see who could get to the office first. He'd beaten her the first day, obviously, so she'd shown up at six thirty the next morning, only to find Carter already in the elevator, waving at her with a satisfied smirk as she'd booked it across the marble lobby in her stilettos.

She'd only been an arm's length away when he'd let the elevator doors swish closed.

This morning, she'd actually bested him. He'd strolled into their shared office at 5:45 a.m., only to find her already at her desk, editing Daphne's latest installment of her fiction column. *Five forty-five.* If she drank more than half a martini tonight, she was going to fall asleep right here at the table.

"He's also entirely too sure of himself," she added, hugging Sabrina a little closer. "It takes him less than three seconds to approve layouts from the fashion department. One look, and he immediately says yes or no."

Addison couldn't fault his taste, though. Every pictorial he'd worked on this week was undeniably stunning. Two days ago, he'd led a photoshoot at the Metropolitan Museum of Art featuring brides in blush-pink gowns posing with Monet paintings, and the outtakes had been so gorgeous that Addison had marched straight to the break room and crammed a sample slice of lavender-infused wedding cake into her mouth. Sabrina had scrambled around her feet, licking up the rage-crumbs as they hit the floor.

"We can add stubborn to the list, too. Once that man sets his mind to something, there's no talking him out of it," Addison added for good measure. "You guys honestly have no idea."

Addison sure did, though. After nearly an entire week of working in such close proximity, she could predict what color tie he'd wear every day with 99 percent accuracy. She'd also known exactly what he'd order for lunch today—a steak and steamed vegetables. When she closed her eyes at night, she could sometimes hear the distinct rhythm of his fingertips tapping away on his keyboard. *Click clack click.* He always hit the enter key with extra enthusiasm. *CLACK.*

But she wasn't going to think about that right now. This was Martini Night, her much-deserved break after dealing with the additions of both Carter and Sabrina in her life. Thank goodness only one of them was present at the moment.

Everly and Daphne watched her as she sipped her drink, both of their foreheads crinkling in unison.

"What?" Addison asked, looking up from her glass. The only thing that would've improved upon the wedding cake martini would be if it came with a side of actual cake.

"No offense, hon." Daphne bit her lip. "But it sort of sounds like you're describing yourself."

"You can't be serious." Addison very nearly snorted. "He's a perfect *Payne* in my backside. Get it?"

See? She was making jokes. That's how delightful she was, as compared to her stuffed shirt officemate.

Daphne regarded her through heavily lashed eyes. "You really can't see it, can you?"

"Workaholic?" Everly made an invisible tally mark with a flick of her pointer finger. "Check."

"Confident and determined—check and double check," Daphne said with a nod.

Addison's neck grew even hotter. "Trust me. We're nothing alike. For starters, I'm not related to our boss."

Although, it wasn't as if Carter spent much time with Colette at the office. Addison hadn't seen them alone together even once. And she wholeheartedly doubted that they ate dinner together or shared a good binge-watch after working hours. She just couldn't see it. For all she'd come to know about Carter over the past few days, she knew exactly zero information about his personal life. It was almost as if he didn't have one.

Addison felt herself frown. Maybe they really were more alike than she'd realized.

No. She needed to get that idea right out of her head. *Not possible.*

"Seriously. You don't understand. He's…he's…" Addison's tongue tripped over itself. Why couldn't she seem to put her dislike for him in words? "He's…"

"Here," Daphne said, shooting a meaningful glance over Addison's shoulder.

Addison shook her head. "That's not what I was going to say."

"No, I mean, he's *here*. At Bloom. He just walked in the door." Daphne's gaze darted toward the entrance to the bar again, and her blue-green eyes went as wide as saucers. "And don't look now, but he's with Colette."

"What?"

If Sabrina hadn't been sitting in Addison's lap, she would've dived straight under the table.

What was *he* doing here? It wasn't enough that she already spent the majority of her waking hours with the man. Now he had to insert himself into Martini Night… and with their boss!

Unacceptable.

Martini Night was a sacred tradition for the *Veil* girls only. Everly and Daphne's husbands showed up every now and then, but those occasions were few and far between. Recently, Henry and Jack had started their own Thursday night tradition—pizza night at Jack's penthouse. Henry, Holly Golightly and the twins were there tonight, as per usual. Jack's daughter Olivia loved doting on the twins and had already volunteered to be their regular babysitter once she was old enough.

Addison suddenly wished she was there right now too, chowing down on a slice of pepperoni pizza and cuddling with her infant nieces. Maybe she should just quit publishing and go to work at a doggy day care or something. Oh, that's right, she couldn't do that, because she was a terrible doggy foster mom. Sabrina had Addison wrapped around her furry little paw.

Also, Addison would never, ever give Carter the satisfaction of conceding defeat.

Her gaze flitted toward the entrance of Bloom, where pink-and-white flowers hung from the ceiling and a Christmas tree made from pale pink feathers stood in the corner. Sure enough, there stood Carter Payne, looking as masculine as humanly possible amid Bloom's ultrafeminine, Instagrammable decor.

"What are you doing? I told you not to look." Daphne nudged Addison with her elbow, and her wedding cake martini sloshed dangerously close to the rim.

Addison could say nothing in defense of her actions. It was just that whenever Carter was around, she felt a hum of awareness coursing through her that was difficult—if not impossible—to ignore. She kept telling herself it was simply because she was always on high alert around him, like a gazelle in a nature documentary every time a lion prowled onto the scene. But even that explanation infuriated her because she was no fragile, helpless gazelle. She was supposed to be the lion, dang it.

Carter's gaze collided with hers in an instant, as if he sensed her presence every bit as much as she noticed his. A wave of relief washed over her. *Good, it's not just me.*

And then Carter's mouth curved into a smile so imperious that it sent a chill up and down her spine. He may as well have roared right there in the crowded bar.

Addison's pitiful gazelle heart thumped wildly in her chest as Carter lifted a single eyebrow, like he knew precisely what she was thinking.

Who's the lion now?

It figured.

Carter had finally managed to arrange some time away from the office with his aunt, and the bossy, enigmatic thorn in his side had turned up at the same exact place. If Addison hadn't already been seated at a table when he and Colette arrived, Carter would've been tempted to believe that his nemesis had followed them. He wouldn't have put it past her. Addison was laser-focused on beating him out for the editor-in-chief position—so laser-focused, in fact, that it almost made the competition fun.

She hadn't expected to see him tonight, though. The deer-in-the-headlights expression on her lovely face said it all, and Carter couldn't help but feel a surge of triumph at catching her off guard. It took a lot to throw Addison off her game. He'd take his little victories where he could get them.

Carter took a seat opposite his aunt in a pink velvet cocoon that passed as a cushy armchair. After spending fifty-plus hours this week in an office that resembled the inner depths of a bridal bouquet, he'd somehow managed to go around the block and find a location with an even more romantic aesthetic.

"This place is stunning. I can't believe I've never been here before, given that it's so close to the office," Colette said as her gaze swept over their surroundings— the glossy high-top tables near the bar, the sumptuous velvet seats lining the walls, the feathery pink Christmas tree near the entrance.

Carter had never seen so many shades of pink in one place. Bloom was a bar, but it was apparently the sort of bar that necessitated batting pink carnations away from your face while making your way to your table. No wonder Addison was here. Beneath her uber-professional exterior beat the heart of a true romantic, even if he had a feeling she would've denied such a label in a hot second. It showed in the litany of editorial comments she made on the articles and pictorials she edited.

Add more description here—tell us about the expression on the groom's face.

Too dry. It's a wedding. Let's make our readers feel *something.*

And Carter's personal favorite, *more pink, please! This entire shoot should look like it's been overlaid with a* Le Vie en Rose *Instagram filter.*

She listened to French music in her headphones and kept a vase of pink peonies on her desk. The candle situated beside her laptop was labeled *Afternoon in Paris.* Definitely a romantic…and Carter was perhaps beginning to understand why her friends had looked him up and down and stated, "It's got to be the French thing." Maybe being labeled a Cronut wasn't such a bad thing, after all.

Still, how was it that in a city of eight million people, Carter couldn't make a move without bumping into Addison England?

A romantic might say it was fate, his thoughts whispered as he stole a glance in Addison's direction.

But Carter was no romantic. Quite the opposite, according to the women he'd dated in the past. Carter wasn't sure he completely agreed. He had priorities, that's all. And until he landed in an editor-in-chief position, work came in at number one. After all, he'd learned from the best.

Colette Winter had been more than just an aunt to Carter. After he lost both of his parents at the tender age of fifteen, she'd been his mother and father all rolled into one. And at the moment, she was looking at him as if he'd morphed back into a petulant teenager.

"You haven't heard a word I've been saying since we sat down. What on earth could be so interesting on the other side of the room?" Colette's gaze flitted toward Addison's table just as a large party of patrons moved toward the bar, obscuring the view.

"Nothing." Carter smoothed down his tie. Was Addison on a *date*? He'd been so caught off guard by the sight of her that he hadn't noticed who she was with, and now he couldn't see a thing. His jaw clenched as he directed his attention back to his aunt. "Just taking it all in."

Their server conveniently showed up before Colette could question him further. While she ordered something from their special Christmas cocktail menu, Carter snuck another glance in Addison's direction. It was no use. The crowd was only getting bigger. For all he knew, she could've already left.

Alone, or with a date? That was the question.

"I'll have a Manhattan with an orange twist," he said. For some reason, the thought of Addison enjoying an evening with another man made Carter want something good and strong. "Thank you."

Colette studied him through narrowed eyes after the server left. "You seem tense."

"Do I?" He let out a quiet laugh. "I can't imagine why."

She sat back in her chair. "Let me guess—you're upset about the editor-in-chief position."

Upset was only the tip of the iceberg.

"For years you've been telling me that you wanted me to take over the magazine someday. *Years*," he said.

Carter didn't even know where to start. Back when he'd been a freshman in college and she'd talked him into switching his major from business to journalism? The time she'd dropped everything she was doing to surprise him on campus when he'd been named editor-in-chief of the university paper? The disappointment that had been etched in every line on her face when he'd told her he was moving to France after graduation instead of joining *Veil* right away?

He'd known how disappointed his aunt would be, and he'd tried his best to explain that he needed to make his own way in the world first. He was in no way turning his back on his "birthright," as Colette liked to call it. They were the only family that each of them had left. Carter had always known how much *Veil* meant to her. Coming to live with her after the accident had turned both of their worlds upside down. Colette had always been there for him, but she also devoted so much of her heart and soul to the magazine that Carter had always joked that *Veil* felt like his sibling. He'd spent his adult life working at other publications halfway across the world, but aside from Colette, Carter knew *Veil* better than anyone else ever could. He'd always considered it an honor that his aunt had chosen him as her successor—such an honor that he'd wanted to prove himself first. He'd wanted to *earn* it. Colette deserved that much, and so did *Veil*.

"I just…" He shook his head. He was so tired all of a sudden. Constantly trying to one-up Addison all week was beginning to take its toll. "I don't understand. Why am I here? Moreover, why didn't you tell me about Addison?"

Colette reached across the table for his hand and squeezed it tight. "Carter, my dear. You know how much I love you. If I'd told you about Addison, would you have gotten on that plane and come back home?"

No. He didn't have to think about his answer. It was a given.

He cleared his throat instead of saying it aloud.

"That's what I thought." Colette nodded and squeezed his hand even tighter. "Listen, there's a method to my madness. I promise. All will seem right in the end. You're just going to have to trust your favorite aunt a little while longer."

"Favorite aunt?" Carter arched an eyebrow at her. "You're my only aunt."

They were the only members of the family left, which went a long way in explaining why Carter had always been willing to pick up where Colette left off. She'd built *Veil* into an institution, and one day, it would transcend that lofty status and become their family's legacy. Little by little, year by year, memories of his mom and dad had been slipping away. Devoting himself to *Veil* was the only way that Carter knew how to make sense of the loss. He wanted...*needed* to leave something behind—something real and permanent.

"Touché," Colette said with a laugh, but there was a sadness around her eyes that told Carter she was thinking about their family too. Everyone they'd loved and lost.

Had he really been so ready to go back to Paris and leave this all behind? Maybe. But that didn't matter anymore. He was here. He'd stayed, even when Colette had seemed to go back on her word. Now, all he could do was trust her...

And he would.

Because that's what family did.

Chapter Seven

"Thanks for staying. I realize the others needed to go, but how am I supposed to leave when my mortal enemy is here with our boss?"

Addison swirled her drink. Her *third*, which was beginning to feel like a mistake now that she was talking to Sabrina as if the Cavalier understood a word she was saying.

Pathetic.

She pushed the martini glass away, stood and gathered Sabrina into her arms. Addison may have lost every competitive edge in her quest for the top of the masthead, but she still had her dignity. Trying to spy on Carter and Colette from the other side of the bar was impossible. Addison hadn't had a clear view of their table for over an hour, and despite the YouTube tutorial on lip reading that she'd just watched on her phone, she didn't have the first clue what they were talking about.

"Is this seat taken?" someone behind her asked—the fourth person in the past half hour to do so. Yet another reason she needed to give up on her weak attempt at corporate espionage and go home. Bloom was about to host its yearly Christmas movie trivia contest and the empty spaces at her high-top table for four were prime real estate.

"No, I was just—" She turned around to tell the stranger he was welcome to her seat, but her throat clogged when she realized the man was no stranger. It was Carter.

"Leaving?" He reached to give Sabrina a scratch under her chin. The dog responded by squirming free of Addison's arms so she could throw herself at Carter. Weren't dogs supposed to be loyal? Addison's canine knowledge was admittedly limited, but she was pretty sure their alleged loyalty was supposed to be their most famous personality trait. "So soon? The night is young, Cruella."

Not for someone who got to work this morning at five forty-five.

"Of course it's you," Addison said, injecting as little emotion into her tone as humanly possible.

"Don't pretend to be surprised. I know perfectly well you saw me when I walked in earlier," Carter said as he lowered himself onto the barstool that Everly had occupied up until an hour ago. "Just like I know you're dying to know what Colette and I talked about this evening."

"I couldn't care less," Addison lied.

She wasn't fooling anyone. Even Sabrina's puppy-dog eyes seemed to look at her with a heavy dose of disbelief. Carter studied her for a beat, clearly unconvinced, and then his blue eyes flitted to the empty barstools around the table.

"Are you and this dog that doesn't belong to you here all on your own tonight?" he asked without quite meeting her gaze.

"No." *Not that it's any of your business.* "The rest of our party went home already."

A muscle in Carter's jaw ticked. "Your date left you here alone?"

Her date? Was he joking? "Why all the questions? As you pointed out, we saw each other earlier tonight. Did you really not see who else was sitting here?"

The muscle flexed again, this time hardening into a visible knot. He ignored her question and patted the seat next to his. "Sit. Stay."

"Charming. Are you talking to me or the dog?" Addison hiked her Louis Vuitton farther up onto her shoulder.

She had zero intention of spending her free time with Carter Payne. As soon as she managed to wrestle Sabrina away from him, she was going to go straight home and enjoy the Ladurée macaron samples she'd swiped from the break room while submerged in an aromatherapy bubble bath. Self-care at its finest.

"Excuse me." Ron, the bartender who regularly served the *Veil* girls, stopped beside the table carrying a tray loaded down with a stack of paper. He shot a curious glance at Carter and then swiveled his attention toward Addison.

"I'm so sorry, Addison. Ordinarily, you know I could let you stay as long as you want, but the trivia contest crowd is bigger than we anticipated. I'm afraid you and your—" Ron eyed Carter up and down "—*date* can only sit here if you're playing along."

"He's not my date," Addison said, perhaps a little too emphatically.

Carter's eyes flashed. "We're playing," he said flatly.

Addison glared at him.

"Come on, it'll be fun. You win, I'll tell you all about my conversation with Colette. I win, you tell me about your date," Carter said, and despite the easy grin on his face, something about his expression seemed strained.

He seriously thought she'd been on a date?

It certainly seemed that way. What she couldn't figure out was why he even cared. Unless…

A forbidden thrill skittered through her. He was *jealous*. How had she not seen it? Carter's feelings were written all over his annoyingly handsome face, and Addison didn't need a YouTube tutorial to tell her that he was giving off definite green-eyed monster vibes.

Wasn't this an interesting turn of events? Addison toyed with a lock of her hair and then tucked it more firmly behind her headband, an oversized silk number in red holiday plaid.

"You know what?" She plunked her handbag down on the table. "That does sound fun."

The flutter in her belly told her that staying wasn't such a great idea. She shouldn't care a lick if Carter seemed jealous at the thought of her on a date with another man. She *definitely* shouldn't have been so giddy at the prospect. Addison had more adrenaline coursing through her veins than a kid on Christmas morning.

But if there was one thing she loved, it was a challenge. Addison knew every bit of dialogue in *The Hol-*

iday by heart. She and the *Veil* girls held a Christmas romcom movie night every December. They made hot cocoa, Christmas Crunch popcorn dotted with green and red M&Ms and danced along with Hugh Grant in *Love Actually.* Carter really thought he could best her in a holiday movie trivia contest?

Bring.

It.

On.

"Okay, then." Ron peeled two trivia contest score sheets off the stack of paper on his tray. "I'm assuming you're not playing as a team."

"As if," Addison said, reaching for one of the score sheets.

The corners of Carter's eyes crinkled. "Did you just quote Cher Horowitz from *Clueless*?"

Addison stared at him, open-mouthed. How did he know both the first and last name of the character Alicia Silverstone played in a movie from 1995? *Clueless* was a classic, but still.

"What? A guy can't be fluent in romcom?" Carter shrugged one shoulder and loosened his tie.

Who was this man, and what had he done with the stuffed shirt she shared an office with? *Under duress*, Addison reminded herself. *You have no choice in the matter.*

Yet here they were, together in a crowded bar on a Thursday night with nary a paper clip in sight. This was decidedly worse than their temporary closet truce. At least that had taken place on *Veil* property.

"Just surprised, that's all," she said as Sabrina curled herself into a contented ball on Carter's lap. Then the dog sighed, as if visions of sugarplums were dancing in her furry head, and despite herself, Addison went a little swoony.

"Surprised?" The corner of Carter's mouth lifted as Ron announced that the trivia contest was all set to begin, and then he leaned closer to whisper in her ear. "Or scared?"

A ribbon of heat curled down Addison's spine, like a smooth strip of shiny red satin on an unexpected Christmas gift—the sort of present that was such a surprise that it took the recipient's breath away.

Both. She swallowed hard, and somewhere deep down, she knew that the delicious swirl of foreboding she felt low in her belly had nothing to do with a silly trivia contest. *Definitely both.*

One hour, twenty trivia questions and two more wedding cake martinis later, Addison sat beside Carter, cheeks sore from laughing so hard.

It had started straightaway when Ron returned to their table to take their drink orders and Carter eyed Addison's martini glass and said he'd have whatever she was having. Within minutes, there was a fresh wedding cake martini in Carter's hand, and for a brief moment, Addison considered giving him a heads-up. She was certain Carter had no idea what he was about to consume since, to the naked eye, the *Veil* girls' signature drink resembled a regular vodka martini. But why give him any additional information he hadn't asked for? This was war, after all.

A single sip was all it took. Carter's eyes watered,

and he managed to choke the drink down while Addison collapsed into giggles.

"You did that on purpose," he said, mouth puckering as he examined his glass.

"I did nothing of the sort. You ordered a wedding cake martini all on your own," Addison laughed again, prompting Sabrina to switch places and climb into her lap, tail wagging with excitement.

"A wedding cake martini? Why am I not surprised?" Carter took another sip and smacked his lips. "I have to say, now that the shock has worn off, it's not half bad."

The man knew his romcoms and gamely drank Addison's favorite girly cocktail. If she hadn't disliked him so thoroughly, she might have been charmed.

Before she had a chance to remind herself to keep her guard up—because hello, this wasn't a date, even if it was beginning to feel like one—Ron rattled off the first trivia question. It was about *The Holiday*, and boom! Addison knew the answer before he'd even finished reading the question aloud.

"Yes!" She scribbled the answer on her score sheet, taking extra care to shield her paper from Carter's view.

When she shot him a triumphant grin, his eyes twinkled. "I see you tackle pub quizzes with the same sort of intensity that you do everything else."

"Obviously." She tapped her pencil on the table in a nervous tempo. "Why do something if you're not going to give it one hundred percent?"

Carter's eyes went soft in a way that made her heart beat hard in her chest. "That's my girl," he said under his breath as he scrawled his answer on his paper.

What an odd choice of words, Addison thought as

she bit her lip. She wasn't his girl. She should probably point that out to him, but she couldn't seem to force the words out before Ron read the next question.

That time, it was Carter who seemed to know the answer right off the bat. He'd finished writing his answer and had already thrown down his pencil and raised his arms in a ridiculously premature gesture of victory before Addison could come up with a reasonable guess. Right then and there, she should've been worried about the outcome of this seemingly innocuous competition. Under normal circumstances, she would've employed her trademark focus to simply block him out while she buckled down on what really mattered: winning.

But these were hardly normal circumstances. For once in her life, Addison wasn't sitting at her desk or a conference table working on a *Veil* piece or feature article. She was at a bar, playing Christmas trivia with a dog on her lap and a man sitting next to her—a man who didn't seem the slightest bit intimidated by her ambition, a man who charmed her and infuriated her in equal measure, a man who somehow seemed to make butterflies take flight in her belly whenever he was near. Which was *all the time*, seeing as he was her work husband, and she was his work wife.

None of that seemed to matter much as the night wore on, because Addison actually found herself having fun and she and Carter battled it out to see who could answer the questions first. The entire quiz was a constant back-and-forth with their pencils flying so fast that Addison's handwriting was nearly illegible. That *never* happened.

"You're going down, sweetheart," Carter said, polishing off his wedding cake martini while Ron collected the score sheets.

"Keep telling yourself that, Cronut. I'm the queen of Christmas."

His gaze flitted toward her plaid headband, and he arched a brow. "I see you have the crown to prove it."

"Are you making fun of my headband?" Addison gasped, because that would really be going too far.

"I wouldn't dare." He winked at her, and again, she had to force herself to remember they weren't spending time together because they wanted to.

Why were they here together, again?

"Ladies and gentlemen, the scores have been tabulated." Ron came out from behind the bar holding a gaudy gold trophy topped with a holographic ugly Christmas sweater above his head.

Tomorrow morning, Addison was going to plop that thing on the edge of her desk directly in Carter's line of vision.

"Can I get a drumroll, please?" Ron shouted.

Everyone cheered and drummed their hands on the tabletops. A giddy electricity skittered through Addison—the sweet, sweet hum of anticipation.

"The winner is—" Ron paused dramatically.

Addison's gaze fixed with Carter's. The poor guy. He looked as happy and confident on the outside as she felt on the inside.

"—Carter Payne!"

Everything seemed to move in slow motion as Addison tried to make sense of what she'd just heard. Had Ron really just called out Carter's name? He'd *won*? How was that possible?

She blinked and tried to make sense of the swirl of activity around her—the cheering crowd, the victorious grin on Carter's face, the silly trophy in Ron's hands as he walked toward their table…

She felt like she'd just been pelted with a wet snowball, right in the face. She'd really and truly lost?

Then, just as the mortifying news was beginning to fully sink in, Ron let out another shout. "But wait! That's not all. We have another winner, folks! That's right, you guys. For the first time ever, we've got a *tie* in the annual Bloom Christmas Trivia Contest. Give it up for our other winner, Addison England!"

Addison gasped and snapped her head up to beam at Carter. Her heart pounded hard as their eyes met and held. Her breath hitched and she went tingly all over, as if there was a sprig of invisible mistletoe hanging over their table. She nearly glanced up to double-check, but she couldn't manage to tear her attention away from Carter, who was looking at her as if they shared some strange, enchanting secret. Like they were the only two people sitting beneath the canopy of dreamy pink flowers at Bloom. Funnily enough, he didn't seem all that surprised at the sudden turn of events…or even disappointed.

Not even when his dimple flashed as he shook his head and muttered under his breath.

"Son of a Nutcracker."

Chapter Eight

They'd tied.

Carter might not have believed it, if not for the careful placement of the trophy they'd won together. The silly gold statue sat square in the middle of their table—half on his side, half on Addison's. Neither of them had so much as touched it in the moments since Ron placed it there, along with another round of celebratory wedding cake martinis.

They hadn't touched their drinks either, which Carter chalked up to the surprising results of the pub quiz. Addison, in particular, seemed thrown by the results. She'd been ecstatic when she'd realized Carter hadn't beaten her, but now that the celebratory atmosphere had died down, the competitive wheels in her head had begun turning again. Carter could practically hear them spinning away as she sat there gnawing on her bottom lip, glaring at their shared trophy with an adorable little crinkle in her forehead.

The woman was relentless. It was exhausting...

And far more alluring than Carter wanted to admit. If all those nutty holiday movies about alternate timelines were really true, there was probably a different version of Carter out there somewhere who'd arrived in New York earlier this week and stepped into his job at *Veil* as the confirmed future editor-in-chief. No silly contest, no shared office, no Addison. That version of Carter didn't have to get to the office at obscene hours just to get a jump on his competition, nor did he engage in ridiculous games of one-upmanship like stealing his coworker's espresso cup. He didn't have to, because his future at the magazine was already set in stone. As oblivious as he was successful, that fantastical version of Carter had no idea what kind of chaos he was missing out on.

The real Carter almost felt sorry for him.

"Are you thinking what I'm thinking?" Addison said, shifting her gaze from the ugly Christmas sweater atop the trophy to Carter.

Those doe eyes were going to be the death of him. It was getting harder and harder to maintain a proper level of antagonism when he felt like he was locking eyes with Bambi. The fact that the absurdly cute dog in her lap had its chin resting on the edge of the table didn't help matters.

"I don't know." Carter shrugged and reminded himself they weren't playing reindeer games. They were two professionals up for the same job—a job that a million journalists would kill for. "Try me."

Addison leaned forward, wrapping him up in her strawberries-and-cream. "What if this happens at work? What if we tie for the promotion?"

She said *tie* like it was a dirty word, and Carter couldn't help but laugh. Until he remembered what his aunt said at dinner...

Listen, there's a method to my madness. I promise. All will seem right in the end. You're just going to have to trust your favorite aunt a little while longer.

Addison's doe eyes narrowed at him. "What is that look on your face right now? Do you know something? You do, don't you?"

"I assure you, I'm just as clueless as you are," he said.

Addison shook her head. "Not buying it, Cronut."

"You're really going all in on that nickname, aren't you?" Carter sat back in his chair, unfastened his cuff links and began rolling up his sleeves. He'd been wearing his pressed Oxford shirt for going on sixteen hours now, thanks to the crazy hours he and Addison had been working in an attempt to outdo each other.

Addison's gaze dragged slowly to one of his forearms, and her eyes went dark and liquid for a moment before she blinked hard and cleared her throat. "Consider it payback for calling me Cruella for almost the entire week. And stop trying to avoid my question. Tell me what you know."

"I wish I could. Alas, I'm not privy to any secret information. If I had any sort of look, it was simply because I was thinking about something my aunt said earlier tonight." He paused a beat. Were they really going to do this? Share personal information? Carter hoped so. He still needed to know if Addison had been here on a date. The thought had been nagging at him all night, far more bothersome than the pub quiz tie. "Colette told me I needed to trust that there was a method to her madness. That's all."

Addison tipped her head back and groaned. Carter loved seeing the unguarded side of her. He had a feeling that not many people did.

"That's about as clear as mud. Did she say anything else?" She blew out a breath, shoulders sagging. "Never mind. You don't have to tell me."

Carter's jaw clenched. "Of course I do. We had a deal, and I'm a man of my word."

Her nose wrinkled. "But I didn't win."

"The trophy sitting in front of you says otherwise." Carter nudged it closer to her.

She gave the trophy a playful push back toward his side of the table. "Neither of us won. We tied."

"Which means we both won." He leaned forward, clasping his hands in front of him. "I'll go first. Tonight wasn't a business dinner. Colette is my aunt, and this evening was the first time we've had a chance to get together alone, just the two of us, since I've been back."

"So it was simply a family thing?" Addison eyed him dubiously.

"Yes. I know you have a certain idea about my aunt, and I'm not going to try and convince you otherwise because it's not entirely untrue." Carter wasn't blind to Colette's faults, but she was the only family he had left. "But we're close. Colette and I have a unique relationship."

It was all he'd intended to say, more than enough to satisfy their deal. But for reasons he didn't care to think about, he kept going before Addison could interrupt.

"From the time I was fifteen onward, she was my guardian. My parents both passed away in a private plane crash, and afterward, Colette took me in."

There, he'd said it. He'd brought up the big bad thing that every single one of his ex-girlfriends had tried to get him to talk about, even though he refused to go there. Whenever they'd pushed, he ended things. The past was the past, and Carter preferred it to stay there.

But Addison had let herself be vulnerable with him more than once already. Granted, a few of those times had been against her will, but he'd been the one to witness those moments. Not her *Veil* friends, not whomever she may or may not be dating, but Carter. Being vulnerable and allowing others to see her softer side didn't come easy to Addison. Carter understood this perhaps more than anyone else, because he was the same way. Maybe that's why he let his guard slip.

Or maybe, as crazy as it seemed, he simply felt like he could trust her. She'd never hesitated to be real with him, and Carter wanted to be real with her too. Losing his family at such a pivotal age had changed Carter. He'd gone into self-protection mode, closing himself off like a book and pouring all his focus into controlling every facet of his life. Something about Addison made him want to let go…just a little. Just enough to remember what it felt like to live in the moment.

Or perhaps he'd simply had one too many of her fancy cake-flavored cocktails. Probably that.

"Oh, Carter." Addison's big brown eyes went soft— so soft that Carter's chest immediately went tight. "I didn't realize. I—"

"How could you?" Carter shrugged, already retreating back into himself.

But in true Addison form, she wasn't going to let him. "I know. And I also realize that couldn't have been easy to share. Trust me, I know, because when I was younger, I went through something similar. My dad passed away right after I graduated from college. I was older than you were when you lost your parents, but it still turned my entire world upside down. I can't even imagine losing both my mom and dad. I'm so sorry that happened to you."

I'm sorry.

It was something people said all the time, as if by rote. *I'm sorry for your loss.* Carter typically nodded and brushed his family tragedy off as something that happened a long time ago, something that no longer had anything to do with him. He'd treat the topic as a conversational speed bump and say whatever it took to move on.

He couldn't do that with Addison, though. She understood loss in the same way that he did. She understood it deep in the marrow of her bones. They'd been forged by the same fire. No wonder they were so fully adept at pushing each other's buttons.

"Do you ever think that maybe we're more alike than you want to admit?" he asked before he could stop himself.

Their conversation was venturing into dangerous territory, and he knew it, but it was also the thought that kept him up at night when he was lying alone in his hotel room at the Carlyle and pretending that his preoccupation with Addison England was purely professional.

She looked at him for a long, silent moment without saying anything, and it was all the answer he needed.

Then she deftly changed the subject. "I think I finally understand what's going on here. Colette wants you involved with *Veil* because it's her legacy, doesn't she? It's her way of showing how much she loves you. And here I am, getting in the way of things. How bad do you hate me right now?"

"Something tells me I hate you the same amount that you hate me," Carter said, and the ache in his chest was clearly readable in his tone.

Addison audibly swallowed, and he traced the movement up and down the slender column of her throat. They were both suddenly saying more with their silence than they were with their actual words.

"None of this means I'll win, Addison. In the end, Colette will do what's best for *Veil*. You know that," he said.

"And what if we tie?" She shot a meaningful glance at their Christmas contest trophy. "That could actually be her plan—the 'method to her madness.' She could fully intend to make us co-editors-in-chief."

Carter shook his head. "That's not a thing."

Never in his entire career had he heard of two names at the top of the masthead, side by side. That would be a recipe for disaster, even for two people who got along.

"I promise you it's not. I'd resign first," he said, and he meant it.

"Me too. No question." Addison couldn't appear to nod fast enough. "Maybe we should form a pact—no matter what happens, only one of us gets the job."

Carter considered the suggestion. It was a no-brainer.

Magazines didn't have two top bosses. At the same time, he wondered if they'd resorted back to talking about work in order to avoid something else. Something deeper that neither of them was ready for, least of all with each other. It was a move straight out of the workaholic playbook.

"I'd agree to that," he said and stuck his hand out to shake on it.

"Good. Consider it done." Addison reached around Sabrina to slide her palm against his.

The moment their hands met, warmth surged through Carter. He loved how soft her skin felt against his. It made him want to do something wholly inappropriate and out of fashion, like press a tender kiss to the top of her hand like they were a couple from an old black-and-white movie.

That would've been crazy, though. So instead, he let her go and dropped his hand to the tabletop. Addison did the same, and the sliver of space between the tips of their fingers crackled with electricity. Carter felt like he was only millimeters away from a shock on par with the one he'd gotten from a faulty string of Christmas tree lights as a kid.

"Need I remind you about the terms of our *other* deal?" he asked as casually as he could manage, which was likely not casual at all.

A smile danced on Addison's lips all of a sudden. "Oh, right. You wanted to hear about my date."

Carter tried to clear his throat, but it came out as a grunt. *Smooth. Real smooth.* "Go ahead. Tell me all about Mr. Right."

How was it possible to feel jealous of a man he knew nothing whatsoever about?

Addison rolled her eyes. "At the risk of repeating one of your favorite quotes, as if. I wasn't on a date earlier. I was here with Everly and Daphne. Bloom is our usual Thursday night hangout."

All the muscles in Carter's body seemed to relax at once. She hadn't been on a date, after all. Not that it was any of his business, but still. Maybe now he could get a half-decent night's sleep for once.

Then he looked down and realized Addison's fingertips were inching slowly toward his.

He glanced back up and fixed his gaze with hers. "So there's no Mr. Right, then?"

"Hardly. I don't have the greatest track record in that department, I'm afraid. I gave up on dating a while back. There will be time for that sort of thing later, once my career is firmly in place." Meaning, once she'd nabbed the job they both wanted, which didn't seem as irksome as it should when Carter realized they were now holding hands, their fingers loosely intertwined.

"Honestly, I'm not really cut out for a relationship. At least that's how it seems. I'm either too independent, too busy or just generally too much," Addison said quietly, and Carter knew those weren't merely words she'd pulled out of thin air. She was quoting past boyfriends. He knew it, because he'd heard the same things from women he'd dated in the past. She shrugged, but when she smiled at him, her bottom lip gave a telltale wobble. "I guess you could say that most men find me intimidating."

And there it was again—a glimpse of vulnerability that made Carter's gut tie itself up in knots. Like the moment a groom lifted the veil from his bride's face.

I'm not most men.

The words danced on the tip of his tongue, sweetly forbidden. It took every ounce of Carter's willpower not to utter them out loud.

"I'm sorry," he said instead, but the sentiment felt woefully inadequate when he wanted to say so much more.

Addison untangled her fingertips from his and slid her hand back toward her lap. Her smile stiffened into the one she wore at the office—the mask of cool professionalism she showed to the world at large. If what she'd just shared with him had been some sort of test, he'd just failed spectacularly.

"It's fine," she said.

It *wasn't* fine. Neither was the fact that whatever intimacy had developed between them over the course of the evening seemed to be slipping through Carter's fingers like a delicate snowflake, too fleeting and precious to grab hold of.

"I suppose we're even now," she said, and the fake cheer in her tone rubbed him entirely the wrong way.

The night had started with a silly bet, but they'd moved beyond that. At least, he thought they had.

"Looks that way," he said tightly, and he told himself this was for the best.

He wasn't anyone's Mr. Right, least of all Addison's. The second they gave in to the undeniable attraction swirling between them, they'd both be sure to regret it. They each had too much at stake to risk over a casual holiday fling.

What if it wasn't casual, though? What if it was everything you never knew you wanted?

Carter pushed back from the table and stood. He needed to get out of here and put some distance between him and the woman who was dead set on beating him out of his dream job, the one he'd spent his entire life preparing for. He needed to shake off all of those silly Christmas romcoms and keep his feet firmly planted in the real world like he always did.

Most of all, he needed to remind himself why he'd come back to New York to begin with—to take over *Veil*, not to lose his head over Addison England.

"See you tomorrow, Cruella," he said as he reached for their trophy.

When Addison realized he intended to take it, she tried to grab it, but she wasn't quick enough. Carter swiped it off the table just in the nick of time.

She glared at him in typical Addison fashion, and Carter winked in return. Then, with a quick pat to Sabrina, he strolled out the door and into the frosty December night, grateful for the way the chill of winter seemed to settle back into his bones.

Chapter Nine

Fashion closet. Fifteen minutes!

The emergency text pinged on Addison's cell phone just as she'd finished her third proofreading pass over the vision board she'd created for her monthly pitch meeting with Colette.

Correction: *their* Wednesday pitch meeting, as in hers and Carter's.

On the second Wednesday of every month, Addison met with the editor-in-chief to pitch new ideas for covers and feature articles. Ordinarily, she loved the one-on-one time with Colette, but of course that sacred little luxury was now a thing of the past. Today's pitch meeting, like everything else in Addison's life, would now be a competition between her and Carter Payne. They'd both been instructed to come armed with their best idea for a feature article and accompanying pictorial for the

Veil digital site. Whichever one Colette liked best would go immediately into production and be splashed across the *Veil* home page right before Christmas.

Addison had been working on her presentation night and day ever since Colette's email outlining the parameters for the pitch had landed in her inbox on the Monday morning following the pub quiz at Bloom. She'd been grateful for the assignment, actually. It gave her something to focus on other than the shiny gold trophy that now occupied a place of honor in the office she and Carter shared. That night had been so unexpected… so *fun*…that without a pressing reminder of what they both had at stake, Addison might have let her thoughts linger a little too long on everything Carter had shared with her. Even some of the things he *hadn't* said had found a way to get under her skin.

I guess you could say that most men find me intimidating.

Addison wasn't sure why she'd felt the need to give voice to one of her most personal insecurities. Maybe it was the way their hands fit together so perfectly, like winding her fingers through Carter's felt like the most natural thing in the world. Or maybe it was how a new connection simmered between them once she'd learned more about Carter's childhood, almost like fate had held a mirror up to her soul. Addison didn't fully understand what had happened between them that night. All she knew for certain was that the moment she'd whispered those tremulous words and given Carter a secret glimpse into her private, innermost feelings, it was as if she could hear his thoughts as clear as if he'd spoken them out loud.

I'm not most men.

But that's not what he'd said. Instead, he'd simply dropped his gaze and told her he was sorry. At first, Addison had almost thought she'd misheard him. Then, when she'd realized how badly she'd wanted him to say something else—something that told her whatever inappropriate feelings she was starting to have for him weren't purely one-sided—she'd slid her hand back to her lap and tried her best to tamp down her disappointment.

It had been more than disappointment, if she was really being honest. The lump that lodged in her throat as Carter got up and walked away had left her reeling. Addison never put her heart on the line like that. Everything she'd told Carter about her past relationships had been one hundred percent true. If anything, she'd downplayed what a disaster her dating life had truly become. Why she'd allowed herself to think, even for a moment, that Carter might be different from the other men she'd known was a mystery she couldn't begin to fathom—especially when he was the absolute last man on earth she should find attractive. *Dead* last. Worse than all her other ghosts of boyfriends past put together.

He'd done her a favor, really. Now she could fully concentrate on what was most important—*Veil*. No more flirting, no more holding hands, no more wondering what if.

What if she and Carter had met under different circumstances? What if they both weren't up for the same promotion? What if Addison really could have it all—a career, a partner, a family of her own? She was burying those questions back into an imaginary heart-shaped box and throwing away the key.

"Someone seems intent on getting in touch with you," Carter said from behind his desk.

Was it her imagination, or did their office seem to shrink more and more each day? Addison may as well have been sitting in the man's lap.

"Pardon?" she asked, pushing the thought as far from her consciousness as possible.

"Your phone has been blowing up for the past quarter hour." His gaze narrowed. "Have you really not heard it?"

She hadn't—not since the first fashion closet SOS. Addison had been too busy *not* thinking about Carter to notice that her phone had chimed three more times.

Fashion closet. Ten minutes!

Fashion closet. Five minutes!

Fashion closet. Now.

She'd missed an entire dramatic countdown, and before she even had a chance to respond and say she was on her way, another message popped up in the group chat.

Addison? Where are you? Is everything okay?

No, everything was not okay. Clearly.

"I have to go," Addison said to Carter. She stood, and Sabrina immediately followed suit, hopping off of her doggy bed to dance circles around Addison's feet.

"Now?" Carter looked up from his laptop, brow furrowing. "You realize our pitch meeting is in an hour, don't you?"

"Don't pretend you wouldn't love it if I was a no-show," Addison said.

"What would be the fun in winning by default?" A corner of his mouth lifted.

Quel liar. Carter would love upstaging her, no matter how he went about doing it.

"I have a feeling you'd find a way to live with it," she retorted.

Carter let out a low laugh that seemed to scrape Addison's insides and turned his attention back to his computer screen as another text landed in the group chat.

Do we need to send out a search team? What has he done to you?

Addison blew out a breath. She wished she knew how to answer that last question. She was still trying to figure that one out for herself.

On my way, she tapped out, freshly painted nails clicking on the tiny screen. Addison had indulged in an at-home manicure the night before in preparation for the important meeting with Colette. Instead of her usual blush pink, she'd gone with a more festive option—Love at Frost Sight by Essie. It was a snowy, winter white with just a touch of sparkly ice blue they'd recently highlighted in the magazine. She still hadn't had time to even think about getting a Christmas tree, but at least her nails had a dash of holiday spirit.

"See you at the meeting," she said, squaring her shoulders and heading for the door.

Carter's mouth twisted. "Can't wait."

Addison paused for a beat, then turned back to grab her laptop so she could take it with her.

"You don't actually think I'm going to try and spy on your presentation while you're gone," Carter said as his smile slipped.

"A girl can't be too careful."

His gaze hardened, and all of his fierce concentration was suddenly focused on Addison.

So he was angry now? Disappointed? *Good*, she thought. *Join the club.*

Addison held the laptop more closely against her chest and turned to go, Sabrina prancing right on her heels.

"Finally," Everly said when Addison got to the fashion closet a full five minutes late. In all the years they'd been meeting in their semi-secret spot, no one had ever arrived past the designated time. "We were beginning to think Carter was holding you hostage."

Nope, just a teeny, tiny piece of my heart, along with the majority of my common sense.

Not anymore, though. Addison just needed to get through the pitch meeting, and the rest of the month should be a breeze. The presentation she'd put together was perfect for the digital site. It was Christmassy, romantic and exactly what their readers—most of whom were based in New York City—would love this time of year.

"Sorry. I got distracted," she said as Sabrina shimmied toward Holly Golightly, her doggy double. The two Cavaliers touched noses, and their tails wagged in perfect unison. "I'm here now, though. What's up?"

"Look!" Daphne thrust a thick square of card stock etched in gold toward Addison. "The official invitation to the Fashion Media Awards just arrived via courier."

"Oh, Daph. That's wonderful! You and Jack must be thrilled." Addison threw her arms around her friend in a tight hug.

Known in the industry as the Oscars of fashion journalism, the Fashion Media Awards were held every year at the Rainbow Room just ten days before Christmas. *Veil* had been nominated a few times, but the magazine had never won one of the coveted trophies. The honors typically went to fashion magazines with a more general scope, like *Vogue* and *Elle*. This year, Daphne and her husband Jack were nominated in the Best Feature Series category for a four-part undercover series they'd written for *Veil* about an exclusive wedding etiquette class called Elegantly Engaged. The series had famously gone viral, but more importantly, it had also been the impetus for Daphne and Jack's romance. Being nominated for a Fashion Media Award was the icing on top of a very special cake.

Daphne beamed at Addison. "We are! Colette is too, of course. She's reserved an entire table for *Veil* at the award ceremony. She gave me specific instructions on who she wants to attend. Jack and me, obviously. Everly and Henry. Colette and Marshall Leighton…"

Addison nodded. Marshall Leighton was the CEO of Harry Winston, one of the magazine's biggest advertisers. Colette never dated socially. If an event required a plus-one, she always brought an important business associate.

"…and you and Carter." Daphne's smile stretched even wider.

"Me and Carter?" Addison's stomach flipped. "Why are you saying our names like we're a couple?"

"I'm not, and I'm sure that's not what Colette meant either. It's just that the tables only seat eight, so there's not really space for either of you to bring a plus-one. And both of you should be there since you're the magazine's co-deputy editors," Daphne said.

"Of course." Addison nodded. She loved Daphne like a sister, so naturally she'd do anything for her, including sitting beside Carter Payne all night at a black-tie event. She'd better end up on Santa's nice list this year, though, with a shiny new promotion under the tree on Christmas morning.

"Now that the guest list is settled, we need to talk about the most important thing of all." Everly spread her arms out wide, encompassing the closet and all of its glittering contents. "What are we going to wear?"

Carter's jaw clenched as he glanced at the digital clock on the upper right-hand corner of his computer screen. The pitch meeting with Colette was scheduled to start in less than fifteen minutes, and there was still no sign of Addison and her little canine mini-me. Where had she gone in such a hurry? He couldn't fathom what could be more important to her than the meeting she seemed to be on the verge of missing.

Mind your own business. Addison England is not your problem.

Except she was. Quite literally. If someone had forced Carter to sit down and make a list of every problem in his life, Addison's name would occupy each and every slot.

She was a big girl, though. A fully grown, professional woman who didn't need a lick of help from the likes of him. She'd risen all the way to deputy editor without Carter around to make sure she was on time for important pitch meetings. What did he care if she was late. Or, horror of horrors, missed the meeting entirely? As Addison had so bluntly put it, he should love it if she was a no-show.

Which was precisely why he needed to make sure she was there.

It rankled Carter that she still saw him like that—like he wanted to beat her at all costs—even though he knew he only had himself to blame. He'd been the one to pull away from her at Bloom. After days of thinking about Addison and nights of dreaming about her, just when things had turned real between them, Carter had walked away. Because that's what he always did when his relationships with women moved beyond the superficial.

He closed down.

There was a reason the things Addison had told him about her dating history sounded so familiar. *Too busy... too competitive...too independent.* Carter had heard them all before too, and now he'd gone and proved them to be true with the one woman who seemed to understand him like no one else could.

Carter didn't want to be that way with Addison, though. He told himself it was because she was safe.

Whatever happened between them could never last, simply by virtue of their circumstances. It was okay to show her who he really was, deep down inside, because once Christmas was over, so were they. They'd agreed. Even if they tied and Colette tried to make them share the job of editor-in-chief, it would never happen. They'd made a pact that only one of them would get the job.

Part of him wondered if there wasn't more to his need for Addison to see the real him, but Carter didn't have the time or desire to pull at that thread. Those sorts of thoughts were best left unexamined when Christmas was just right around the corner.

The bottom line was that he refused to win the promotion by default. Regardless of Addison's opinion of him, that's not who Carter was. There was no way she was going to be late to the pitch meeting, even if he had to drag her to Colette's office himself. Of course, in order to do that, he'd have to locate her first.

Carter's gaze cut toward her workstation, and that's when he spotted her ginormous handbag, still sitting in its usual spot beside Sabrina's plush dog bed. The bag was big enough to fit the Cavalier inside, plus Addison's entire collection of padded headbands. Carter wondered every single day what she kept in there, along with how she managed to avoid tearing her rotator cuff from hauling it around everywhere she went. If the bag was still here, Addison hadn't left the building, full stop.

Which meant there was only one place she could have possibly disappeared.

Carter pushed away from his desk, grabbed the tablet that contained his video presentation for the pitch meeting and marched down the hall toward the fashion closet. This time, he didn't hesitate in the slightest. He balled his hand into a fist and banged on the door until someone yanked it open.

Addison. *She* was that someone, although it took Carter several long moments to realize who exactly he was looking at, distracted as he was by the preponderance of sparkle and fluff filling the doorway.

"Carter, are you okay?" she asked, forehead crinkling in concern.

"I…um…" Carter could barely speak.

Addison was dressed in a wedding gown. At least he thought that's what it was. It was a strapless white satin number that hugged every curve, with an elaborate chiffon overskirt trimmed with a black organza ruffle. Jet-black crystals and whimsical embroidery trimmed the rest of the gown, hence his confusion. Maybe it wasn't a wedding dress. Carter hadn't been at *Veil* long enough to become an expert in bridal fashion. All he knew for certain was that he'd never seen anyone or anything as stunningly beautiful as Addison swathed in black-and-white chiffon.

She reached for his forearm and gave it a tug. "Come in. You're beginning to scare me."

That made two of them. Carter could feel his heartbeat pounding in his throat. Is this what it felt like to have some sort of coronary event? What was wrong with him?

"You're beautiful," he said, clutching his chest as if doing so could tamp down the ache he felt just looking at her.

"What?" Addison blinked, but the way her cheeks

flushed as pink as carnations told him she'd heard him loud and clear.

"You're always beautiful," he corrected, jamming a hand through his hair. He couldn't think straight. What was he doing in the fashion closet, again? He glanced around in search of a reason, but it was like being slapped in the face with a hundred yards of white tulle. Wedding gowns everywhere, but Carter only had eyes for Addison. "That dress is a stunner, to be sure. But it's you who's taking my breath away right now, not the gown."

He swallowed a beat too late. He'd said too much, and there was no use stopping now, because the truth was already out there.

They'd both been dancing around the truth for days, and he'd gone and broken their unspoken rule. He'd said the quiet part out loud. He wanted her. He'd *always* wanted her, right from the beginning. The more he'd gotten to know her, the more intense the longing had become. And now, much to his dismay, Carter wanted Addison with more than just his body. After years of dormancy, his heart had foolishly jumped into the mix.

It was almost as if he'd been sleepwalking in the years since his parents passed away. Then, Addison had tumbled into his path in a whirl of contradictions. Ambitious, but tender. Confident, but also shy in her own special way. Strong, and at the same time, achingly soft. And Carter had been shaken awake, blinded by her dazzling light—as mesmerized as if she'd been the Christmas star, shining bright against a velvety night sky. Try as he might, looking away was becoming next to impossible.

"Surely you know I find you attractive, Cruella," he said in flagrant violation of probably each and every sentence of the *Veil* company policy guidelines. Carter couldn't be sure because he still hadn't read them in their entirety, but he knew enough to realize when he'd said something inappropriate to his coworker...

With whom he was actively competing for head of the entire magazine.

Addison regarded him, eyes blazing bright. "No, actually. I don't. Things between us are admittedly—" she swallowed "—complicated."

Carter stepped closer, cupping her jaw and tilting her face upward so she had no choice but to meet his gaze head-on. "Then allow me to make them a bit more straightforward: you drive me crazy, in every way possible. I can't stop thinking about you."

She stared at him for a long, loaded moment, and just as he was about to mentally draft his resignation letter, she rose up on tiptoe and pressed her lips to his.

The kiss was soft at first—tender in a way that seemed to break Carter's heart and then put it back together all at once. Its own contradiction.

But then Addison opened for him, and the kiss deepened until all doubts and all restraint melted away, leaving him with one true certainty.

This.

All their little games had been punctuated by surprisingly authentic moments that had led up to *this*—the single most spectacular kiss of Carter Payne's life.

And then it ended just as quickly and unexpectedly as it had begun.

"Addison, it's almost time—" Everly came flying

around a rack of wedding gowns, followed in close succession by Daphne.

Carter only caught a glimpse of them as his eyes drifted open, but it was enough to register the shock on both of their faces as they came to a stumbling halt.

Everly held up her hands. "Oh, my gosh. I'm so sorry. I—"

Addison reeled away from Carter so fast that he nearly fell forward into a mountain of nearby tulle.

"It's fine," she blurted. "We were just—"

She glanced at him, pleading with her eyes for him to complete the sentence with something reasonably believable.

"Consulting about the pitch meeting," Carter said as he attempted to right himself while Sabrina and her office doggy buddy Holly scampered past him. What was going *on* in this closet? Was there anyone left, either human or canine, in the office proper?

Daphne snorted. "Consulting…right, that's totally what it looked like."

Everly jabbed an elbow into Daphne's side. "We really didn't mean to interrupt. I was just looking for Addison. The pitch meeting that you're, um *consulting* about is going to start in just a few minutes."

Addison, who'd been stunned into silence since her friends burst onto the scene, gasped. "The meeting!"

Right. That.

The all-important pitch meeting had somehow slipped Carter's mind the second he set eyes on Addison in the black-and-white ball gown. And then, she'd kissed him into a stupor.

"What time is it?" Addison grabbed his arm.

Think, man.

Carter yanked his phone out of his suit pocket and glanced at it. His jaw clenched as he looked back up and met Addison's panicked gaze.

"We're officially one minute late."

Chapter Ten

Last month, if someone had told Addison she'd be sitting across from Colette at the next pitch meeting with her chest heaving, dressed in a ball gown, she never would've believed it. Not in a million years. Not even a trillion, or a zillion, or whatever it was that came after a million.

Even worse, she'd been *late*. Tardiness was the worst possible faux pas at *Veil*, akin to showing up at a wedding right smack in the middle of the part where the minister asks if anyone objects to the union of the bride and groom.

Speak now or forever hold your peace.

Wouldn't that be nice? Addison *wished* she could speak. She certainly had plenty to say, starting with the fact that she hadn't had a moment's peace since Carter Payne took up residence in her office...her life...her every waking thought. She no longer had a shred of peace to hold on to, thank you very much.

But Colette was Carter's aunt and his surrogate mother. Of course Addison couldn't say those things. So instead she folded her hands in her lap and tried her best to catch her breath while Colette regarded the two of them with cool irritation.

"How nice of you two to join me—" Colette glanced at her silver Cartier tank watch, a gift from the famous jewelry store's public relations department "—five full minutes after our meeting was scheduled to begin."

More like three minutes, after Addison and Carter's mad dash from the fashion closet. But Addison wasn't about to correct her, and neither was Carter, apparently. He sat quietly in the chair beside her with a perfectly inscrutable expression on his chiseled face. Cool, calm and collected, as always.

Meanwhile, Addison could feel a splotchy, red rash blossoming on her chest, her lips were bee-stung, and her legs felt like noodles. She longed for a paper bag to breathe into. Colette was talking, but the words seemed to go in one of Addison's ears and straight out the other.

She'd *kissed* Carter. And oh, what a kiss it had been.

"Excuse me." Colette's assistant strode into the office, doing a double take as she took in Addison's attire. She blinked and refocused on their boss. "Colette, I've got the rep from Oscar de la Renta on the phone for you. I know you're in a meeting right now, but he's about to board a transatlantic flight to London and I thought you might want to speak to him before he takes off."

"Yes. Thank you." Colette nodded and aimed another frown at Addison and Carter. "This is an important call. If I go take it in the conference room, can I trust that you two will be here when I return? No more disappearing on me?"

"Absolutely." Addison nodded, although she longed to dart back to the closet to get her laptop. In the rush to get to the meeting, she'd left it behind.

"Take your time." Carter drummed his fingers on the tablet in his lap, because he'd managed to remember his tech. Carter: 1, Addison: 0. "We're ready to proceed whenever you are."

Colette left the office, clicking the door closed behind her, and it immediately felt as if she'd taken every bit of the oxygen with her. Addison couldn't seem to catch her breath as her gaze collided with Carter's. She could feel his eyes moving over her face, every bit as real as a caress.

"Your aunt is going to fire us both," Addison whispered.

"No, she's not. She can't. We're the future of the magazine, remember," he said.

"Only one of us is the future of the magazine," she corrected. They had a deal—no matter who got chosen for the editor-in-chief position, one of them had to go, period.

"You're right. Either way, she can't fire both of us, and technically, you got here first. I was later than you were." The corner of Carter's mouth twitched as if he was trying not to smile at her.

"Only because you held the door open for me." Addison cleared her throat. "Thank you for that, by the way."

He winked. "Anytime, Cruella."

Addison's heart turned over in her chest, and that's when she knew she was in trouble. She couldn't do this.

It was bad enough that she'd kissed him, but she was beginning to think she might be developing feelings for him. *Real* feelings, and that absolutely could not happen.

"I'm sorry I kissed you," she lied.

Carter flinched. If Addison had blinked, she might've missed it. "I'm not."

She shook her head. "Please don't say that. You *can't* say that."

"I just did."

Addison closed her eyes. She couldn't keep looking at him while she pretended the kiss hadn't meant anything. "Carter, please. It was a mistake, and we both know it."

"Do we?" His voice went soft—as soft and gentle as a feather bed. It was all Addison could do not to let herself sink right into it.

She opened her eyes and leveled her gaze at him, determined to make him see reason. Of course the kiss had been a mistake. They simply needed to agree to forget all about it, pretend it never happened and get back to business.

Addison could do that, couldn't she?

Before she could fully wrap her head around that idea or say another word to Carter, the door flew open, and Colette entered the office. She took her seat behind her desk and steepled her hands like she always did at the start of a pitch meeting.

"Now, then," Colette said, ready and waiting to be dazzled. "Let's move on."

Addison let Carter give his presentation first. As much as she hated the fact that he had his tech all ready to go and she was basically going to be flying by the seat of her pants, choosing to go last still seemed like the better option. She wanted her ideas to be fresh in Colette's head when the editor-in-chief made up her mind about the direction of the digital site for the rest of the month. Letting Carter get the final word seemed far too dangerous to contemplate.

But Addison hadn't anticipated just how nervous sitting through his pitch would make her feel. The second he flipped his tablet around and Colette's eyes lit up at the first slide of his presentation, Addison's heart sank all the way to her glittery Kate Spade mules. The heel of each shoe was a round acrylic snow globe with a tiny porcelain wedding cake inside. Addison had spotted them one day a while back at Bloomingdale's, and all the *Veil* girls immediately bought a pair. She'd worn them today thinking they might bring her good luck, and now here she was, about to give her pitch dressed in a gown from the fashion closet.

Even worse, she could barely concentrate. Carter could've been talking about dressing zoo animals up as brides for all she knew. All she could seem to think about was his reaction when she'd said they both knew good and well that their kiss had been a mistake.

Do we?

Those two little words had left her breathless. She felt like a bridal figurine that had wobbled off the top tier of a wedding cake and couldn't seem to find her way back to where she belonged.

She blinked hard and willed herself to focus.

"My concept for the December feature is inspired by *Vogue*'s use of celebrities in lieu of fashion models on the covers of their print magazines," Carter said as a collage of fashion magazine covers featuring well-known actresses flashed onto his screen. "*Vogue* was the first magazine to start using celebrities as cover models, and their readership numbers instantly skyrocketed."

Colette nodded thoughtfully as her gaze swept over the collage. Everything Carter was saying made sense, with one notable exception.

"That will never work for us. We feature brides on our covers. I'm not sure readers will buy into a famous celebrity in a wedding gown unless she's really engaged to be married," Addison said.

Colette immediately agreed. "I'm afraid Addison has a point."

Before Addison could celebrate that tiny victory, Carter continued, completely unfazed.

"I'm not suggesting mega-celebrities. My idea is simply inspired by that concept." He tapped the screen, and the next slide came into view.

This time, it was a moving image instead of a still picture. A ballerina twirled across a darkened stage, dressed in a long, romantic tutu with a gossamer veil draped over her head. She looked almost otherworldly— a bride floating between dimensions. A shiver coursed up and down Addison's spine as pale blue fog slowly enveloped the stage floor, swallowing the ballerina's pointed feet.

"Oh my, that's quite lovely," Colette said, leaning closer to the tablet. "Who is she?"

"Her name is Nina French, and she's a principal dancer for the Manhattan Ballet, right here in New York City," Carter said.

Colette leaned back in her chair. "Ah, I see. A *local* celebrity."

"Wait, I know her." Addison knew the dancer looked familiar. "She teaches at the barre fitness studio where I take class a few times a week."

"That's perfect. We already have an established relationship with her." Carter nodded as if the entire matter was settled, even though Addison had yet to present her idea. "Nina French has the starring role in *Giselle*, and as you can see, the ballet has strong bridal visuals. She's just famous enough to pique the interest of our readers without being too well-known. Her role in *Giselle* will match perfectly with a wedding gown pictorial. She can wear her pointe shoes and model five or six looks from our top advertisers."

"I like it," Colette said. Even her shiny bob seemed to have somehow gotten bouncier all of a sudden.

Addison wanted to disagree, but she couldn't do so in good conscience. Carter's idea was fresh, new and compelling. Addison hadn't seen a single other bridal magazine do anything like it, dang it.

"This is good, Carter," she said quietly.

She had to give credit where credit was due. They might be in direct competition with one another, but Addison had never been the type to try and undermine a colleague. As much as she wanted to beat Carter, she intended to do so fair and square.

"Since Nina and I have already met, I'd be happy to reach out to her on behalf of the magazine," Addison added.

Carter smoothed down his tie. "Thank you. I'd really appreciate that."

"*If* we decide to proceed with your feature concept, that is." Addison shot him her most saccharine smile. Surely he didn't think she was going to give up on the pitch meeting so easily.

Carter's smile widened. Of course he didn't think she was ready to pack up her ball gown and go. He knew her better than that—a fact that made Addison go all fluttery inside, despite her best efforts to the contrary.

"On that note—" Colette turned toward Addison "—I'm interested to hear what you have in mind for the digital site, Addison."

She took a deep breath. This was it—her chance to show both Carter and Colette that she had what it took to run this place. No one was better suited than she was to take over the helm of *Veil*.

"Would you like to use my tablet?" Carter pushed it toward her.

Addison paused for a moment. How civilized they'd suddenly become, after days of coffee cup wars and trying to beat one another to their respective desks. Anyone watching might have believed they were well-suited to share the top job.

No way. Addison lifted her chin. *Never going to happen.*

"Thank you, Carter." Her presentation was on the server. She could easily pull it up, but she wanted to do this one hundred percent on her own. "But I've got this."

Her concept was good—no, not good. It was perfect. She didn't need flashy visuals to make her point. The idea could stand on its own.

"For the mid-December digital feature, I propose we do a pictorial with an accompanying article called *How to Elope in New York City at Christmas.* Manhattan consistently ranks number one in the entire country for tourism during the holidays. Christmas in New York is iconic, and *Veil* has never done a story on holiday elopements before."

Colette was already sitting up straighter in her chair, signifying her interest. Addison had her boss right in the palm of her hand.

"We've got snow in the forecast next week, so it would be the perfect time for a bridal photo shoot at some of the city's most beloved Christmas locations. The pyramid of giant red ornaments on Sixth Avenue. The steps of the public library with the lions, Patience and Fortitude, dusted with snow and wearing their traditional wreaths around their necks. The Cartier flagship store on Fifth Avenue, wrapped in its spectacular red ribbon and tied with a bow."

Addison swallowed at that last one. The last time she'd taken in the sight of the Cartier store all dressed up for the holidays had been the night she'd first met Carter—the day her life had been turned upside down. Had that evening unknowingly been the inspiration behind her idea for the pictorial?

The prospect rattled her a bit, but she pressed on, describing each scene in vivid detail, along with an accompanying checklist for couples who wanted to tie the knot in the city's most dreamy holiday locations. Addison knew every single step by heart. Getting married in Manhattan was as easy as pie, which made her pitch all the more appealing. Anyone could elope in New York with little to no planning in advance. They just needed to get a license, find an officiant and a witness. Boom, done.

"How to Elope in New York City at Christmas." Colette nodded, eyes shifting toward the window overlooking the streets below. A yellow cab flew past with a Christmas tree tied to its roof, and her lips curved into a smile. "It's perfect."

Addison felt herself brighten, like a star atop a glittering holiday tree. But alas, her quiet celebration was short-lived.

"These are both excellent ideas. Kudos to you both. Let's get to work on this right away," Colette said, and then spun toward her computer as if the meeting had finished and everything was said and done.

Addison and Carter exchanged a glance.

"Excuse me, but—" the set of Carter's jaw tensed, as hard as a diamond "—get to work on what, precisely?"

Addison cut straight to the chase. "Which feature are we going with?"

"Both of them."

"Both of them?" Addison and Carter echoed simultaneously.

"Yes. As I said, you've each done excellent work. Carter's concept is new and splashy. Addison's will no doubt become an evergreen feature that will get clicks for years to come. You've presented me with the best of both worlds. There's really no reason to choose. If we work hard and hurry, the team can roll out both features well before Christmas." Colette's eyebrows arched until they all but vanished behind her thick layer of blunt-cut bangs. "Understood?"

Addison forced her lips into a smile and nodded. Beside her, Carter's posture stiffened, and frustration rolled off him in waves. Of course they understood. Their boss had just made things crystal clear. It was a draw. Neither one of them had won, and neither had lost.

In the latest cutthroat battle for the promotion to editor-in-chief, Addison and Carter had tied.

Again.

Chapter Eleven

Two days later, Addison was enjoying a rare moment of solitude at her desk in the office she shared with Carter when a cupcake slid into view beside the photo layout she was going over with a magnifying loupe.

A telltale candy daisy sat atop the cupcake's generous swirl of baby-pink frosting. Addison would've known that daisy anywhere. It was the signature cupcake topper of New York's famed Magnolia Bakery—also known as Daphne Ballantyne's favorite place on earth.

Sure enough, when Addison's gaze drifted upward, she found Daphne smiling down at her. Her pink-highlighted updo was extra glittery today. She must've spent some serious quality time with her hair bedazzler before work this morning.

"Hi, there." Addison put down the loupe and picked up the cupcake. It smelled divine, a heady combination of sugar and vanilla that made her mouth water. "What's this?"

"Just a little afternoon treat." Daphne dragged Carter's wheeled office chair out from behind his desk and sat down in it directly opposite Addison. "I thought you might need a pick-me-up, so I popped over to the bakery on my break."

Of course she had. There was probably a groove worn into the pavement between the *Veil* office and Magnolia Bakery.

Not that Addison was complaining about it.

"Thank you. This is a wonderful surprise." She peeled back the paper liner on the tiny cake and took a bite. The buttercream frosting melted in her mouth, and she sighed...until the full meaning of Daphne's words sank in. "Wait a minute. Why would I need a pick-me-up?"

And just like that, Everly suddenly appeared in the doorway holding a cardboard carrier containing three steaming coffee cups wrapped in pink decorative sleeves. "Good afternoon!"

Addison eyed the coffees. There was no way that Everly had just coincidentally made a midafternoon trip to the cute coffee truck around the corner at the exact same time Daphne decided a cupcake run was in order. Something was definitely up.

"Fancy meeting you here," Everly said to Daphne as she placed the coffee carrier on Addison's desk. She bent to unclip Holly Golightly's collar from her leash so the Cavalier could wiggle her way over to Sabrina's dog bed. The two pups greeted one another with wagging tails and then curled up together like matching commas. "Looks like we both had the same idea."

"Indeed we did," Daphne said, plucking a coffee cup from the tray and placing it in front of Addison beside what was left of her cupcake.

Cupcakes and sugary sweet lattes. The double whammy. Whatever had happened, it must have been big.

"You two are scaring me," Addison said as she took a cautious sip of her drink.

Everly propped herself against the edge of Carter's desk and aimed a questioning glance at Daphne. "She hasn't seen it yet?"

Daphne shook her head. "Apparently not."

The cupcake was beginning to feel like lead in the pit of Addison's stomach. "Someone needs to tell me what's going on."

Daphne motioned toward Everly with her coffee cup. "You do it. You're family."

"We're *all* family," Everly corrected. It was the truth— Daphne was like a sister to both of them. Addison didn't know what she'd do without her *Veil* girls.

Even if they were driving her the tiniest bit crazy right now.

"Please, you guys," she groaned.

"It's really not that serious." Everly waved a hand, as if the mysterious situation wasn't so dire as to require copious amounts of sugar and caffeine.

"No big deal at all," Daphne said, focusing intently on her coffee cup.

Addison was going to lose it. She might have to stifle a scream with a cupcake if they didn't get on with it and tell her what was going on.

"The proofs from Carter's ballerina shoot were uploaded to the server about thirty minutes ago," Everly finally said.

Daphne pulled a face. "They're kind of spectacular."

"Oh." Addison's heart began to gallop wildly in her chest. *Probably just the sugar*, she told herself. A bald-faced lie. "How spectacular?"

Everly winced. "Really, really spectacular."

Great. Addison had followed through with her promise and helped Carter snag the city's most well-known ballerina for his pet feature project, and somehow, that good deed was coming back to bite her in her backside.

She jabbed at her keyboard until the file containing the proofs popped up on her screen. Then she clicked and the first image alone took her breath away.

It was grainy and hadn't been properly lit or re-touched. A photo proof was the pictorial equivalent of a rough draft—just something to show the proposed layout and fashion details for Colette's final approval before proceeding with the rest of the shoot. Colette typically responded with a terse *yes* or *no* in the margins, along with her initials. She rarely posted any actual feedback, either positive or negative.

This time, however, she'd typed STUNNING in a digital post-it note pasted right on top of the first picture, followed by a smiley face emoji. Addison couldn't believe her eyes. Since when did Colette use *emojis*?

She tried to imagine an ongoing family text message exchange between Carter and his aunt, littered with little cartoon symbols. Hearts, smileys and yellow faces laughing until they cried. Impossible. Addison simply couldn't fathom it. Colette and Carter both seemed like the type to text with full punctuation, and she would've bet her entire salary that neither one of them even knew how to locate the emoji keyboards on their phones. But there it was—a smiley face—right there on the *Veil* server, mocking Addison until tears threatened to spill down her own, real-life face.

She slammed her laptop closed. "How is he *so good* at this job?"

"He's good at it, but he's not better than you are," Daphne said.

Everly nodded. "Agree. He's exceptional at art direction, but the man knows nothing about weddings. The other day, he walked into the beauty department, picked up a pearl-tipped bobby pin and said, 'what is this?' I think he thought it was a letter opener."

A *letter opener*?

Addison would've laughed out loud if she didn't already feel like crying.

"I appreciate your efforts at cheering me up, but I'm starting to seriously worry." Her bottom lip slipped between her teeth. She could barely bring herself to utter the unthinkable out loud, but the competition between Carter and her was approaching its fever pitch. "What if he wins?"

"He won't. He *can't*," Daphne said.

"Daphne's right. You've earned this." Everly reached to give Addison's hand a squeeze. "Now *you're* scaring *me*. I'm not sure I've ever seen your confidence this shaken before."

Addison didn't know what to say. How could she put into words the effect that Carter seemed to have on her? She wasn't sure of anything anymore—not professionally and not personally. Not after that kiss.

In truth, though, her confusion had started even before she'd thrown herself at Carter in the fashion closet. The more time she spent with him, the more fluttery and unsettled she became. Who *was* she?

Daphne studied Addison through the former beauty editor's thick layer of eyelash extensions. "Does the fact that we recently caught the two of you in a steamy lip-lock in the fashion closet have anything to do with the odd look on your face right now?"

Everly kicked Daphne's shin with the pointy toe of her prim ballerina flats. "We're not supposed to mention that, remember?"

Addison had waved off each and every one of their attempts to discuss The Kiss. Maybe she should talk about it, though. Pretending it had never happened clearly wasn't working.

"It's fine. We can talk about it," Addison said, swallowing an enormous gulp of her latte—liquid courage of the caffeinated variety.

"Finally." Daphne leaned forward in her chair. "How hot was it, exactly? On a scale of holiday-related heat… are we talking a single, scented tea-light candle or a full-size Christmas tree strung with twinkle lights?"

"Neither. It was actually more along the lines of that crazy house in *Christmas Vacation*," Addison said and then dropped her head in her hands.

Everything would have been so much easier if she simply hated Carter. Was finding him despicable really too much to ask? They were rivals, after all. Wasn't that supposed to be the natural order of things?

"I knew it!" Daphne did a little dance in her chair.

Everly nodded. "We had a feeling there was more

going on between you and Carter than you wanted to let on."

"There's nothing going on." Addison tightened her grip on her coffee cup. "Carter and I agreed that the kiss was a mistake."

Daphne gaped at her. "I don't understand. How can a kiss hot enough to cause a citywide power shortage be a mistake?"

"A *fictional* citywide power shortage," Addison corrected.

"You're avoiding the question, sis." Everly sighed, and her eyes filled with so much concern that Addison had to look away. "It's okay if you like him, you know. It's more than okay. I can't remember the last time you were seriously interested in someone."

"I'm not good at the relationship thing. I think that much has already been established," Addison said quietly.

"That's because you've never been with a man who was good enough for you. You deserve someone who's just as smart, ambitious and passionate as you are, Addie. And call me crazy, but Carter Payne fits that bill to a *T*."

Addison could hardly believe her ears. Since when had her sister defected to hashtag #TeamCronut? "You're forgetting one tiny detail—he's also out to steal my job."

"There are other jobs," Daphne said and held up her hands before Addison could argue. "I switched from beauty editor to an entire new position, and I couldn't be happier. I'm just saying that sometimes hopes and dreams change. The future might not be what you've always planned. It could be even better."

"Also, you're not bad at relationships. You're the best big sister a girl could ever want. You took care of me when Mom couldn't. You're my best friend, my family and my rock, all rolled into one. My babies couldn't ask for a better auntie and role model." Everly's eyes shimmered with unshed tears all of a sudden. She was going there—straight to the place where they always seemed to do their best not to go. The past. "So don't you dare say you aren't good at relationships. You have more love in your little finger than most people have in their entire bodies."

"She's right, you know," Daphne said. "You're always there for every single person in your life. Maybe it's time to think of yourself, for once. What do you really want, Addison?"

Addison opened her mouth to respond, but nothing came out. How was that possible? Her entire professional life had been mapped out since the day she started at *Veil*.

"Snow," she finally said, because it was the only thing that came to her—the one thing she was absolutely certain she needed. "I want it to snow. Tomorrow is the elopement photo shoot, and I need the entire city to look like a snow globe. It's the only way I'll be able to top Carter."

Everly looked at her long and hard. "That's it? *Snow?*"

Addison hated disappointing her little sister, but did Everly really think she was going to throw away her entire future based on one little kiss?

It's more than that, and you know it. Addison swallowed hard. A horrible lump had formed in her throat, and her eyes were beginning to burn. She just needed to stay the course until Christmas Eve. Come Christmas morning, this would all be over, and life would go back to normal. She'd probably never have to see Carter again for as long as she lived.

Addison blinked against the tears that were gathering behind her eyes. *There's no crying around wedding gowns*, she reminded herself. Never mind that there wasn't a Vera Wang in sight or that her *Veil* girls had already debunked that particular mantra.

"Snow. That's it. That's all I want," she said with enough conviction that she almost believed it. "Just please pray for snow."

Carter bowed his head against a fresh wave of snow flurries as he climbed the steps of New York's marriage bureau building the following morning. A *Veil* camera crew was already setting up shop near the gilded entrance, but Carter had it on good authority—namely, the minute-by-minute schedule that Addison had posted to the magazine's server—that the first photos of the day would be taken inside, where the models would pose as a couple applying for their marriage license. Once the faux paperwork was done, the shoot would move outdoors, just as it would with an actual wedding. After the requisite shot next to the bronze city clerk sign, the freelance crew *Veil* had hired would pack up and move from one Manhattan holiday landmark to another.

It was an ambitious project—far more intense than Carter's shoot the day before—and the day was sure to be made more challenging by the weather. The snow had come out of nowhere. The last time Carter checked, the forecast called for light flurries, which would've been perfect for the look Addison was going for. But Mother Nature had other ideas, apparently. The ground was already covered in a thick blanket of white, and the surprise snowfall showed no signs of stopping. It was as if someone had waved a magic wand over the city and transformed it into a winter wonderland overnight.

Carter held up a hand at the camera crew and then fought against the wind to push through a set of heavy, decorative doors. The city clerk's office was located in a historic building that looked straight out of an F. Scott Fitzgerald novel. Addison couldn't have conjured a more picturesque setting for an activity as mundane as filing for a marriage license. She'd struck gold today…

So long as the weather didn't spin completely out of control. Or Addison herself, which seemed like a real possibility as Carter rounded the corner at a sign pointing the way toward the marriage bureau counter.

"When do you think Delilah will be in? We had an appointment. I confirmed twice yesterday." Addison scrolled through her phone until she found the email she was looking for and then held it up to the man working the lone window at the counter that appeared to be open for business. "See?"

The man behind the counter—Joe, according to the nameplate at his station—held up his hands. "Ma'am, I'm sorry. I'm sure if Delilah were here, she would be happy to accommodate you, but as you can see, I'm the only one working the license desk today. Perhaps you haven't heard, but we're in the middle of a snowstorm."

Joe gestured toward the small window behind him

where flurries danced against the glass. Carter felt himself wince.

"Addison," he said in a low tone as he came to a stop just behind her, but she didn't appear to notice. She was on a mission, as per usual.

"Not a storm." She shook her head. "Just a light dusting. It's atmospheric. It's *lovely*."

"It's a hot mess is what it is," Joe corrected. "The subways are running on a modified schedule. Delilah lives in Queens. You do the math."

Carter cleared his throat and stepped up to the window, shoulder-to-shoulder with Addison. "Perhaps you can help us instead, Joe? *Veil* has a generous budget, and we'd be happy to compensate you for your trouble."

Addison gave a start and then looked at him askance. "What are you doing here?"

"I'm helping," Carter said and handed her a steaming cup of hot cocoa with extra marshmallows. He'd picked up two of them from a pop-up Christmas market on his walk from the office, intending to enjoy the other one himself. Instead, he placed the second cup on the counter and nudged it toward the frustrated clerk. "Right, Joe?"

Joe eyed the cocoa. He gave it a wary sniff, and his eyes lit up. "Is this from that place down the street with the red-and-white striped tents?"

"Sure is." Carter grinned. "And it's all yours."

Addison blinked. "What is even happening right now?"

"What's happening is that Joe here is going to make sure we get your pictures taken as quickly as we can so you can get the outdoor shots done before the models freeze to death." Carter raised his brows at Joe.

The clerk took a sip of cocoa and finally relented with a nod.

"See?" Carter gave Addison a gentle shoulder bump. "I told you I was helping. Problem solved."

Her lips twitched into a reluctant smile. "I could've handled it on my own, you know."

"I know, just like I could've probably secured Nina French for my feature spread. But you helped out because you wanted to, and now here I am to do the same." He leaned closer to whisper in her ear, and a lock of her dark hair brushed against his cheek, sending a shiver of longing coursing through him. "We talked about this, remember? About how doing it all yourself can get lonely sometimes…must we go through this dance every time, Cruella? Let me help you."

"Fine, but only because I helped you first." She stared longingly at her cup of cocoa and finally let herself take a sip. "My gosh, this is delicious."

He winked at her. "You're welcome."

Joe waved at them from behind the counter. "Yoo-hoo. I thought you were in a hurry to get this snowball rolling." He waggled his eyebrows. "*Snowball*… see what I did there?"

Carter snorted, and Addison elbowed him in the ribs.

"Indeed we do." She flashed Joe a smile. "Very cute, Joe. We're all set to start as soon as the models get here. It should be any minute now."

"The models aren't here yet?" Carter swiveled his gaze toward the corner of the room where a fashion assistant from the magazine stood next to a collapsible rolling rack full of bridal gowns and tuxedos. The assistant shrugged.

"No. They aren't scheduled to arrive until nine." Addison handed Carter her drink so she could dig around in her massive handbag for her tablet. She scrolled through her checklist, as if she hadn't committed every last item to memory. "It says right here. Nine a.m."

"Lady, it's nine fifteen," Joe said right before he tipped his head back to drain his cup of cocoa.

Panic flickered in Addison's gaze. "It is?"

Carter glanced at his watch. "Afraid so, but hey. Don't panic. If the subways are running a modified schedule, they're just running a little behind. They'll be here."

"Do you really think so?" she asked.

"Yes. If the models were going to be a no-show, you would've heard from their agency by now."

As if on cue, Addison's cell phone began to ring. She plucked it out of her oversized tote, took one look at the name of the caller and went as white as one of the fluffy designer bridal gowns hanging off to the side, ready and waiting to be photographed for her feature article.

She swallowed, took a deep breath and looked up at Carter with an expression that made his gut tie itself up in knots. "It's the modeling agency."

Chapter Twelve

Addison was going to need something a little stronger than hot cocoa—even if said hot cocoa was the best Christmas beverage she'd ever tasted.

"The models aren't coming," she heard herself say, but she still hadn't managed to wrap her head around the news.

How could this be happening? Today was one of the most important, if not *the* most important, days of her entire career and it was rapidly turning into a disaster.

"It's fine," Carter said with a conviction she wanted so desperately to believe. "We can figure this out. Everything's going to be okay."

Despite herself—and despite the fact that her fiasco of a feature article was beginning to feel like a snowball rolling downhill, growing bigger and more ominous by the second—Addison allowed herself to relax. Ever so slightly.

Carter's presence was a relief, which made no sense whatsoever. But Addison was too stressed to question it, so instead she let herself bask in the warm glow of his reassurance…even when everything was spiraling out of control.

He held out his arms, an invitation. Without hesitation, Addison stepped right into them. When he captured the paper cup from her hands, she grabbed onto the lapels of his coat and dropped her head against his chest and took a long, ragged inhale. She closed her eyes as she let herself melt into him. It felt so good to let go, to let someone else share her burden—not just anyone, but *him*. Carter Payne, who against all odds, seemed to understand her like no one else could. She was tired of fighting so hard to keep him at arm's length. So she gave in and let him comfort her. Just for a second…just long enough for her to breathe again.

"Why do you need models?" someone asked. It was Joe, who apparently grew more cooperative when gourmet hot chocolate was involved. "Can't you two do it? You're a couple, right?"

Addison's eyes flew open.

"Um," Carter said.

That single, awkward syllable was all it took for her to come to her senses.

"No," she blurted as she backed away from Carter and adjusted her headband. Today's was luxe white velvet, covered with pearls of various sizes. She'd snagged it from the fashion closet the day it had arrived from Lele Sadoughi. "We're work colleagues."

Carter's eyes went steely. He spoke to Joe but kept his gaze fixed with Addison's. "Definitely not a couple."

"Could've fooled me." Joe snorted. "You look just like every other couple who comes in here all lovey-dovey, ready to apply for their marriage license."

Addison didn't think the current situation could get much worse, but that did it. The words hit her like an arrow, straight to her heart.

"He has a point, you know," Carter said, and a muscle in his jaw ticked.

Addison's face went warm. If a snowflake had landed on her cheek, it would've sizzled. "What are you trying to say, Carter?"

Were they really going to do this here? After weeks of pretending they weren't developing feelings for each other, had Carter just decided to bare his soul in the Manhattan marriage bureau?

Addison didn't know whether to panic or swoon.

"I'm saying we could step in for the models. I've seen you in a sample wedding gown, and you looked better than anyone on the magazine's pages," Carter said.

Addison should've been flattered, but disappointment crystalized inside her like ice. He was throwing her a lifeline, but judging by the way she suddenly couldn't seem to speak, it wasn't the one she wanted most of all.

Daphne's voice invaded her thoughts, dragging her back to their conversation yesterday in her office. *What do you really want, Addison?*

For the first time in her entire adult life, she was at a loss. She hadn't planned for any of this.

"Joe seems to think we can fake being in love as well as two hired strangers from a modeling agency." Carter slid her a guarded look. "What do you think?"

I think this is the worst idea anyone has ever had.

I think I never should've asked the Veil *girls to pray for snow.*

Most of all, I think pretending to be your bride might just kill me.

She gave him a tight smile and squared her shoulders, channeling her inner Colette Winter, editor-in-chief. "I think we don't have much of a choice."

Addison changed clothes in the cramped two-stall bathroom of the city clerk's office, wondering all the while how many genuine brides had done the same. Loads of them, probably. Couples came to this building every single day to apply for marriage licenses, and if they chose to do so, all they had to do was head farther down the hall to exchange vows.

It's just a building, she told herself as the wardrobe assistant fastened the row of tiny satin-covered buttons that ran the length of her spine. *And this is just a photo shoot.*

She wasn't sure why stepping into the lace-covered gown had made her instantly feel like an imposter. During her tenure at the magazine, Addison had tried on too many wedding dresses to count. She and the *Veil* girls did it all the time, purely for fun. They had access to the most exquisite couture gowns on the market, the fashion closet was their home away from home, and playing dress-up as an adult was a seriously underrated activity.

But this felt different. She wasn't about to prance in front of the full-length mirror in the fashion closet and twirl in front of her girlfriends. She was about to step out of this bathroom, place her hand in Carter's and apply for a marriage license. And every single second that followed—every stolen glance, every rebellious beat of her heart, every brush of Carter's lips against hers—would be captured on film.

The camera doesn't lie. Wasn't that what people always said? How could she go through with this, knowing the entire world would see right through her? Colette. Everly and Daphne. The entire *Veil* staff.

Carter.

Her throat went dry. He'd know. He'd see the way she looked at him in the pictures, and he'd know that he meant more to her than an annoying obstacle she was dead set on eliminating. Somewhere along the way, he'd become important to her, and now, for the very first time, putting on a wedding dress didn't feel like playing dress-up. It felt meaningful. It felt sacred. It felt exactly like slipping on a bridal gown was supposed to feel.

"You're ready," the wardrobe assistant, Chloe, said.

Addison blinked. She'd never be ready for this, but she didn't have much of a choice. It was either play bride and groom with Carter in front of the cameras or concede and let him walk away with her promotion.

"Thank you for your help." She offered the assistant a shaky smile. "How do I look?"

"Honestly? Like a million bucks." Chloe gave Addison a final once-over and reached out to smooth the voluminous layers of the gown's tulle princess skirt. "Too good to waste on a fake marriage license at the city clerk's office."

Addison felt sick. "Thanks...I think."

"Come on." Chloe held the bathroom door open to make way for the dress. "We're already behind the jam-packed schedule you created, and it's really coming down out there. I know we need the marriage bureau photo because it's the first step in the elopement process, but the real magic is going to be the outdoor shots."

Chloe was right. Addison didn't have time to indulge in an existential crisis, so she gathered the puffy layers of the dress's skirt in her hands and made her way back to the hallway. Chloe trailed behind her, juggling a lint brush and emergency sewing kit in one hand and a makeup bag in the other. They hadn't had time for hairstyling, so Addison had just left her fancy headband in place. The outdoor shots would be the perfect opportunity to show a bridal veil floating on the icy breeze, but for now, they just needed to get one useful photograph.

When they rounded the corner and the marriage bureau counter came into view, Addison spied Carter already dressed in a tuxedo. Ready and waiting. He had his back toward her, but she could tell from the tense set of his shoulders that he wasn't any happier than she was about the current situation. There'd been an edge to Carter ever since Addison had corrected Joe's assumption that they were like all the other "lovey-dovey" couples that came here looking for a marriage license.

Fine. Let him be annoyed. Addison could use a little breathing room.

But then Carter turned around, and the instant he set eyes on her, his expression changed. His blue eyes glittered—not with irritation this time, but with something different...something that made Addison go weak in the knees. He looked like every gobsmacked groom in the video compilation she'd put together for the *Veil* site last year that showed men getting emotional as they watched their brides walking down the aisle.

Breathe, she told herself. *This is all just make-believe.* But then Carter clutched his chest and gave her a smile so soft around the edges that she wasn't quite sure what was real and what was pretend anymore. And a tiny part of her—the brave, carefree part that almost moved to Paris once upon a time—no longer cared. She just wanted to hold on to the moment, to stop time and make the snowflakes whirl toward the ground in slow motion so she could remember that look on Carter's face...*for as long as we both shall live.*

She came to a stop just a whisper away from him— so close that she could see the way his eyes darkened as his gaze swept over her, could hear the slight catch in his throat. She felt her lips part, and all the things she hadn't allowed herself to say to him were right there on the tip of her tongue...

Until a flash of light exploded nearby, startling them both back to reality. Addison swayed on her feet.

"That was it. That's the shot," the photographer said. "We got it already."

"I—um. Wait, no." Addison gave her head a firm shake. She was supposed to be directing this photo shoot, for crying out loud. "We need a photo of the bride and groom filling out the wedding license paperwork."

The photographer shrugged. "Whatever you say. You're the boss, and you've got me booked for the entire day. But trust me—we're never going to top that first picture."

"The shoot is supposed to tell a story," she said, repeating her words from the pitch she'd given Colette.

Thank goodness she'd practiced it so often, because concentrating in this heady atmosphere was next to impossible.

"Go ahead, then." The photographer aimed his camera at Joe's workstation.

Carter reached for her hand and wove his fingers through hers as she walked toward the counter in a daze. He took his place beside her, and Addison felt like she was in a fever dream. The photo crew seemed to fade into the background, and she was barely aware of the pen in her hand or the scratch of ink against paper as she completed the paperwork. The sound of the camera's shutter barely registered in her consciousness, but she was hyperaware of the weave of the fabric of Carter's tuxedo and the way his silver cuff links twinkled beneath the photographer's mono-lights. He signed the bottom of his form with a flourish, and when at last she glanced up to meet his gaze, he winked at her. It was so quick that even the camera missed it—just a private message for her and her alone. She held it close, like a secret penny tucked into a bride's left shoe on her wedding day.

"Work colleagues," Joe said from behind the counter. He blew out his cheeks and huffed. "Yeah, right."

It's only a dress.

Carter's inner thoughts were beginning to sound like a broken record.

He'd first tried out the phrase back at the city clerk's office when his eyes had nearly fallen out of his head at the sight of Addison in the high-necked lace princess gown she wore while they pretended to secure a marriage license. Then he'd repeated it once they'd moved to the public library to take photos with the marble lions that flanked either side of the steps leading up to the grand building. Patience and Fortitude had already been covered in a thick blanket of snow, with the balsam fir Christmas wreaths around their thick stone necks only halfway visible. It made for a striking visual. The photos were sure to be some of the most memorable in *Veil* history. But then Addison had walked toward him from one of the building's three arched entrances, and all at once, the lions, the wreaths, the snow vanished from his periphery. He only had eyes for her.

It's only a dress, he'd repeated as he took in the sight of Addison's form draped in an airy chiffon gown paired with a white fur stole draped over her shoulders and tied with a smooth satin ribbon. Addison's bare, porcelain arms had been covered in goose bumps as they had their picture taken, walking hand in hand up those iconic steps. But Carter's veins flowed with a heat that warmed him from the inside out.

And so the day went—from one snow-covered Manhattan landmark to the next, and each location, Addison changed into a different gown.

It's only a dress, Carter repeated to himself each and every time, but who was he kidding? It wasn't the dress.

It was *never* the dress. It wasn't even what the dress symbolized…not really. It was Addison. Seeing her dressed as a bride—*his* bride—had shaken him to his core, over and over again at five different shooting locations. Somehow, it never got any easier.

He thought he'd been prepared after stumbling upon her in a ball gown in the fashion closet when he'd gone looking for her before their pitch. How foolish he'd been. That little incident had led to a kiss. How could it have possibly prepared him for remaining anything close to levelheaded while pretending to be her groom?

Now, here they were, at the final location on the shot list. Carter just needed to get through one more picture, and then he could go back to his hotel and bask in his bachelorhood. Unfortunately, this last shot involved more than just posing together in wedding clothes. For the final photo, Addison had booked a model to pose as a wedding officiant to appear in the picture with them while they took their "vows."

To make matters worse, they were shooting the photo on the snowy street corner where the Cartier flagship store was located, wrapped like a Christmas gift in its famed red ribbon made of lights and tied with a spectacular bow—the exact spot where Carter and Addison had attended the party on the night they'd first met.

Carter glanced up at the store's flashy red awnings and the big crimson bow as he suppressed a shiver. The weather had gone from bad to worse, and Manhattan was like a snow-covered ghost town. The city looked as if someone had upended a sugar bowl over it. Everything sparkled, and the empty streets and closed stores only added to the intimacy of their surroundings. If this had been a real wedding, it would've been just what Carter would've wanted. None of the usual stress that usually accompanied a big, splashy ceremony and so often made brides and grooms forget the real purpose of the occasion. Just two people focused entirely on their union and their promises to love, honor and cherish one another…

Until death do us part. Carter exhaled a frosty breath. *Or until one of us gets promoted, whichever comes first.*

"Bride incoming," the photographer called as a lone taxi crawled its way down a snowy and barren Sixth Avenue. "Let's get this last shot done so we can wrap this up. We'll be lucky if we can all get home tonight."

Home. Where was that, again? Carter still hadn't called a broker or even begun to look for an apartment in New York. He was living out of a suitcase at the Carlyle until the job situation was resolved, and for reasons he didn't want to contemplate, he was continuing to dodge calls and emails from his former boss at *L'homme.* For the entire month, he'd had one foot in New York and the other in Paris. Home was beginning to feel like a foreign concept.

The taxi came to a stop, and Carter opened the back door to help Addison out of the car. She'd changed into yet another bridal white gown at the lone open coffee shop on the block, and this time, her ensemble seemed all the more realistic with the addition of a bouquet. His chest squeezed tight as he took hold of her hand.

"Ready to get married?" she asked after he'd lifted her to her feet. Her cheeky grin told Carter she'd meant it as a joke, but when their eyes met, the smile wobbled off of her face.

He gave her a hand a squeeze. "I'm ready if you are."

She nodded and took a deep breath. It felt too real—all of it. And while the pictures were no doubt going to be a huge success, this entire day was seriously messing with Carter's head. Addison's too, judging by the way she suddenly seemed to be doing her best to avoid looking him directly in the eyes.

"I'm surprised your model showed up for this last shot," Carter said as the photographer consulted with an elderly man dressed in a black suit and a white clergyman's collar.

"He didn't. This guy isn't a model. He's the real deal," Addison said.

Carter smoothed down the lapels of his tux as they took their positions. "Where on earth did you find a minister willing to fake-marry us in the middle of a snowstorm?"

"Joe from the marriage bureau found him for us. That hot cocoa you gave him worked some serious magic. I owe you one." Addison tucked a lock of her dark hair behind her ear. The frigid wind was wreaking havoc with her updo, but she'd never looked lovelier. Wisps of hair whipped around her head in a furious halo. "I owe you big time, in fact. Thank you, Carter. I don't know what I would've done without you today."

"It was nothing. I'm sure if I hadn't been here, you could've found some other lucky guy to marry you," he said with a shrug.

"Somehow I doubt that." She rose up on tiptoe and pressed a kiss to his face, lips warm against his cold cheek. "Seriously, thank you."

"Anything for my bride," he said, rubbing his hands against her bare shoulders. She had to be freezing in her strapless satin gown. "Now let's get hitched before we both catch pneumonia. If we die out here in the cold, neither one of us gets that promotion."

Addison smiled up at him, eyelashes tipped with snow. "In sickness or in health, that job is mine."

Heat curled down Carter's spine, despite the chill in the air. *Let it snow,* he thought. *Let it snow, let it snow, let it snow.*

"In your dreams, wifey."

Chapter Thirteen

Addison was frozen to the bone by the time the photo shoot was over. All she wanted to do was get home and soak in a scalding hot bubble bath for an hour. Maybe a week. Possibly a year.

But as the taxi driver they'd used for the shoot was so insistent on telling her, getting anywhere outside of a five-block radius was a pipe dream.

"You seriously can't take me home?" She leaned into the open driver's side window of the cab, teeth chattering. "I don't live too far from here, and the trains stopped running hours ago."

"Unless it's a straight shot and I don't have to pass more than four intersections to get there, it's too far." The driver waved his arm, encompassing the snow-covered streets and sidewalks. "Look around, lady. We're in white-out conditions."

"Addison, where's your coat?" Carter stomped toward

her, shrugging out of his wool overcoat as the snow on the ground swallowed his footsteps.

"I sent the wardrobe girls home hours ago, and I think they accidentally took it. All I've got are the clothes I wore to the office this morning." She held up her Louis Vuitton, stuffed to overflowing with garments, her tablet and the Polaroids the photographer had taken as test shots all day. "And now I can't seem to get a ride home."

Carter draped his coat over her bare shoulders just as a gust of wind whipped the chiffon skirt of the wedding gown she was wearing into a fabric tornado. She nearly went airborne, like a giant, bridal snowflake.

He opened the door to the taxi's back seat and practically growled, "Get in."

She shook her head. "I can't. The driver said he won't go farther than just a few blocks."

He arched a brow. "Addison, either get in, or I'm going to pick you up and put you in the back of this cab myself. I'm staying at the Carlyle, and it's just down the street. You're coming with me. We'll get you a room, and then we can both defrost."

It wasn't a bad idea. Not that Addison had much of a choice in the matter.

"Fine, but only because a luxury hotel room sounds lovely at the moment, and not because you've suddenly gone all growly and alpha male on me." She did her best to cram her dress into the car and slide onto the back seat.

"Duly noted." Carter sat down beside her and batted a puff of tulle away from his face.

The ride to the hotel took five times as long as it would've on an ordinary day. The cab's back end fishtailed more than once, and Addison was suddenly grateful the cabbie had refused to take her home. She'd been so focused on the elopement feature and making sure they had a variety of usable images that she hadn't realized quite how bad the storm had gotten.

She burrowed into the warmth of Carter's coat. It smelled like all the familiar scents she'd come to associate with him—dark espresso beans, winter pine and the French lavender she loved so much.

She turned toward him, biting back a smile. "Did we just do a wedding photo shoot in an actual blizzard?"

The corner of his mouth hitched into a half grin. "We sure did."

"Who even does something that crazy?"

He reached over to brush a strand of her windswept hair from her eyes. "The most relentless, stubborn…"

"Hey. Watch it, Cronut." She gave him a playful jab to the ribs.

"Ouch. I wasn't finished." His gaze turned tender. "The most relentless, stubborn and beautiful…"

A shiver coursed through her that had nothing to do with the cold.

"…editor-in-chief in *Veil* history," he concluded with a tap to her nose.

Addison gasped. "Are you bowing out? Was that your concession speech?"

"Not on your life. It was just a prediction. You can wipe that ridiculous grin off of your face." He rolled his eyes, but before he swiveled his head toward the window, Addison was certain she spied a ghost of a smile on his lips.

She grinned to herself for the entire rest of the cab ride.

Her happy mood took a serious hit, however, once she and Carter stood face-to-face with the front desk manager at the Carlyle.

"I'm sorry. What did you just say?" Addison wrapped Carter's coat tighter around herself. People in the lobby were already beginning to stare and ooh and aah as if she and Carter were real newlyweds.

For once, being mistaken as Carter's bride was the least of her worries.

"We're fully booked." The manager peered at his computer screen. "I apologize for the inconvenience, but I'm not seeing any availabilities at all. We've been inundated with people stuck in the city due to the snowstorm."

For the millionth time that day, Addison cursed herself for telling the *Veil* girls to pray for snow.

"Addison, it's okay. Let it go," Carter murmured.

She laughed, despite the fact that she was officially stranded. "Was that an intentional *Frozen* reference, or was it purely accidental?"

"Accidental." He smirked. "It was on point though, wasn't it?"

"As much as I'm enjoying this little exchange, how can I let it go? Where am I supposed to sleep tonight—here in the lobby?" She waved a hand toward the Carlyle's glittering foyer and stifled a yawn. Now that the most challenging photo shoot of her career was over, she was beginning to realize how exhausted she was.

"Oh no, ma'am. I'm afraid I can't let you do that," the front desk manager said.

"It was just a joke." *Sort of.* Addison drummed her fingernails on the smooth marble reception desk. "Are you sure there's no availability at all? Not even a tiny twin bed tucked away in the attic or something?"

"I'm afraid not." The manager brightened. "But the good news is that our honeymoon suite is free tomorrow night! Shall I put you down for our Wedded Bliss Package? It includes breakfast in bed."

"Okay, let's go." Carter took Addison by the hand and dragged her away from the desk before she had a full-on meltdown.

It took a second for her to realize they were headed toward the elevators. "Where are we going?"

"To my room. You're staying with me tonight. No arguments." He jabbed the *up* button with his free hand and tightened his grip on Addison with the other, as if he expected her to turn runaway bride on him.

The elevator doors swished open, and they stepped inside.

Carter met her gaze in one of the lift's mirrored walls. His eyes were as fierce a blue as she'd ever seen them. "Was that too growly and alpha male for you?"

His gaze seared into her.

Warm at last.

"On the contrary." She drew in a long breath and told herself the impromptu arrangement was purely for convenience's sake. This was a bona fide emergency. "It was perfect."

An hour later, Carter and Addison sat on opposite sides of his king bed, clad in plush, white hotel robes with their legs stretched out in front of them.

When they'd first stepped inside his room, the air had felt supercharged with electricity. They'd lingered for a few, awkward seconds, hand in hand, gazing at one another as if they didn't already spend nearly every waking hour together. Then Carter had muttered something about ordering room service, because if he hadn't come up with a purpose to occupy his racing thoughts, he would've acted on every forbidden impulse that had raised its naughty head when Addison had given him that look in the elevator.

It was perfect.

Her words danced in his head as he reached for another French fry. The energy between them had turned flirtatious the moment they were alone together. It was becoming a habit, and damned if Carter could remember why flirting with Addison England was a bad idea.

She'd disappeared into the bathroom while he'd ordered the food and emerged wearing the robe, warm and relaxed from a bath. Then she'd taken one look at the bed and burst out laughing. Nearly every square inch of the luxe bedding was covered with silver serving trays.

"Is there anything on the room service menu that you *didn't* order?" she'd asked.

Carter had simply shrugged and said he wasn't sure what she'd wanted. It was the truth, as was the fact that he'd unconsciously managed to build a wall of food to separate them while they watched television together.

"The pizza is delicious," Addison said, holding her hand out for the remote control. "But this reality show has got to go. Isn't there a Christmas movie or something on?"

He surrendered the remote. "Feel free to scroll through all ten thousand channels. I'll be over here on my side of the bed eating my body weight in junk food."

"Sure you will. I've seen you in those European-cut suits of yours. Something tells me you don't indulge in junk food on the regular." She aimed the remote control at the television and began flipping from one channel to the next.

"Careful there. Ogling me at the office is grounds for an HR report."

Addison gave him a sideways glance. "As if HR wouldn't have a field day with what's going on right here, right now."

"Tonight is completely innocent," Carter countered. "This bed is a no hanky-panky zone."

"Hanky-panky? What century did you borrow that phrase from?" Addison laughed, and when an old black-and-white movie flashed onto the television screen, she gasped with delight as if she hadn't just mocked his use of retro vocabulary. "Carter, look! It's *Sabrina*!"

He loved seeing her like this—casual and carefree. Dare he think it? Relaxed. "*Sabrina*, as in your dog of the same name?"

"Yes," she said, and then she caught herself. "I mean, no. She's not my dog. Is it crazy that I miss her, though? Everly kept her for me today since I was going to be so busy with the photo shoot."

"Admit it. You're keeping that little monster."

"Only until Christmas." She pointed a sliver of pizza crust at him for added emphasis.

He stole the crust out of her hand and took a bite out of it. "Tell me something, Cruella. What happens *after* Christmas?"

Her forehead scrunched. "What do you mean? With the dog. Or…"

With us?

Neither of them wanted to say it, but they were both thinking it. The question had been nagging at Carter for a while now. Surely it had crossed Addison's mind a time or two.

If it had, she pretended otherwise and aimed her attention back toward the television. "*Sabrina* is my favorite movie of all time. Have you ever seen it?"

Carter followed her gaze to the screen, where a waiflike Audrey Hepburn was perched in a tree, spying on an elegant house party that spilled out onto the lawn of an opulent mansion. "Not that I can remember."

"Oh, we have to watch it, then. It's so dreamy. When Everly and I were little girls, our mom used to watch Audrey Hepburn movies with us all the time. *Breakfast at Tiffany's* was always Everly's favorite, but mine was *Sabrina*. Audrey plays the chauffeur's daughter, and she's in love with one of the Larrabee brothers who live at the main house. He thinks she's just a silly kid until she goes off to Paris and comes back transformed into a graceful, worldly woman."

"Have you ever been?" Carter asked, thinking about her fondness for macarons, the French music she loved so much and all the other telltale signs in their office that there was a Francophile in residence.

"To Paris? No, I haven't. I was supposed to move there right after college graduation, but then…" Her voice drifted off.

"You lost your dad," Carter said. So much about Addison was starting to make more sense now.

"Yes, so obviously my plans changed. My family needed me, and it wouldn't have felt right moving so far away. I still keep up with my French, though. Just in case." She turned soft eyes on him. "Tell me about it. Is Paris as magical as it seems?"

"In a lot of ways, yes. I think you'd love it. You should go." *We should go...together.*

Addison's face flushed, as if she could read his mind with perfect clarity. "If the editor-in-chief job doesn't work out for you, do you think you'll move back?"

"I'm afraid that ship might've sailed. My former editor at *L'homme* already offered me my old job back, and I turned him down. They're not going to keep the position open forever." Carter purposefully averted his eyes, but it was too late. Addison was already onto him.

She narrowed her gaze at him. "Are you telling me that email you got from *L'homme* during the staff meeting on your first day at *Veil* was a job offer?"

"Maybe." He looked up at her. "Okay, yes. It was."

"I don't get it. You were obsessively checking your phone during that meeting. Why didn't you say yes?"

He let out a laugh. How was he supposed to answer that question? Did she want the truth, or an answer that would be easier to swallow?

"And miss out on all the fun we've been having these past few weeks?" he said, aiming for light and breezy. But the truth had a way of shining through. Didn't it always?

"Carter." Addison audibly swallowed. "Did you turn the job down because...of me?"

Maybe it was the fact that they were miles away from the office and the pressures of *Veil*. Maybe it was the way the hair at the nape of Addison's neck was still damp and curly from her bath, and Carter had wanted to twirl a lock of it around his finger all damn night. Or maybe it was because he still couldn't shake the feeling of standing beside her in front of a preacher earlier.

Whatever the reason, Carter decided it was time to tell Addison the truth. "You captivated me. You still do, Cruella. How could I leave when we'd barely gotten started?"

Her breath caught in her throat, and those big, brown eyes of hers looked at him as if she was seeing him for the very first time. Then she asked him a question that seemed like it came out of the blue. "Do you want to hear my favorite line from *Sabrina*?"

He nodded. "Very much."

He wanted to know everything about her—each and every one of her secret dreams and her deepest desires.

"Sabrina's father is worried she's going to get her heart broken, and he tells her that no matter how much she changed in Paris, nothing about her circumstances has changed. She's still the chauffeur's daughter, and she's still reaching for the moon. And Sabrina says the most perfect thing I've ever heard."

Carter angled his head closer to her—close enough to inhale her clean soap and strawberry scent. Not touching her was becoming almost impossible. "What does she say?"

"She says, 'No, Father. The moon is reaching for me.'" Addison shoved aside the empty plate that sat between them and crawled into his lap. Her face leaned toward his, and at first, Carter thought she was going to kiss him again like she'd done in the fashion closet, but instead, her lips brushed against his jaw, and she whispered, "Be my moon, Carter. Just this once."

He gave the tie of her robe a gentle tug and slipped his hands inside, reveling at the softness of her skin against his fingertips. "Are you sure about this? I need you to be sure."

She nodded. "I'm sure. Maybe we just need a few ground rules, though."

Of course she wanted rules. It was classic Addison, and that was fine with Carter. In that moment, she could've pulled out a fifteen-page contract, and he would've signed it with his own blood without reading a word of it if it meant she wanted to spend the night in his bed.

"This is just a time-out. Once the snowstorm is over, we'll never speak of it again," she said. "Deal?"

It was the most absurd thing Carter had ever heard, but if that's what it took to make her feel safe, he was all in.

He nodded. "Deal."

Then, there were no more words as lacy snowflakes continued to fall on a sleepy Manhattan. There was only touching and discovering and loving…as time stood still. Just for a night.

Chapter Fourteen

Fashion closet. ASAP!

Addison went straight from Carter's hotel room to the *Veil* office the following morning, all the while thanking her lucky stars that she worked at a magazine with its own beauty and fashion departments. Using the stockpile of cosmetics samples that advertisers were constantly sending over, and the fancy, Hollywood-style makeup mirror in the fashion closet, she managed to make herself look presentable enough to hide the fact that she'd spent the night snowed in with her office nemesis.

Was he still her nemesis?

Addison wasn't sure anymore. She wasn't sure of anything. She and Carter had agreed that their arrangement had been for one night only, but beyond that... nothing.

This is why people who are up for the same promo-

tion shouldn't sleep together, she told herself as she twisted her hair into a messy chignon—emphasis on *messy*. But even as the memory of Carter's lips against her collarbone and his hands moving tenderly over her most secret places sent a shiver down her spine, she knew that spending the night in his bed was the least of her problems. She hadn't just given her body to him for a night. She'd let him inside her heart, and it was a lot harder to set time restrictions on feelings than it was on certain physical activities.

You can't love him. She jammed a pearl-tipped bobby pin into her updo. Somehow, it did absolutely nothing to lessen the messiness. *You absolutely cannot.*

She froze in front of the mirror as her reflection stared back at her, wide-eyed.

Who said anything about love?

"Addison?" Everly pushed through the door, accompanied by Holly and Sabrina prancing at the ends of their matching Tiffany blue leather leashes. They were dressed in tiny canine puffer coats—also Tiffany blue—because of course they were. "How did you get here so fast? The weather has really cleared up, but the roads and sidewalks are still a mess. I think most everyone is going to be late today."

Daphne burst into the closet right on Everly's heels. "I'm here! What's the emergency?"

The postal service truly had nothing on the *Veil* crew. Neither snow, nor rain, nor heat, nor gloom of night would prevent them from responding to an urgent fashion closet text.

"I'm so glad you're both here, you have no idea." Addison held her arms out and Sabrina made a beeline straight toward her. She gathered the dog into her lap and smoothed down her copper-colored ears, tipped with little bits of snow and ice. "You too, Sabrina. Let's get you out of this coat, and I'll give you a proper brushing."

Daphne's eyes shone with amusement as she watched their exchange. "You're totally adopting that dog, aren't you?"

Why did everyone keep saying that?

"We're not here to talk about my foster dog. Something happened yesterday," Addison said in what might be the understatement to end all understatements. "Actually, a lot happened yesterday. I'm not even sure where to start."

Everly and Daphne both shed their coats and plopped down on the silk damask ottoman, already hanging on her every word.

"Just start at the beginning," Everly said.

"Whatever it is, we'll help you deal with it." Daphne nodded. "Unless this involves the new software system, because I still haven't gotten a full handle on that yet."

Of course she thought Addison's problem was work-related. Wasn't it always? Maybe Daphne and Everly were right. Maybe she really did need to expand her horizons beyond *Veil*. Then again, she'd done exactly that last night, and now she couldn't even think straight. Personal lives were vastly overrated.

"Well, I guess it all started when Carter showed up to help at my elopement photo shoot yesterday," Addison said. So far, so good.

"That was awfully nice of him," Daphne said.

Everly pressed a hand to her heart. "I like him, Addie.

I know you don't want to hear that, but I do. And I'm beyond certain that *he* likes *you*."

She truly had no idea.

"What happened next? Anything exciting?" Daphne gave a little shrug.

Addison just needed to spit it out, didn't she? "I guess you could say that. First, the models for the shoot didn't show up, so Carter and I had to pose for the pictures ourselves. We basically spent the entire day playing bride and groom."

"Okay, wow." Everly's jaw dropped, and it took her a second to close it back up again. "That is definitely a lot. I can see why you wanted to talk this out."

Addison swallowed. "There's more."

Daphne crept so close to the edge of the ottoman that she almost teetered off of it. "How much more?"

"By the time the shoot was finished, the entire city was shut down. I couldn't get home, and Carter is still staying at the Carlyle, which was just down the street. But they were completely booked because of the storm, so I had to spend the night in Carter's room. We watched *Sabrina*, and he told me that after he first got here, his former boss offered him his old job back in Paris, but he turned it down…because of me." Addison let out a breath. She'd been talking so fast that her tongue was tripping over itself. "And then I'm pretty sure you can guess what happened next."

Everly squealed so loud that Holly and Sabrina both sat up and cocked their heads.

Daphne's face split into a wide grin. "You are truly an overachiever of the highest order. We told you to get a life beyond work, and you went all in."

Addison couldn't believe her ears. They actually thought last night had been a *good* thing. It was hands-down the worst decision she'd ever made, and that included the ill-advised Jennifer Aniston *Friends* haircut she'd gotten in junior high school.

"This is not a laughing matter. It's a disaster," she said, even though nothing about last night had felt remotely disastrous at the time. On the contrary, it had been sort of perfect. So perfect that Addison almost wanted to ask her *Veil* girls to pray for snow again. This wasn't a Christmas movie, though. No amount of wishing or praying or hoping could turn back the clock. "It's also over."

Everly shook her head. "How can it possibly be over already?"

"Because it never really started to begin with. Whatever happened between Carter and me wasn't even real. It was just a bit of Christmas magic, like being trapped in a snow globe." Addison did her best to put on a brave face, but even Sabrina looked unconvinced.

Why did this conversation have to take place when they were surrounded by a plethora of wedding gowns? Somehow, that made it so much worse.

Addison stood, turned her back on the closest rack of bridal wear and began sifting through a selection of midi-length cocktail dresses. "I need to find something to wear to work today. I can't go back out there in the same pencil skirt and headband I wore yesterday morning before I left for the shoot."

"So that's it? You and Carter are just going to pretend that last night never happened and go back to business as usual?" Daphne plucked a carnation-pink silk dress with pleated detailing off the rack and shoved it toward Addison.

It was a lovely dress, and Kate Middleton had worn one just like it a few weeks ago, but the prospect of wearing it failed to lift Addison's mood one iota. Goodness, she really had it bad, didn't she? "That's the plan. I'm going to focus on work and try to go back to pretending he doesn't exist."

"That's going to be awfully hard, given what day it is," Everly said.

Addison's hands shook as she slipped the dress over her head and worked to fasten the long row of fabric-covered buttons down the front. "What are you talking about? It's the third Wednesday of the month. There are no meetings on my schedule at all."

"You're forgetting that life doesn't end at the close of business." Daphne handed her a pair of silver stilettos to pair with her borrowed work outfit. "The Fashion Media Awards are tonight. Everly and Henry are bringing the twins over to the penthouse beforehand. My dad and Jack's mom have graciously agreed to babysit Olivia and the babies. Feel free to bring Sabrina over too. The more, the merrier."

Addison's heart sank as she stepped into the shoes. "That's tonight?"

No, please no. Anything but that. She was happy for Daphne and Jack. They had a great chance at winning the top prize for their undercover series. She just needed a day to collect herself first…or possibly hibernate like a polar bear.

Wait, polar bears didn't hibernate, did they? They just partied it up in the snow without a care in the world, much like Addison had done, and now she was about to pay the price.

"It's tonight, all right." Everly's eyes sparkled. "And don't forget—Carter is your date."

"I'm really sorry about this," Addison said as Carter placed his hand on the small of her back and led her into the Rainbow Room later that evening.

"I know. You said that already in the cab on the way over here." He gave her a tight smile, and she got the impression that he wasn't any happier than she was to be on a date together this evening. "A couple of times, actually."

"I'd forgotten about tonight, and the timing is admittedly awful." She glanced at their surroundings.

The timing may have been disastrous, but the location of this exercise in awkwardness was stunning. Located at the top of Rockefeller Center, the Rainbow Room was steeped in old-style New York glamour. A sparkling chandelier hung in the center of the elegant space, and massive evergreen centerpieces dotted with red holly berries decorated the round tables where award nominees and their guests were seated. The Rainbow Room's real showpiece, though, was its view overlooking the glittering Manhattan skyline. Addison never grew tired of seeing the city like this. From up high, it looked every bit as magical as she thought Paris must be. Even more so tonight, with the Empire State Building lit up in red and green for the holidays.

"It's okay, Addison. I'm happy to be here with you," Carter said.

Butterflies swirled low in her belly as she tried to

interpret whether he was happy to be there in a professional way or in an afterglow-type way. She honestly couldn't tell. What kind of mess had she gotten herself into with all of her talk about ground rules?

"Addison! Carter!" Everly waved at them from a table on the other side of the room. "Over here!"

The *Veil* gang was already paired off and assembled—Everly and Henry, Daphne and Jack, Colette and Marshall Leighton from Harry Winston. A yellow diamond solitaire the approximate size of a golf ball hung around Colette's neck, no doubt a party favor on loan for the night from her escort.

"Hi, everyone." Addison bent to kiss her *Veil* girls on the cheek while Carter pulled out her chair.

"How's the date going?" Everly whispered with a waggle of her eyebrows.

"Stop it," Addison said through a clenched smile. "Everyone will notice."

"You're fine. Colette doesn't have a clue. She's blinded by the boulder hanging around her neck. Do you think she'll show up to the office tomorrow in a cervical collar?"

Laughter bubbled up Addison's throat as she took her seat, and Carter's eyes danced while the overhead lights dimmed.

"Ladies and gentlemen, welcome to the 36th Annual Fashion Media Awards, celebrating the best in fashion journalism," a slender woman dripping in couture said from the podium.

Addison leaned toward Carter and whispered, "Why are you looking at me like that?"

A waiter passed by carrying a tray of champagne

flutes, and Carter selected two of them—one for him, and one for her. "It's just nice to see you laugh, that's all. You've been quiet as a mouse all day. I was beginning to think last night had been a figment of my imagination. No regrets?"

None. Zero. Nada.

"No regrets," she said, because it was true. No matter how many times she told herself that making love with Carter had been a mistake, she couldn't bring herself to believe it. Even if things between them had gotten exponentially more complicated—literally overnight.

"But do you really want to talk about last night *here*? Now? Our boss—your *aunt*—is seated less than three feet away." Not to mention the presence of the fashion goddess herself, Anna Wintour. The *Vogue* table was situated smack in front of the podium. They always swept the awards. "You're impossible, as per usual. We had a deal."

"That's right. I almost forgot. 'Never speak of it again.'" Carter winked at her in the darkness. "Dramatic much?"

She punched him in the leg as the award emcee called out the names of the nominees for the first award. And as the night went on, Addison thought that maybe they could actually do this. Maybe dating Carter wasn't a completely far-fetched, impossible idea.

The celebratory mood must have been getting to her. Their table was buzzing with anticipation as Daphne and Jack's category crept closer. While the winner in the category immediately preceding theirs gave her acceptance speech, Carter typed out a text message on his cell phone, hidden beneath the table.

Within seconds, Addison's iPhone vibrated. She glanced down at it, and Carter's name lit up her screen, followed by a text bubble.

Have I told you how gorgeous you look tonight? Nice dress.

Addison grinned at him, and he blew her the quickest, sneakiest kiss imaginable. She'd worn the white satin ball gown with the black crystal detailing that she'd been trying on when she kissed him in the fashion closet and subsequently had been forced to wear to their pitch meeting. Carter clearly recognized it.

"And now, in the category of Best Feature series, the nominees are…" The emcee gave a dramatic pause.

"This is it!" Addison grabbed Carter's arm, suddenly nervous for her friends. It was a long shot, but Daphne and Jack deserved that award. The fact that their undercover series had been the catalyst for their real-life romance would make the win even more meaningful.

Addison's gaze swiveled toward Daphne, but she and Jack were too busy making lovey-dovey eyes at each other for her to notice.

The emcee recited the names of the nominees, and the entire *Veil* table held its breath when she unsealed the envelope.

"And the winner is…" This was torture. "Daphne Ballantyne and Jack King of *Veil* Magazine."

They'd done it! They'd won!

The room exploded into a roar of applause, and around Addison, her table mates rose to their feet, whooping and hollering while Daphne and Jack made their way to the podium. It took her a second to realize that Carter was still seated. She bent to tug him to his feet, but he wasn't paying attention.

His gaze was glued to his cell. His face, ashen.

"Carter, what's wrong?" Addison sat, and as she did so, she noticed an incoming email notification scrolling across the screen of her phone.

"It's addressed to both of us. Don't look at it. Just wait until after the ceremony." Carter made a move to steal her phone, but Addison was too fast for him.

Whatever was in that email had obviously thrown him for a loop. If he thought she wasn't going to read it right away, he was nuts.

"Addison, seriously," he said. The edge to his voice was beginning to scare her.

She tapped the message and began to read.

Dear Ms. England and Mr. Payne,
We regret to inform you that in the confusion surrounding the recent snowstorm, our office mistakenly filed paperwork that we now understand was only meant to be a prop for a fashion photoshoot.

Please be advised that your marriage was certified as of yesterday, and you are now legally married.

We apologize for any inconvenience this has caused.
Happy holidays!
Very sincerely,
The Office of the City Clerk
Manhattan

Chapter Fifteen

"Married." Daphne's gaze remained glued on Addison as she reached for her wedding cake martini and took a sip so large that it made her eyes water. "I definitely didn't see this coming."

"Neither did we," Addison said, and then corrected herself when she realized she was speaking in the collective—as if her marriage to Carter existed in the real world instead of just on paper. "I mean, neither did I."

Thank goodness this evening was the *Veil* crew's regularly scheduled Martini Night at Bloom. Addison had spent the better part of the preceding twenty-four hours in a daze. She'd never needed a wedding cake martini or a girls' night so badly in her life.

Her mind just couldn't stop reeling. After the award ceremony, she'd picked up Sabrina from Daphne and Jack's penthouse and hadn't breathed a word about her accidental marriage. She needed a plan first, or maybe just a night to convince herself she wasn't stuck in a bad dream. Alas, here she was, in real life, a married woman. A married woman who once again needed her *Veil* girls to tell her that everything was going to be okay.

Addison had always prided herself on being self-reliant, but since the calendar flipped to December 1, she'd been in full-blown crisis mode. When had she become this person?

Possibly around the time you became Mrs. Carter Payne.

She nearly choked on her drink. Good grief, that was her legal name now, wasn't it?

"What are you and Carter going to do?" Daphne asked.

That was the million-dollar question, wasn't it?

Last night, they'd agreed to sleep on things and talk about their "problem" in the morning. Addison had tossed and turned so much that Sabrina eventually crawled to the foot of the bed to get some actual shut-eye. In the clear light of day, things still seemed more confusing than ever.

"We're going to get the marriage annulled, of course. Carter has a lawyer friend who he thinks might be able to get it taken care of." Throughout the entire workday, they'd exchanged a grand total of two sentences: *Would you like me to call my attorney friend to see if he can help? Yes, please.* The rest of the day had been business as usual. "It was all just a big mistake."

Addison's money was on Joe at the marriage bureau's office. This had to be his fault.

"Everly, you've gone awfully quiet," Daphne said, turning toward Addison's sister. "You seem to be having even more trouble digesting this news than the rest of us are."

Everly sat up straighter on her barstool. "I was just thinking—and don't kill me, Addison—but what if this wasn't a mistake? What if it's fate?"

"There's no such thing as fate," Addison countered.

Everly raised an eyebrow. "You realize you sound exactly like Meg Ryan's character in *Sleepless in Seattle*, don't you?"

Daphne gestured at Everly with her martini. "She's right. You do."

Addison's love of romcoms was going to be the absolute death of her this holiday season, wasn't it?

"*Sleepless in Seattle* is a movie." Undoubtedly Nora Ephron's best, but that was beside the point. "This is real life, and fate doesn't exist. If it did, that would mean Dad's car accident all those years ago was all part of some cosmic plan. I can't believe that, and I know you don't either."

Losing her father had been the most devastating moment of Addison's life. She'd long since given up on trying to make sense of it. Merely surviving it had taken everything she had.

"You're right, I don't. Fate doesn't mean that bad things can't happen, though. Tragedy is part of life. But if we're really lucky, fate steps in and helps heal those wounds by bringing the perfect person into your life—the one individual who truly understands what you've been through, who loves you just as you are. Not despite your faults or your struggles, but in part, because of them." Everly's eyes went so tender that Addison almost wanted to believe her. How wonderful it would be to just give in and trust that Carter had swept into her life for a reason that didn't involve stealing her job. She just couldn't do it. Once upon a time, maybe. But Addison was older and wiser now. She'd stopped believing that if she reached for the moon, the moon would reach right back in return. "That's how you know you've found your perfect match."

"My heart." Daphne sighed. "This is actually better than *Sleepless in Seattle*."

"This isn't Seattle. It's New York City." Yes, Addison knew that half of the aforementioned movie technically took place in Manhattan, but she needed to shut down this conversational detour at once.

Thankfully, her phone pinged with an incoming text, putting an end to the romcom references. She slipped her cell out of her bag, and her pulse quickened when she saw that the message was from Carter.

"We have a meeting with the lawyer tomorrow during lunch," she said as a terrifying knot lodged in the back of her throat. "Perfect."

She typed a thumbs-up emoji in the text box, and then deleted it. What was the proper response to an invitation for a lunchtime annulment?

Daphne's brows rose. "Tomorrow? That's really soon."

"What's the hurry?" Everly rested her hands on the table and spoke calmly and quietly, as if trying to reason with a child…or a younger sibling. Oh, how the tables had turned. "Maybe you need to slow down and think about this for a while. Can't it at least wait until after Christmas?"

Addison just needed for it to go away. The sooner, the

better. The longer she was married to Carter, the more real it would feel.

"Are you crazy? I can't be married to him."

"Oh, honey." Daphne's eyes flashed over to Addison, and the corner of her mouth curled. "You already are."

The following afternoon, Carter sat beside Addison on a small sofa in his college friend David Holt's office as they took turns relaying the crazy story of how they'd accidentally ended up married. The irony of having to insist they didn't really want to be husband and wife while sitting together on a love seat, of all things, wasn't lost on him. Every time Addison's thigh brushed up against his, he had to remind himself that it had all been just a crazy mistake.

An annulment made perfect sense. They'd never intended to marry each other. If they could undo it with a simple set of signatures on a one-page legal document, they absolutely should. It wasn't as if they'd ever had a real marriage. What was it that ministers always said at the beginning of wedding ceremonies?

Marriage should not be entered into lightly, but reverently...deliberately...

Carter had never entered into anything less deliberately or reverently in his life. Which begged the question...

Why did ending it feel so wrong?

"I'm happy to help you with this," David said. He held up his hands. "Under these nutty circumstances, an annulment is quick and easy. We might even have a chance of getting you two unhitched before Christmas."

"Really? That quickly?" Carter couldn't bring himself to aim a sideways glance in Addison's direction.

Instead, he focused on the Christmas tree that stood in front of the window in David's massive corner office. The tree wasn't technically a tree, but an elaborate pyramid of large, leather-bound law books, stacked at odd angles to look like one. A string of white twinkle lights was wrapped around it, and a bundle of mistletoe sat atop the whole pile.

He stared at the mistletoe until the cheery cluster of greenery and berries grew blurry.

"By Christmas? That would be—" Addison paused, and Carter could've sworn he detected a hitch in her voice "—wonderful. Thank you so much."

David took a pen from his jacket pocket and scribbled a few things onto his yellow legal pad. "Don't thank me yet. It's not a done deal until I file the necessary paperwork and get in front of a judge. I'm friendly with some of the judges in family court, though. Their schedules tend to be more relaxed this time of year, so there's a good chance I can get this on the docket right away."

"Great," Carter heard himself say.

So, so great that the prospect is making my gut churn.

"I just need to ask you both a few detailed questions so I can get started on the Petition for Annulment." David clicked his pen, and the sudden noise made Addison jump.

Carter finally turned to look at her, but she kept her gaze glued to David's yellow legal pad. He wanted nothing more than to take her hand in his and tell her not to worry—they were in this together, just like every other crazy thing they'd been through this month.

But that wasn't true this time, was it? Ending a marriage was the very opposite of togetherness, even when that marriage was accidental.

"Let's start with your legal names, birth dates and the specific details surrounding the wedding ceremony," David said.

Addison went first, rattling off the information he needed. The lawyer took copious notes, even writing down a description of Joe at the marriage bureau for good measure.

"Good, good. Again, this should be really cut and dried. It sounds like a paperwork error run amok. There's no judge in the state who would refuse to grant you an annulment." David shrugged. "So long as the marriage wasn't consummated, obviously."

He glanced up and did a double take when he realized that both Carter and Addison had gone as still as stone.

"I'm sorry," Addison croaked. "What did you just say?"

"I think you heard me the first time." David aimed his pen back and forth, pointing to Addison and Carter and then back again. "You two said you were coworkers. The marriage wasn't consummated, was it? If so, we've got a problem. A big one."

"Then we might have a problem," Carter said quietly. He'd never been the type to kiss and tell, but there was no avoiding the question. Especially not if he and Addison were going to be expected to appear in court and talk about their relationship under oath.

"It didn't count, though." Addison shook her head so hard that Carter half expected her headband to fly across the room. Maybe he should duck, just in case. That thing was so embellished with colorful gemstones that it could probably poke an eye out. "We were snowed in."

David's forehead creased. "So was the rest of the city."

"I know, but we were stuck together in one hotel room. I was wearing a *wedding dress*," Addison said.

A valid point. Seeing her dressed as a bride hadn't helped matters. Carter wasn't about to jump in with more commentary, though. Addison appeared to have plenty to say, all on her own.

"There's got to be some sort of exception to that rule. Special circumstances, maybe? We had an agreement that it was only a onetime thing, just until the snowstorm was over."

David gave a solemn nod. "Ah, the snowed-in exception."

"Yes!" Addison clapped her hands. When the corner of David's mouth twitched, her gaze narrowed. "Is that a thing?"

"In romance novels, yes. Real life? Not so much." David let out a laugh, shrugged and tossed his legal pad onto the coffee table. "Look, I can still help you, but an annulment is out of the question. You've been intimate, and that means you no longer qualify. Legally, the assumption is that on some level, you must have legitimate feelings for one another."

The silence that fell over the room was deafening. Addison let out a shaky exhale, and Carter had to close his eyes for a second before he said something he'd never be able to take back—something he knew good and well that Addison didn't want to hear.

"I'm not saying that's what's going on here. That's just the legal assumption." David cleared his throat. "Why don't we all just take a breath and figure out where to go from here. An annulment is off the table, but there are other options."

"Sounds good. Let's choose one and wrap this thing up," Carter said. He suddenly wanted to be anywhere but sitting in his friend's office going over the myriad ways to end his marriage with a woman he couldn't stop thinking about. At Christmas, no less.

David nodded. "Then I'm not going to sugarcoat it. In my professional opinion, what you two want is a quickie divorce."

The *D*-word was a punch to Carter's gut. He'd known it was coming, but even so, it all but knocked the wind out of him.

A divorce sounded so grave. So *permanent*. Carter didn't object to the concept of divorce, in general. But they weren't discussing it in the general sense. Far from it.

"Say the word, and I'll draw up a Petition for Divorce, along with a simple settlement agreement that says there was no commingling of assets and you each leave the marriage the exact same way you came into it," David said.

Fat chance. There was no way Carter was walking away from this with his soul intact, no matter what the paperwork said. He'd changed. *They'd* changed. And whether or not they ever saw each other again after Christmas, Addison would always be a part of him.

"Is that what you want?" David asked, gaze shifting between them.

"Yes," Addison said.

At the same time, Carter shook his head. "No."

"No?" Addison turned toward him, eyes blazing. "Did you just say no?"

The effort it took to hold his tongue was monumental. But Addison's big doe eyes had gone panicky, like a deer caught in headlights. This wasn't the expression of a woman who wanted to stay married to him. Even if she had feelings for him—even if she'd fallen head over heels in love with him—the thought of being his wife was clearly more than she could handle, and Carter knew why.

He'd felt the same way for as long as he could remember. Love meant losing control. Love meant allowing yourself to be vulnerable in every way possible, and making it permanent, making it *real*. It meant being a family. It meant a lifetime of Christmas Eves and finding shelter in each other during a storm, not just for a night. And one day, it would mean losing each other when tragedy came to call.

The end was inevitable. That's just the way life was. Better to face it now, by choice, than later when it had even more potential to bring you to your knees.

Carter understood. He really did. He just didn't feel the same way anymore. After a lifetime of keeping his heart under lock and key, he was ready to wrap it up like a Christmas gift and give it away.

"That came out wrong. I said no, but I meant yes," he lied, because as much as he wanted her, it couldn't be like this.

Not until she was ready...

But Christmas Eve was only days away, and in the end, one of them would win, the other would lose and they might never see each other again. Until then, he'd give her whatever she wanted, because the magazine wasn't the most important thing to him anymore. Addison would've told him he'd lost sight of the prize...

But Carter knew better.

Chapter Sixteen

As fate would have it—not that Addison had started believing in fate, because she very deliberately hadn't—the divorce papers arrived at the office via messenger on the very same day that the *How to Elope in New York City at Christmas* feature went live on the Veil website.

One minute, Carter and Addison were sitting at their respective desks, each staring at an enormous, blown-up photograph of the two of them in wedding attire on their computer screens, and the next, a courier knocked on their opened door.

"Yes?" Addison said without tearing her gaze from her laptop.

Had Carter really looked at her like that?

The photograph she'd selected as the main image to accompany the story was the one the photographer had taken when she'd exited the tiny bathroom at the city clerk's office—the picture he'd snapped of Carter's reaction to seeing her in the first wedding gown of the day. She remembered the photographer's grin and his satisfied smile with perfect clarity.

That's it. That's the shot. We've got it.

It wasn't until she'd seen the moment captured on film that she fully grasped how right he'd been. Addison had wanted a collection of images that told a story. Well, this photo alone said it all. The wonder in his eyes…it stole the breath right out of her lungs every time she saw it. Never in her life did she think a man, or anyone, would look at her like that…would see her the way that Carter did.

She'd recognized the photograph as something special the first time she'd seen it—as a tiny thumbnail on a contact sheet the photographer emailed her. Then again, as a hi-res image on the design layouts. But now that it was splashed across the *Veil* homepage just under the magazine's banner, it looked almost like a piece of art—a painting that might hang in a museum.

Addison couldn't stop looking at it. This had been her wedding day. It had all been such a crazy mistake, but no one would've believed it, judging by the photographic evidence. Addison wasn't sure she believed it anymore either.

"Yo." The courier waved a flat manila envelope in the air. "I've got a delivery for a Carter Payne and Addison England from the Law Offices of David Holt. It's marked Personal and Confidential, so the receptionist sent me back here. Someone needs to sign for it."

Addison finally dragged her attention away from the computer and her gaze immediately collided with Carter's. Surprise splashed across his face, followed im-

mediately by the inscrutable mask he wore so often—
the wall he erected around himself when he wanted to
keep the world at arm's length. Addison hadn't seen it in
days, and its sudden reappearance made her want to cry.

"I've got it," Carter said as he smoothed down his tie
and pushed his chair away from his desk.

Thank goodness, because Addison suddenly couldn't
seem to move. Or speak.

They were really doing this. Getting *divorced*. She
knew the papers were supposed to be coming in any day,
so she couldn't fathom why their appearance had been
such a shock. It was the right decision, she reminded
herself. She and Carter didn't belong together. They
weren't soul mates, like Meg Ryan and Tom Hanks in
Sleepless in Seattle. Addison had never even wanted to
be swept off of her feet like that.

Even so, it had been fun while it lasted. For one
snowy day, she'd had the time of her life.

"Thank you," Carter said after he'd scrawled his name
on the receipt and the courier handed him the envelope.

"Sure thing, man. Merry Christmas," the courier said.

And a happy divorce! Addison's thoughts screamed.
She thought she might be sick.

Carter sat back down and slid the papers from the
envelope. It was all there in black and white—the legal-
ese that would forever separate their brief, unintentional
union. As she and Carter reviewed the documents, wedding language kept running through her mind on a loop.

*What God has joined together, let no man put asun-
der...*

Carter offered her a pen and slid the signature page
toward her. "Shall we?"

She'd rather have taken hold of a live snake than pick up that pen.

"You first," she said with a tremor in her voice.

His eyes bored into her, and then the mask slipped—just long enough for her to get a glimpse of the same man whose face was featured on the *Veil* digital site. The real Carter.

Then he averted his gaze and bent to sign his name in the space indicated on the paperwork.

Addison looked away until she heard him huff out a breath.

"What is it?" she asked, holding her breath as she waited for him to say something.

"The pen doesn't work." He tossed it into a nearby trash can where it rattled against the metal with a clang.

A coincidence?

Or fate?

You don't believe in fate, Addison reminded herself. Then she promptly told her inner thoughts to shut the heck up.

"Maybe we should do this another time," she said.

Carter nodded. "Agreed."

He slid the papers back into the envelope and tossed it onto his desk. Neither of them moved a muscle. They just stared at the envelope like it was a hot potato.

"Anyone around here could mistake that for something work-related." Carter's gaze slid toward Addison. "It might be a good idea to keep it out of sight for the time being."

She nodded. "Absolutely. It's our personal business."

Carter lifted a brow, prompting her to pick up the envelope and stash it out of sight, but she still couldn't bring herself to touch it. A small smile played on his lips as he reached for it and placed it in the top drawer of their shared credenza. Out of sight, but not quite out of mind.

They did the same dance every day.

Shall we? he'd ask. And every time, Addison would find an excuse not to sign the papers. *I have a meeting in the fashion department. I need to take Sabrina for a walk. I just painted my nails, and I don't want to ruin my manicure.*

The excuses grew more implausible by the day, until late in the afternoon on Christmas Eve.

"David texted me this morning and said there's an available slot on the docket the day after Christmas. All we have to do is sign the papers, and he'll arrange the rest." Carter's gaze flitted toward the credenza. "Shall we?"

Was he calling her bluff, or were they really staring down the barrel at an available court date? Addison regarded him, heart pounding. Sabrina roused herself from a nap on her dog bed and came to sit on the pointy toe of her stiletto.

Then a legitimate excuse waltzed into their office in the form of the editor-in-chief's assistant. "Colette needs to see you immediately."

"Both of us?" Sabrina pranced around Addison's feet as she stood.

"No, just you, Addison," the assistant said.

Odd, Addison thought, and then the significance of today's date hit her. *Christmas Eve...the big promotion.*

How could she have possibly forgotten?

Addison did her best to arrange her features into a serene, confident expression, but out of Colette's view, her right foot jiggled uncontrollably.

The *Veil* holiday party was in less than two hours. She'd planned on going home and taking Sabrina for a walk before she dashed back out to the party. If this meeting lasted longer than half an hour, she might have to change into her Christmas dress in the fashion closet and bring Sabrina along to the festivities at Balthazar, the SoHo brasserie where *Veil* always held its annual holiday party.

There was no way Balthazar allowed dogs, though. It was a restaurant. She might've finally hit the wall when it came to toting Sabrina around everywhere.

Addison bit the inside of her cheek and ordered herself to concentrate as her boss took a seat opposite her and folded her hands neatly on top of her desk the way she always did when she had something important to say. The needy foster dog should be the absolute farthest thing from Addison's mind right now. This was *it*, wasn't it? This was the moment she'd been waiting for all month. She'd assumed Colette was going to make an announcement about the editor-in-chief job at the party but judging by the serious look in her boss's eyes, Addison had assumed wrong. Even the freshly trimmed, razor-sharp edges of Colette's bob haircut seemed to mean business.

"First of all, Addison, I want to commend you on a job well done this month. The elopement feature is a runaway success. We haven't had this much engagement on the digital site since Daphne and Jack's award-winning undercover series." Colette smiled, but Addison still wasn't sure whether the news was good or bad. She felt like she was perched at the very top of a roller coaster, teetering back and forth while she waited for the inevitable plunge.

Good news for her would mean bad news for Carter, and vice versa. Like it or not, he was her *husband*—at least for the time being. Admittedly, that complicated things. There was no logical reason why it should, but somewhere along the way, logic had taken a back seat in Addison's meticulously ordered life. Now here she was, on the brink of her biggest success or most crushing failure, and all she could seem to think about was the man she'd accidentally married and her needy little dog...

Neither of whom genuinely belonged to her.

"Thank you. Carter and I are both thrilled with the response to the digital site this month," Addison said, speaking for the both of them as if they were some sort of unit. Business partners...lovers...man and wife.

Against the odds, they'd somehow been all three over the course of the past few weeks. And now that the moment Addison had been waiting for had finally arrived, she wasn't sure where she and Carter stood anymore. The lines had become so blurry they were nonexistent.

"As you should be." Colette nodded, then tilted her head and regarded Addison with a knowing gleam in her eyes. "I'm sure you're wondering why I called you here this evening, though."

"You could certainly say that, yes." Addison smiled— or at least she tried to, but her mind kept going back to the divorce papers, still sitting unsigned in a manila envelope in the top drawer of the credenza in the office she shared with Carter.

It was like they were playing a game of marital chicken,

each one waiting to see who would crack first. Since the photos of their accidental wedding day had gone live on the *Veil* site, neither one of them had gone anywhere near the manila envelope. It remained exactly where they'd left it a few days ago. A bomb waiting to detonate. Why did she get the feeling that whatever was about to transpire would be the spark that set everything ablaze?

"Then I won't keep you in suspense any longer. Congratulations, my dear." Colette stood and offered Addison her hand.

Addison somehow managed to get to her feet, even though her heart felt like it might beat right out of her chest. The excitement swirling in her belly was so intense that it almost felt like dread.

"I'm pleased to offer you the position of editor-in-chief…" Colette paused to give Addison's hand an extra squeeze. Then she smiled as wide as a department-store Santa, ready to grant each and every one of the wishes on Addison's Christmas list. "…of the brand-new French edition of *Veil*."

Colette's mouth kept moving, but Addison couldn't seem to understand any of the words coming out of it. She stood there, shocked into silence, vaguely aware of shaking her boss's hand and the little snippets of French peppering Colette's repeated congratulations.

"Toutes nos félicitations." Colette finally ended the handshake, smoothed down her skirt and sat back down. "Paris is especially lovely during the holidays. You couldn't be moving there at a better time."

Addison felt like the wind had just gotten knocked out of her. *Quel surprise.* Paris? Really?

After all this time?

"I'm sorry, Colette. I just…" She plopped down into her chair without an ounce of Audrey Hepburn's grace or elegance. "I'm having a hard time wrapping my head around what you're saying. All of it. Could we start over again?"

S'il vous plaît.

"I realize it's a shock, but it's also a dream come true, yes?" Colette aimed a meaningful glance at Addison's French manicure. "I remember everything that goes on at this magazine, my dear. It was quite some time ago that you sat in the same spot where you're sitting right now and told me how you'd planned on moving to Paris for a year, but due to family circumstances, all you wanted was to be hired as my assistant. Did you think I'd forgotten?"

Addison swallowed. She couldn't even remember sharing that intensely personal information during her initial job interview at *Veil*. Clearly, it had left an impression.

"And did you think I hadn't noticed all the days you came into the office early to do your French lessons at your computer?" Colette's gaze flitted to Addison's artfully styled bangs. "And the French-girl fringe, the red lipstick and your fondness for macarons?"

She'd made her point, and Addison didn't know whether to be impressed by her boss's keen observational skills or embarrassed by the number of times she'd hoarded the macaron samples Ladurée regularly dropped off in the break room.

"The board of directors has been in discussions about adding a French edition of *Veil* for years now. A few months ago, they made the decision to proceed, and they tasked me with choosing my replacement here in New York upon my retirement as well as selecting someone with the necessary experience and leadership skills to head up the new office in Paris." Colette leaned back in her chair and steepled her fingers. "Fortunately, I had two people perfectly capable of taking my place, either here or abroad."

"Me and Carter," Addison said, and for the first time since Colette had uttered the words *French edition*, she understood why the two of them had been pitted against each other all month. "Wait a minute, if I go to Paris to run French *Veil*, that means he's staying here, doesn't it?"

"Of course." Colette nodded. "Carter will remain in the New York office as editor-in-chief of American *Veil*. I assured him there was a method to my madness. I never had any intention of disappointing either of you. You both wholeheartedly deserve the job, and you're both getting it."

But they'd be on completely different continents.

"Does Carter know yet?" Addison asked in a voice she scarcely recognized as her own. It sounded very small and very, very far away. Nothing about this meeting was turning out like she'd imagined it might. In her wildest dreams, she never would've guessed what Colette had up her sleeve.

"No, he'll find out at the party when I make the big announcement. I wanted to speak to you first, though. I thought you might need some extra time to prepare," Colette said.

"Thank you. This definitely comes as a surprise. I'm

not sure two hours is enough time for it to really sink in, but I appreciate the heads-up."

Colette frowned. "Oh, no. That's not what I meant. I was referring to preparations for your move. Your flight leaves the day after Christmas. I've booked you in business class, of course. The board of directors has already rented a flat for you just off the *Champs-Élysées*. It's lovely. I know you probably would've liked to choose something yourself, but there's simply no time. You have a very big job ahead of you. The next few years are going to be quite a challenge."

Addison's head spun. Colette couldn't be serious. "I'm moving to Paris the day after Christmas? But today is Christmas Eve."

She couldn't possibly pack up and move to a foreign country in less than forty-eight hours. Logistics aside, what about the rest of the holidays? She still hadn't put up her Christmas tree. She hadn't made time to go ice skating in Central Park. If she left before New Year's Eve, she wouldn't get to kiss Carter when the clock struck midnight.

And she was maybe…possibly…getting divorced the day after Christmas. Could she really squeeze that in before an international flight?

Colette continued, oblivious to Addison's invisible holiday checklist. "The board wants the French digital site up and running by Valentine's Day. The first print issue will drop in June. You'll need to hit the ground running right away. Like I said, it's a big task, but if anyone can do it, it's you."

She was asking the impossible. But that's what Colette had been doing since Addison's very first day at

Veil, and Addison had never failed to deliver. At long last, all of that hard work was finally paying off.

Or was it?

"At first, I'd had Carter in mind for the Paris position. It only made sense, given that he's been working there for years already. But Carter doesn't know weddings like you do, Addison. His editorial instincts are spot-on, but he needs the experience of the rest of the New York editorial staff when it comes to the ins and outs of bridal fashion. You, on the other hand..." Colette pointed at her. "You're fully prepared to build an entirely new *Veil* from the ground up."

She could. Addison knew she could, without a doubt, but she wasn't altogether sure she wanted to.

This kind of opportunity won't come around again. It's now or never.

This is what she'd been working toward for her entire career. It just looked a little different than she'd expected, that's all. Colette wasn't just offering her the editor-in-chief role. She was offering her *Paris*. Addison's future could look just like she'd always wanted it to. Just like Audrey's in *Sabrina*. All she had to do was say yes.

"I'll make the announcement tonight at the holiday party." Colette was already reaching for her handbag, a sure sign the meeting was coming to an end. "Tonight will be a very special evening. You and Carter certainly have a lot to celebrate."

But Addison didn't feel like celebrating. She felt more like crying, and to her astonishment, the tears that threatened to spill down her cheeks weren't of the happy variety.

Colette had given her a genuine Christmas miracle. She'd all but turned back time and served up Addison's lifelong dream on a silver platter. Addison could start over and have everything she'd ever wanted. Everything she'd dreamed of back when she'd been a young girl who'd just graduated from college. Everything she'd lost in the dark days that followed.

But Addison wasn't that young girl anymore. She was a fully grown woman, with a life here in Manhattan—a life that was blossoming and becoming more full than she ever could've imagined. Maybe she'd taken things for granted, but the night of the snowstorm, Carter had lifted the veil from her eyes and shown her who she was. She wasn't just the deputy editor of *Veil*. She was an aunt, a best friend, a foster dog mom. There was more to her life than just work. The *Veil* girls had been trying to tell her as much all along, but it had taken Carter to help her see the truth.

Carter, with his silly nicknames, his soulful eyes and his tender kisses. That night had changed everything. Now, Addison was all those things and more. Now, she was also a wife.

Addison inhaled a ragged breath and steeled herself not to cry, but it was too late. The moment the first tear slipped down her cheek, something broke inside of her.

She didn't want to go. Addison had changed, and so had her dreams. Why would she want to run a magazine without her *Veil* girls? They were supposed to do this together, not on opposite sides of the world.

And how could she leave her darling newborn nieces? Addison didn't want to be a long-distance aunt. She wanted to be the aunt who took the girls to Disney

World and sat front row, center at all of their dance re-
citals. She wanted to read them bedtime stories and buy
them cute little outfits with matching bows for their hair.

And she wanted to keep her dog. Sabrina wasn't the
only one with separation anxiety. Addison was pretty
sure she had it now too, because just the thought of taking the little Cavalier back to the pet rescue made her
sick to her stomach.

Was moving to Paris with a dog a viable option?

Addison didn't know, but it didn't matter. She didn't
want to move to Paris and spend the rest of her life in
an office. One day she'd get there, and when she did,
she wanted to take long walks in the rain, spend hours
just gazing at Monet's water lily paintings, and see the
ballet perform *Swan Lake* at *Palais Garnier.*

She wanted to *experience* Paris, not just work there.

And she wanted to do it with the man she loved, her
husband, right by her side.

"I'm sorry, Colette. The answer is no," Addison heard
herself say even before the words had fully crystallized
in her mind.

Colette blanched. "I don't understand."

Neither did Addison. Not completely, anyway. She
didn't know what her life would look like without *Veil.*
Until this instant, the very idea would have been unthinkable. She didn't even know if Carter loved her back
or what he might say when she told him she wanted to
stay married.

Because that's what she wanted most of all. The truth
had been right there, brimming beneath the surface all
along. Addison had simply been too afraid to admit it,
too scared to go off-script and lose her sense of con-

trol. That control was just an illusion, though. No one could fully control everything that happened to them, no matter how hard they tried. Case in point: the conversation she was currently having with her boss. Addison had planned for this moment for years, and she'd still gotten it completely wrong.

But if the past month had taught her anything, it was that the unplanned, stolen moments in life were the ones that took your breath away—winning a silly trophy, a surprise kiss in the fashion closet, the delicate beauty of a snowfall. For one night, time had stood still for her and Carter, and in that precious space where Addison could finally let herself catch her breath and be fully present, she'd found something more precious than anything she could've ever planned for. She'd found pure Christmas magic.

She'd found love.

"I don't want to move to Paris." Addison shook her head. Her tears were falling freely now, but she didn't care. Things were shaking loose inside of her, and she finally knew the answer to the question Daphne had asked her with such urgency.

What do you really want, Addison?

She wanted to stay right here in New York and build a life with Carter Payne.

"I love my job here at *Veil*, and for years, I've been hoping to be editor-in-chief one day. But I want to do it here in New York. This is where I belong," she said.

A line etched between Colette's brows. "But what about Paris? And your position here at the magazine?"

"Paris will always be there, and I'll visit when the time and circumstances are right." As Audrey Hepburn famously told Humphrey Bogart in *Sabrina*, Paris wasn't for briefcases. It was for living *la vie en rose*. "And as for *Veil*, I suppose I'll have to wait and see what happens now. But that's okay. I'm beginning to realize that sometimes it's best to figure things out along the way."

In a perfect world, Colette would've told her not to worry. Her position at *Veil* was secure. But as Addison knew all too well, this world was far from perfect. She and Carter both couldn't be editor-in-chief here in the New York office.

Nothing had changed, and at the same time, *everything* had.

"Very well, then." Colette gave her a slow nod. "Merry Christmas, Addison."

"Merry Christmas, Colette," Addison said, and then she stood and walked out of her boss's office on shaky legs.

Once in the hallway, she pressed a hand to her stomach and took a deep breath. She was a bit rattled, but happy. She'd done the right thing, and now all that was left to do was tell Carter how she felt. Addison wasn't sure what would happen next. Colette might want to send him to Paris now, and maybe he'd get on that plane the day after Christmas and never look back. But he deserved to know all the facts before he made up his mind, and the fact of the matter was that Addison England was head over heels in love with her husband.

"Carter, I need to tell you something," she blurted after she'd run down the hall and tossed open the door to their office.

Then she stopped in her tracks. He wasn't there. The office was empty, save for sweet little Sabrina, gnawing on a candy-cane-shaped chew bone that Carter must've given her to keep her occupied after he'd gone. The Cavalier dropped the toy as soon as she saw Addison, and then shimmied toward her with her trademark full-body wiggle.

"Hey, there," Addison cooed, as she bent to scoop the dog into her arms. "Where did Carter run off to, huh?"

Sabrina snuggled her little head against the crook of Addison's neck, and for a brief, blissful moment, Addison thought this might end up being the most perfect Christmas she'd ever had.

Then her gaze landed on a manila envelope sitting on the center of her desk, topped with a shiny, emerald-green bow, as if its contents were a present. While she'd been in Colette's office, finally coming to the realization that their unexpected marriage was the greatest gift of all, Carter had decided to give her the one thing he thought she wanted most.

Her freedom.

Chapter Seventeen

By the time Addison showed up at Balthazar, the *Veil* holiday party was in full swing. She'd spent the past two hours obsessively trying to get in touch with Carter while simultaneously attempting to put herself together for the festivities.

By any standards, both endeavors had been spectacular failures. Not only did Carter seem to be ignoring her calls, but she barely had time to throw on a red satin evening gown and toss her hair into a high pony before leaving her apartment. She'd completely forgone a tiny clutch bag and was still toting around her oversize Vuitton bag, complete with the divorce papers still buried at the bottom, green bow and all. Her face was probably still tearstained. Addison honestly had no idea since she hadn't taken the time to glance in the mirror.

She hiked her big purse higher up on her shoulder as she dashed into the restaurant. The hostess shot her an odd look, but Addison breezed past her, headed straight for the large Christmas tree at the far side of the room, flanked by red leather booths filled with familiar faces. Tradition dictated that the *Veil* holiday party was always held on Christmas Eve, and it was always well attended, given that Colette typically chose the occasion to hand out holiday bonuses and announce big staff promotions. She usually did so shortly after the party began, in case staff members needed to leave early for family obligations.

"Oh my gosh, where have you been?" Everly said as Addison found the *Veil* girls near the bar, flanked on either side by their spouses. "You're never late. We were getting worried."

"Did I miss anything? Has Colette made the editor-in-chief announcement yet?" Addison scanned the crowd, heart thumping as she tried to catch a glimpse of Carter. She couldn't find him anywhere, though. Colette sat in her usual spot, just to the right of the Christmas tree, but the seat beside her was empty.

"No, she hasn't." Daphne handed her a martini glass with a mini candy cane hanging from its rim. "Here, you seem like you could use this. Is everything okay? You look uncharacteristically..."

"Frazzled," Everly said with a furrow in her brow.

Daphne nodded. "And a little bit wild-eyed."

"This is the new me. I do things like turn down jobs in Paris on a whim now, apparently." Addison took a gulp of her cocktail. "And show up at corporate holiday parties for the sole purpose of trying to talk my husband out of divorcing me."

Henry coughed into his highball glass.

Jack's gaze flitted toward him. "I think this might be our cue to leave and let the *Veil* girls have some privacy."

"Couldn't agree more." Henry gave Everly a kiss on the cheek. "Come find me whenever you're ready, sweetheart. And Addison?" He offered her a smile so sympathetic that her chest ached. "Everything is going to be okay. Love finds a way, even if it takes a long and winding road to get there. Trust me on this. Merry Christmas, sis."

Sis. Henry had never called her that before. She rather liked it. "Merry Christmas, Henry."

He gave her shoulder an affectionate squeeze as he and Jack made their way through the crowd toward the red leather booth where a few of the other male staff members had gathered. Once they were out of earshot, Daphne took hold of Addison's arm and steered her toward a quiet corner away from the bar.

"What is going on?" she whispered. *"Paris?"*

"Yes, Paris." Addison pulled a face. "Except I said no. So whatever happens between Carter and me, I'm definitely not moving across the world to be editor-in-chief of the new French edition of *Veil*. Colette offered me the position, and I turned her down flat."

Everly's eyes nearly fell out of her head. "There's going to be a French edition of *Veil*?"

"Apparently so, yes." Addison shrugged. "I mean, *oui.*"

Daphne gave her a curious once-over. "You seem awfully nonchalant about turning down an editor-in-chief job. I'm honestly impressed. Who even are you right now?"

I'm Addison England Payne...for now. Those divorce

papers needed two signatures, not just one. And Addison had no intention of ripping that envelope open any time soon.

"I'm not sure who I am, to be honest," she said with a wobble in her voice. Then she looked her *Veil* girls straight in the eyes and told them the only thing that really mattered…the thing she still didn't want to believe. "He signed the papers."

"No." Daphne shook her head. "Not possible. I don't believe it."

"Believe it. He left them in an envelope on my desk topped with a big green bow," Addison said. It was the bow that killed her. Had she really managed to convince him this is what she wanted?

"That doesn't sound like Carter. I know he loves you, Addie." Everly wrinkled her nose. "I'm not sure I'll believe it until I see his signature for myself."

"Feel free. I couldn't bring myself to look." Addison tipped her head toward her handbag, and then remembered why giving her sister unfettered access to her purse wasn't the best idea in the world.

Too late. Everly was already reaching into the designer tote for the papers. She gave a little yelp as Sabrina poked her head out of the top of the bag.

"I told you to hide," Addison whispered. The dog's tail beat against the inside of the purse in a gleeful tempo.

Everly's mouth dropped open. "Addison England, am I seeing things, or have you snuck your foster dog into the *Veil* Christmas party?"

"Shh." Addison touched a finger to her lips. "I couldn't leave her home alone. She was in distress. I'm pretty sure she's picking up on my fragile emotional state. And anyway, your assessment of the situation isn't one hundred percent accurate."

"Could've fooled me." Daphne peered into the handbag. "How does the saying go? If it looks like a Cavalier, swims like a Cavalier and quacks like a Cavalier, then it probably is a Cavalier."

Everly snorted. "Something like that."

"Cute, but what I meant is that Sabrina is no longer my foster dog." Addison couldn't help but smile, even though the rest of her life seemed to be falling apart at the seams. At least she'd gotten this one thing right. "I emailed the pet rescue while I was in the taxi on my way over here, and I told them I want to give Sabrina a permanent home. They responded right away. She's officially mine."

"I called it!" Everly threw her arms around Addison, and Sabrina's tiny head popped out of the bag again so she could cover Everly's cheek with puppy kisses.

Before Addison could put a stop to the commotion and warn her sister that she was about to get them both in serious trouble, someone tapped a knife against a wineglass to capture the attention of the *Veil* staffers.

"Oh boy, here we go," Daphne muttered as Colette stood in front of the Christmas tree to address the party. "I'm guessing Carter got the editor-in-chief job since Colette wanted to send you to Paris."

"Yes, although I still don't see him anywhere. It's weird that he's not here for the big announcement." Addison craned her neck but still couldn't catch sight of Carter anywhere. Where had he gone?

"Welcome, *Veil* family, and merry Christmas." Colette raised a champagne flute in the air. "Tonight is a special evening, and I know some of you have other parties and celebrations to get to, so I wanted to go ahead and share some special news regarding the future of *Veil* as we prepare to ring in a new year."

Addison gazed out over the crowd, and her heart gave a little twinge. She'd worked alongside the people in this room for years. It was hard to imagine working anyplace else. Usually, she sat directly beside Colette at the company Christmas party. It felt so odd to stand apart from the group, no longer sure of her place here. Or anywhere, for that matter.

But her *Veil* girls were right beside her, just like always. And with their support, she could get through anything. It was time to take Carter's advice and learn to accept help when she needed it. The *Veil* crew took care of each other through thick and thin.

"Please join me in congratulating my replacement, the new editor-in-chief of *Veil*," Colette said.

Addison couldn't help but take one last look around. She glanced over her shoulder, but there was still no sign of Carter. Heart pounding hard, she turned back around and found Colette looking straight toward her.

"Addison England." Colette's lips curved into a smile and for the briefest of moments, Addison thought she spied a tear glistening in her boss's eye.

That couldn't possibly be right. *None* of this was right.

"Did she just say my name?" Addison whispered.

"She sure did!" Everly embraced her in a tight hug. "You did it, Addie. Congratulations."

But she hadn't. This was Carter's job, not hers. At least that's what Colette had told her earlier.

Carter's not here, though, is he? No wonder. His absence suddenly made perfect sense.

But how had this happened? Addison couldn't wrap her head around the sudden switch.

Daphne gave her a gentle nudge. "I think you're supposed to go up there."

Everyone in the restaurant was staring at her. Somehow she managed to put one foot in front of the other to take her place beside Colette near the Christmas tree. As soon as she was within arm's reach, her boss took both of her hands in hers.

"Congratulations, Addison. You've earned this." Colette's voice was barely discernible above the cheers and cries of *brava* from the rest of the *Veil* staff.

"Thank you," Addison said. She'd waited for this moment for years, imagined it a million times over. This was what she'd wanted since the very first moment she set foot in the *Veil* office, but a ball of dread formed in the pit of her stomach at the thought of what she might have given up to make it happen. "I suppose this means Carter is moving to Paris?"

"What?" Colette's forehead creased. "No. Carter resigned this evening. He put it all in writing while you and I were meeting about Paris. As soon as you left, I found his resignation email in my inbox."

"He resigned," Addison repeated, doing her best to make sense of what had happened.

Carter had quit before Colette announced her decision. He'd sacrificed himself to make Addison's dreams come true. Could it be possible that he'd taken work out of the equation so they could build something more meaningful…more real. Together?

She wanted to believe it so very much, but if that had been the case, why sign the divorce papers? If anything, his resignation seemed like a parting gift.

"Yes, he did. I have to say, I'm surprised he didn't tell you." Colette leaned closer and lowered her voice. "Given that the two of you are husband and wife."

Of course she knew. Was it possible to truly hide anything from Colette?

"He told me the truth after I read his resignation letter. So much makes sense now. I understand about Paris. You could've told me, you know," Colette said.

"I didn't think it was my place. You and Carter are family."

"And now, so are we," Colette said with a nod.

For now...

Addison's throat closed up tight, but she managed to ask one final question. "What are we going to do about Paris?"

Colette gave an elegant shrug. "It seems as if I need to pack my bags. There's a lot of work to do there."

"*You're* going to head up the French edition?"

"I never really liked that Peloton, you know. I think we both know that I wouldn't be well suited for retirement," Colette said with a gleam in her eyes. "Let's wait and tell the staff about the French edition after the holidays. This is your moment, not mine."

"Thank you so much, Colette," Addison said, and then she did something that she never could've imagined before today—she wrapped her arms around her boss and pulled her in for a hug.

Colette gave a start at first, but then relented and relaxed into the embrace. Addison laughed under her breath. Paris was the perfect "retirement plan" for her workaholic boss. Maybe once she got there, she might even slow down a little. It was possible, wasn't it?

"Excuse me," someone behind Addison said—an aggressively annoyed someone if her tone of voice was any indication.

Addison pulled away from Colette and turned to find the restaurant's hostess glaring pointedly at her Vuitton tote.

Busted.

"Dogs aren't allowed in the restaurant, ma'am. I'm afraid we're going to have to ask you to leave."

Addison winced. "I'm really sorry. I—"

"Just go," Colette said with a flick of her wrist. Then, in an almost imperceptible voice, she added, "You have someplace more important to be, anyway."

A tiny spark of hope glimmered deep inside Addison. "I do?"

"Ma'am," the hostess huffed.

Sabrina's head appeared from the top of the handbag, and she let out a timely woof.

Addison held up her hands. "We're going right now. I promise."

She waved to the *Veil* crew as the hostess escorted her out. Everly and Daphne had joined Henry and Jack in their booth, and for a moment, Addison thought about how wonderful it would be if she and Carter were seated alongside them next year, right here in this very room on Christmas Eve. It was a *Veil* tradition, after all.

A lot could happen in a year, she thought. *Just look how much has changed since the start of December.*

Maybe if she believed hard enough, Christmas Eve

might bring her one last dash of December magic. But it was admittedly difficult to keep the faith when she was being forcibly marched out of the *Veil* holiday party.

"Again, I'm really sorry," she said once she'd crossed the restaurant's threshold and found herself back outside in the cold. "I hope you have a lovely Christmas."

Without a word, the hostess shut the door in her face.

Bah humbug to you too.

"Try not to be offended, Sabrina," Addison said into her handbag. "She must not be a dog person."

A month ago, neither had Addison.

The Cavalier popped her head out again and rubbed her face against Addison's cheek, and the tenderness of the gesture brought tears to her eyes. Maybe crying at the drop of a hat was her new thing now too. Or maybe that was just reserved for days when she had executed divorce papers nestled at the bottom of her bag, all tied up with a bow.

She took a deep inhale and when she opened her eyes, a true Christmas miracle stood in front of her holding a massive bouquet of pink peonies—her favorite flower. She swallowed hard and wondered if she might be hallucinating or experiencing some sort of Scroogian delusion. Or was he really here—the man who embodied her perfect Christmas present and her dream of Christmas future, all rolled into one?

"Carter?"

Carter adjusted the bouquet of peonies in his grip as he took in the sight of Addison standing outside the restaurant like a lost child. It wasn't until he spied Sabrina tucked into her handbag that he realized what was going on.

"Nice dog," he said, biting back a smile.

They were the same words he'd first spoken to her nearly a month ago when he'd stumbled upon her lingering at the entrance to Bemelmans' Bar at the Carlyle. She'd been deep in another dog dilemma then too, and even back then, Carter had known there was something special about her. She'd captured his attention in an instant, and the wild ride that followed had turned his life upside down.

How many times had he asked himself if he'd have done anything differently given the opportunity to go back in time? If he'd known then what he knew now, would he have still spoken to her? Volunteered to puppy sit her dog? Decided to play along with their office games instead of returning to *L'homme* the first chance he got?

In a heartbeat.

If there'd ever been a shadow of a doubt, this moment made things crystal clear. They had a clean slate now—Carter had made sure of it. He'd done everything in his power to make sure tonight marked a new beginning, but as fate would have it, they were starting off on the same foot as they had before.

"Pardon?" Addison said in a shaky voice, following the same script.

She remembers. Carter breathed a little easier. "I was just admiring your dog."

This was the part where she was supposed to tell him the dog wasn't hers, but instead she surprised him. "Thank you. I'm rather fond of her myself."

Carter tilted his head. "Does this mean what I think it means?"

There'd never been a doubt in his mind that she'd end up keeping the dog. Sabrina had Addison wrapped around her little paw. Those two belonged together.

"I adopted Sabrina. How else was I going to get you to stop calling me Cruella?" Addison said.

Her words were light but hurt glittered in her soft brown eyes—a hurt so deep that it nearly brought Carter to his knees. Had he done the wrong thing by resigning? All he'd wanted to do was show her that what they had was more important than the job. He hadn't needed to think twice about giving it up. It belonged to Addison, anyway. She'd earned it, fair and square. Didn't she know that he would've given her the world if he could?

Her gaze flitted briefly to the peonies.

"Why are you here?" she asked flatly.

"I wanted to surprise you. Congratulations, editor-in-chief." He held the flowers out toward her.

When she didn't make a move to accept them, he untucked his other offering from beneath his arm—a gold-rimmed, pale green box of macarons from Ladurée.

Her resistance wavered for a moment, but after a look of pure, unadulterated longing, she blinked and resumed glaring at him.

"The promotion is nice, but please don't congratulate me. I don't care about the job anymore, Carter. *You're* what matters most to me," she huffed. "I love you, you stupid Cronut."

Carter instantly felt drunk with happiness, as if he'd just downed half a dozen wedding cake martinis.

"What are you *smiling* at? I'm furious with you," Addison said.

"But you love me." He felt a smile tug at his lips. "And as it happens, I love you too."

Awe transformed her face…until she remembered she was mad at him. "Wait, if you love me then why do you want to divorce me?"

"You think I want to divorce you? A divorce was never what I wanted. I'm sorry if I haven't made that completely clear. I thought you needed time, and I didn't want to push." Carter shoved the macarons under his arm again so he could cup her cheek. Hope stirred deep in his soul when she didn't pull away. They loved each other. That was all that mattered—not the job, not whatever grave misunderstanding had just happened. His heart belonged to her, to love and to cherish, all the days of their lives. "Sweetheart, why would you ever think that's what I wanted?"

"Because you signed the papers and left them on my desk, topped with a bow," she whispered, as if saying it any louder would've made it true.

"What? No, I didn't." Carter's response was automatic, colored by confusion. And then, when he realized what she meant, he kissed her forehead and held her closer. "Addison, my love, you didn't open the envelope, did you? That was a copy of my resignation letter to Colette."

She drew back to search his gaze. "Really?"

"Really."

"I didn't open it. I just thought…" She shook her head. "I can't believe this. Are you sure you didn't sign them?"

"No. I never had any intention of signing them. The

pen was never really broken, darling. Those papers are still sitting in the top drawer of our credenza, and as soon as I can get my hands on them, I'm putting them through the office shredder, once and for all." He winced. "On second thought, you might have to do that, because I don't work there anymore."

"Gladly." She laughed, and it might have been the sweetest sound Carter had ever heard. His heart squeezed tight as the sadness in her gaze finally disappeared. "I should've opened the envelope. I'm so sorry I didn't, but I guess this means we're still married. We're not even half-divorced, are we?"

"We are one hundred percent husband and wife. I trust that's okay with you?"

"It's the best news I've ever heard." She grinned up at him and wound her arms around his neck. Sabrina immediately took advantage of his close proximity to scramble out of the handbag and launch herself at him, all wagging tail and happy little yips.

"I missed you too, you sweet thing," Carter said, holding the dog close while Addison plucked the bouquet of peonies from his hand and buried her face in the fragrant pink blossoms.

Then she gave his tie a gentle tug, pulling him within kissing distance—a move more effective than all the mistletoe in the world.

"You know, now that you can't call me Cruella anymore, you're going to have to go back to that other nickname," she murmured against his lips.

"Which nickname was that?" Carter gave the corner of her mouth a gentle brush with his lips and a groan escaped him. She was so warm, so sweet—a sugarplum dream. And best of all, she was *his*. Now and forever.

And in the moment before he sealed anew every vow they'd made with a kiss, she offered him a smile more luminous than the Christmas star, shining bright against a world of darkness.

"Wifey."

Epilogue

Veil *Magazine, January Issue*
Wedding Report

Veil*'s own newly minted editor-in-chief Addison England tied the knot—again—at a midnight ceremony on New Year's Eve with former deputy editor Carter Payne. The bride and groom rang in the new year by renewing the vows they famously took in this magazine's December feature pictorial, How to Elope in New York City at Christmas. The second time around, the happy couple were surrounded by close friends and family members as they promised to love, honor and cherish one another at the Shangri-La Hotel in Paris, France.*

The intimate ceremony took place on one of the hotel's iconic marble terraces overlooking the Eiffel Tower, with the bride's Cavalier King Charles

Spaniel Sabrina accompanying her on her walk down the aisle. Everly England Astor and Daphne Ballantyne King stood as co-matrons of honor, with Olivia King and the bride's five-month-old twin nieces serving as flower girls.

Courtiers at Givenchy re-created the ivory lace dress famously worn by Audrey Hepburn at the 1954 Academy Awards ceremony, where the actress won the coveted Best Actress statue for her role in Roman Holiday. *The tea-length gown featured a wide skirt, a bateau neckline with gossamer-thin spaghetti straps and a trim belt with floral lace detailing. Sabrina the Cavalier wore a floral collar crafted from pink peonies. After the ceremony, the wedding party enjoyed an evening of dinner, dancing and a dessert buffet of macarons, Cronuts and champagne cocktails.*

Following a honeymoon in Paris, the happy couple will return to Manhattan where a new era here at Veil *will begin with the bride at its helm as the new editor-in-chief. The groom has recently accepted a position as the founding editor-in-chief at* Mister, *a new American men's magazine by the publishers of the French luxury publication* L'homme.

Veil is thrilled to have played a part in bringing Addison and Carter together, and we wish them every happiness.

* * * * *

Chapter One

Twyla Thompson was thrilled to see a line out the door on the night of *New York Times* bestselling author Stacy Cruz's book signing. This was exactly what Once Upon a Book needed—an infusion of excitement and good-will and the proverbial opening up of the wallet during the holidays for a book instead of the latest flat-screen TV. Even if Stacy's recently released thriller wasn't exactly Christmas material, the timing was right both for her, the publisher and certainly Twyla's family-owned bookstore.

The reading had been short due to subject matter—murder—and Stacy took questions from the crowd. As usual, they ranged from "How can I get published?" To "I have an idea for a book. Would you write it for me?" To "My mother had a *fascinating* life. It should be a book, then a movie starring Meryl Streep." Stacy was a good sport about it all since the Charming, Texas, residents were her friends and neighbors, too.

Twyla, for her part, would never dream of writing a book. She barely had time to read everything she wanted to. Which was basically…everything. The heart of a bookseller beat in her and she recommended books like they were her best friends. Want an inspirational book? Read this. Would you like a tour de force celebrating the power of the human spirit? Here's the book for you. A little escapism with some romance and comedy thrown in? Right here. Want to be scared within an inch of your life? Read Stacy Cruz's latest suspense thriller.

The very best part of Twyla's day was getting lost in the worlds an author created. Her favorite books had always been of the fantasy romance genre, particularly of the dragon-slaying variety. She adored a fae hero who slayed dragons before breakfast. But honestly? She read anything she could get her hands on. Owning her four-generation family bookstore had made that possible. She'd grown up inside these four walls filled with bookshelves and little alcoves and nooks. She read all the *Nancy Drew* mysteries, Beverly Cleary and, when her grandmother wasn't looking, Kathleen Woodiwiss.

Twyla stood next to Roy Finch at the register as he rang up another sale of Stacy's latest book, *Vengeance*, that featured a serial killer working among the political power brokers in DC. Twyla had read it, of course. She could not deny Stacy's talent at terrifying the reader and making them guess until the last page. You'd never expect this from the married, sweet and beautiful mother of a little girl. She was as normal a person as Twyla had ever met.

"Nice crowd tonight," Mr. Finch said. "Too bad Stacy doesn't write more than one book a year."

Too bad indeed. Because while hosting yoga classes and book clubs, and selling educational toys had sustained them, it would no longer be enough. For the past two years, the little bookstore, the only one in town, had been in a terrible slump. Her grandmother still kept the books, and she'd issued the warning earlier this year. Pulling them out of the red might require more than one great holiday season. Foot traffic had slowed as more people bought their books online.

"I've got a signed copy of Stacy's latest book for you." Lois, Mr. Finch's fiancée, set a stack of no less than ten books on the counter by the register. "And I grabbed a bunch of giving tree cards."

The cards were taken from a large stack of books in the shape of a Christmas tree Twyla set up every season. Instead of ornaments, tags indicated the names and addresses of children who either wanted, or needed, a book for Christmas.

"We can always count on you, sweetheart." Mr. Finch rang her up.

It was endearing the way residents supported the Thompson family bookstore. They might have been in this location for four decades, but they'd never needed as much help as in the past two years.

Mr. Finch, a widowed and retired senior citizen, volunteered his time at the shop so Twyla could occasionally go home. For a while now they hadn't been able to afford any paid help. Her parents were officially retired and had moved to Hill Country. Their contributions amounted to comments on the sad state of affairs when a bookstore had to host yoga classes. But the instructor gave Twyla a flat rate to rent the space, and she didn't see *them* coming up with any solutions. They didn't want to close up shop. Of *course* not. They simply wanted Twyla to solve this problem for the entire Thompson family by selling books and nothing else.

"I don't know what I'd do without either one of you," Twyla said fondly, patting Mr. Finch's back. "Or any of the other members of the Almost Dead Poets Society."

Many of the local senior citizens had formed a poetry group where they recited poems they'd written. It had all started rather innocently enough—a creative effort, and something to do with all their free time. Unfortunately, they also liked to refer to themselves as "literary" matchmakers. Literary not to *ever* be confused with "literally." They'd failed with Twyla so far, not that they'd ever give up trying. Last month they'd invited both her and Tony Taylor to a reading and not so discreetly attempted to fix them up.

You're both so beautiful, it's a little hard to look at you for long, Ella Mae, the founder of their little group, had said. *Kind of like the sun!*

The double Ts! Lois had exclaimed. *Or would that be the quadruple Ts?*

Quadruple, I think, Mr. Finch had said.

You won't even have to change the initials on your monogrammed towels! Patsy Villanueva had clapped her hands. *I mean if it works out, that is.*

But no pressure! Susannah had held up a palm.

Twyla didn't own anything monogrammed, let alone towels, but she'd still exchanged frozen smiles with Tony. They'd arranged a coffee date just for fun. Unfortunately, as she'd known for years, Tony batted for the other team. He even had a live-in boyfriend that the old folks assumed was his roommate. It was an easy assumption to make since Tony was such a "man's man"—a grease monkey who lifted engines for a living. And he hadn't exactly come out of the closet, thinking his personal life was nobody's business. He was right, of course. But…

"You really *should* declare your love of show tunes, Tony," she'd teased.

"I'm not a cliché."

"Well, you *could* get married."

"I'm not ready to settle down." He scowled.

Still, they'd had a nice time, catching up on life post-high school. He'd asked after Noah Cahill, and of course she had all the recent updates on her best friend. In the end they'd decided she and Tony would definitely be double-dating at some point.

When Twyla could find a date.

This part wasn't going to be easy because Twyla had a bad habit. She preferred to spend her time alone and reading a book. Long ago, she'd accepted that she wouldn't be able to find true love inside the walls of her small rental. But accepting invitations to parties and bar hops wasn't her style. She wanted to be invited, really, but she just didn't want to go. An introvert's problem.

This was why she'd adopted a cat. But, she worried, if she didn't get a date soon, she was going to risk being known as the cat lady.

"That's the last copy!" Stacy stood from the table, beaming, holding a hand to her chest. "My publisher will be thrilled. I honestly can't *believe* it."

"I can." Twyla began to clear up the signing table. "You're very talented and it's about time people noticed. I just wish you'd write more books."

"So do I, but tell that to my daughter." Stacy sighed. "She's a holy terror, just like her father. Runs around all day, throwing things. I'm lucky if I get in a few hundred words a day."

"That's okay." Twyla chuckled. "We can't exactly base our business plan on how many books you write a year."

Stacy blinked and a familiar concern shaded her eyes. "Are you…are you guys doing okay? Should I maybe ask my publisher whether they can send some of their other authors here for a signing?"

As a bookseller, she knew everyone in the business was suffering, and publishers weren't financing many book tours. Stacy did those on her own dime, hence the local gig. Twyla didn't like lying to people but she liked their pity even less. She constantly walked a tightrope between the two.

"As long as we have another great holiday season, like all the others, we should be fine!" She hoped the forced quality of her über-positive attitude wasn't laying it on too thick.

But Stacy seemed to accept the good news, bless her heart.

"What a relief! We can't have a *town* without a bookstore."

"No, we can't," Mr. Finch agreed with a slight shake of his head. "It would be a travesty."

One by one the straggling customers left, carrying their purchases with them. Not long after, Stacy's husband, the devastatingly handsome Adam, dropped by to pick her up and drive her home. Everyone said their goodbyes.

Mr. Finch and Lois brought up the rear, wanting to help Twyla close up.

"You two go home!" She waved her hands dismissively. "I'm right behind you."

"I'll be by tomorrow for my morning shift promptly at nine." Mr. Finch took Lois's hand in his own.

"Are you sure you don't want to take a break? Take tomorrow off." Twyla went behind them, shutting off the lights. "You worked tonight."

"I'll get plenty of rest when I'm dead," Roy said, holding the door open for Lois.

"Roy!" Lois went ahead. "Please don't talk about the worst day of my life a second before it happens."

"No, darlin'." He sweetly brought her hand up to his lips. "I'll be around for a while. You manage to keep me young."

These two never failed to fill her heart with the warm fuzzies. Both had been widowed for a long time, and were on their second great love.

Which meant some people got two of those, and so far, Twyla didn't even have one.

Twyla arrived at her grandmother's home a few minutes later, having stopped first at the bakery for a salted caramel Bundt cake. She and Ganny usually met for dinner every Saturday night and she always brought dessert. Was it sad that a soon-to-be thirty-year-old single woman didn't have anything better to do on a Saturday night? Not at all. She had her cat, Bonkers, waiting at home. He was mean as the devil himself, but he'd been homeless when she adopted him from the shelter, so she was all he had.

Twyla also had at least half a dozen advanced reader copy books on her nightstand waiting for her. There were also all the upcoming Charming holiday events she'd agreed to participate in because that's what one did as a business owner. Ava had told her about a rare angel investor offering a zero-interest loan to a local Charming business. On top of everything else, Twyla had to prepare an essay this month to be considered. It wasn't as if she didn't have anything else to do. Too much, in fact.

"Hello, Peaches."

Ganny bussed Twyla's cheek. Occasionally she still referred to Twyla by her old childhood nickname. Once, she'd eaten so many juicy fresh peaches from the tree in Ganny's yard that she threw up. It wasn't the best nickname in the world.

"How was the book signing?"

"A line out the door." Twyla followed Ganny into the ornate dining area connected to the kitchen and set the cake on the mahogany table.

Ganny had been widowed twice and her last husband, Grandpa Walt, a popular real estate broker, had left her with very little but this house. It was too big for Ganny, but she refused to leave it because of the dining room. It was big enough to accommodate large groups of people, which she felt encouraged Twyla's parents to visit several times a year.

"It was a good start to the month."

"Good, good. Well, that's enough book business talk for tonight." Ganny waved a hand dismissively. "I've got a surprise for you tonight. An early Christmas present."

"You didn't have to get me anything."

But a thrill whipped through Twyla because her grandmother was renowned for her thoughtful gifts all year long. It could almost be anything. Maybe a trip to New York City, where Ganny had promised to finally introduce her to some of the biggest booksellers in the country. People she'd met over a lifetime of acquiring and selling books. Twyla had wanted to go back to New York for years. She could still feel the energy of the city zipping through her blood, taste the cheesecake from Junior's, and the slice of pepperoni pizza from Times Square.

"Why wouldn't I give my only granddaughter the best present in the world?" Ganny smiled with satisfaction. "He should be along any minute now."

All the breath left Twyla's body. Just the thought of another blind date struck her with a sadness she had no business feeling during the holidays. Everyone in town was conspiring to fix up "poor, sad Twyla who can't get a man."

She could get a man, but she wasn't concentrating her efforts on this.

Please let it not be Tony again. And yet there were so few single men her age left in town. Hadn't her grandmother always told Twyla she'd do fine on her own? If she couldn't find the right man, she didn't need *any* man? Twyla had embraced this truth. She wanted the perfect man or no one at all.

"Life with the right man is wonderful. But a life with the wrong man might as well be lived alone. So many things in life can replace a spouse. Work, travel and books, to start with," Ganny had said.

Twyla, then, *could* lead a happy and fruitful life without ever being married.

"Oh, Ganny." Twyla slumped on the chair. "You didn't fix me up with someone, did you?"

"Of course not, honey!" She patted Twyla's hand. "But speaking of which, you're not going to meet anyone special if you don't get out more."

"I'm just like you. Books are my family."

It seemed to have skipped a generation, because though her father, Ganny's son, had loyally run the family bookstore, it wasn't exactly his happy place.

"Yes, but keep in mind I made myself go out and meet people. It wasn't like it is today. Certainly not. I used to have three dates on the same day. No funny business, of course, but your mother already told me things are different."

Twyla couldn't imagine going out three times in one day. She'd be lucky to go out once every three years. Okay, she was exaggerating. But still. Men weren't exactly lining up to date her. One of them had said she'd look prettier if she'd stop wearing her black-rimmed glasses. Twyla refused to go the contact lens route because if glasses stopped a guy from being interested in her, it wasn't the guy she wanted anyway.

"Fine, I promise I'll go out! But please don't fix me up." Her friend Zoey had bugged her to go out with her and her boyfriend, Drew, and Twyla hadn't yet.

"No blind date. This is someone you actually want to see."

"I can't even imagine."

There was only one "he" she'd like to see, and he was

all the way in Austin, at home with his girlfriend. Probably planning their wedding.

"That's it. I'm having dessert first." Twyla opened the cake box.

The doorbell rang and Ganny rose. "You stay here and close your eyes! Don't open them until I tell you to."

Oh, brother. It was like being twelve again. She clasped her hand over her eyes, but not before taking a finger swipe of salted caramel frosting, feeling…well, twelve again.

"Okay, fine. My eyes are closed."

Twyla heard the front door open and shut, Ganny's delighted laughter, but no other sounds from this "he" man. Nothing but the sounds of boots thudding as they followed Ganny's lighter steps.

"Can I open my eyes now? I would really like to have a piece of cake. Whoever you are, I hope you like cake."

"I love cake," the deep voice said.

Twyla didn't even have to open her eyes to recognize the teasing, flirty sound of her favorite person in the world. She didn't have to hazard a guess because she knew this man almost as well as she knew herself.

And Ganny was right. It *was* the best present.

Ever.

"Noah!"

Twyla stood and hurled herself into the open arms of Noah Cahill, her best friend.

Chapter Two

There were few things in his life Noah enjoyed as much as filling his arms with his best friend. He held Twyla close, all five feet nothing of her. Her dark hair longer now than it had been a year ago when he'd left Charming. Today she was wearing her book-pattern dress, which meant the store must have had a signing. The outfit was a type of uniform she wore for those events. She had a similar skirt in bright colors with patterns of dragons, swords and slayers.

God, she was a sight. The old familiar pinch squeezed his chest. He almost hadn't come home this Christmas, thinking it would be easier. There was already so much he hadn't told her when he normally told her everything.

Almost everything.

Then he'd narrowly missed death, or at the least a devastating injury, and everything changed in the course of days. He would not waste another minute of his life doing a job he no longer wanted to do.

"I thought you weren't coming home this Christmas!" Twyla said, coming to her tiptoes to hug him tight. Her arms wrapped around his neck.

Automatically and before he could stop himself, he turned his head to take in a deep breath of her hair. She always smelled like coconuts. He set her down reluctantly, but he was used to this feeling with Twyla. It was always this way—the push and pull always resulting in the distance he'd created due to guilt.

And loyalty.

"Things have changed."

"Noah isn't just *visiting*," Twyla's grandmother said, sounding pleased. "He's come home to stay."

Bless Mrs. Schilling's kind heart. She'd always been pulling for Noah, against any and all reason, even if he could have told her a thousand times it was useless. He was destined to pine after Twyla forever. What he wanted to have with her would never work and the door had been slammed shut years ago. Now the opening might as well be buried under rubble. Like the roof that nearly fell on him.

"You're here to stay?" Twyla brightened. "But what about your job in Austin?"

"I quit." He held his arms off to the side with a shrug. "It's not for me. Not anymore."

"It's *exactly* you. You've been an adrenaline junkie since you were a boy. How is it not for you?"

Yeah, best not to tell her about the roof that fell inches from him during a building fire. His entire squad had been lucky to escape with no fatalities. Three had wound up with minor injuries.

Noah could have sworn something, or *someone*, had shoved him out of the way. In that moment, with the heat barreling toward him and unfurling like a living thing, he'd felt his brother Will there in the room with him. Will, shouting for him to get out of the way.

His long-dead older brother was telling Noah, in no uncertain terms, to stop trying to be a hero. To, for the love of God, stop rescuing people and start living his own life. Noah had first worked as an EMT, and then later a firefighter in nearby Houston for the past few years. He'd saved some people and lost some, but "imaginary Will" had called it. No matter what Noah did, he'd never get another chance to save Will.

And he was the only save that would have ever mattered. Now it was high time to honor his life instead. Noah may have always felt second best to his much smarter and accomplished brother, but that feeling wasn't one encouraged by Will. His older brother had always had Noah's back. Even on their last day together.

"It was good, for a while, but it's time to move on."

"But—"

"Let's have some of that delicious cake." Mrs. Schilling urged them to take a seat at the table. "We have plenty of time to discuss all this."

"I never say no to cake." Noah took a seat, avoiding Twyla's gaze.

If he looked too directly at her, she'd see everything in his eyes, so at times like these he had a system in place.

Don't make eye contact.

Three serving plates were passed around and Twyla sliced off generous pieces.

"No matter what, we're glad you're home," Mrs. Schilling said. "Aren't we, dear?"

"Yes, of course. It's just such a surprise. So…unexpected." Twyla took a bite of cake.

Using an old trick, he purposely looked at her ear, to make it look like he was meeting her eyes.

"It's a career choice. I have a really great opportunity here."

"Where are you staying?"

It was a fair question since he'd given up his rental when he'd grown tired of the memories that haunted him here and moved to Austin to start over.

"I rented one of those cottages by the beach. Just temporary until I find a place. The place where I'll be living is far less important than what I'll be doing." Noah winked.

This was his biggest news: the culmination of a long-held dream. He'd squashed it for so long after Will's death that he'd nearly forgotten it. But in that fiery building, he'd *remembered*.

"What *are* you going to be doing?"

"Taking over a business here in town." He'd start with the easy stuff first.

"Wonderful!" Mrs. Schilling clapped her hands. "Obviously, I have always loved the entrepreneurial spirit. Why, it's the reason the Thompson family started Once Upon a Book."

"What kind of business? Fire investigation? Teaching safety? You would make a *great* teacher." Twyla smiled and took another bite of cake.

He hoped the news wasn't going to kill her like it might his own mother. But he couldn't live the rest of his life in fear. Or worse yet, accommodating the fears of others.

"No. I'm taking over the boat charter. Mr. Curry is retiring, and he's been looking for a buyer for a year or more."

When his news was met with such silence that he heard Mrs. Schilling's grandfather clock ticking, he continued.

"He actually wants someone local to take it over, so he'll work terms out with me. I have enough hours on the water, so I'll be taking the USCG test for my captain's license. I've obviously already had first aid training and then some. Until I get my license, I'll have Finn's help and he already has his license. Mr. Curry said he'd be around awhile longer, too, if we need help." He filled his mouth with a big piece of cake.

Twyla sucked in a breath, and Mrs. Schilling's shaky hand went to her throat. Other than that, Noah thought everything here would be okay. Nothing to see here. Sure thing. They'd all get used to the idea. Eventually.

Just give them a couple of decades.

"Are you serious?" Twyla pushed her plate of unfinished cake away.

Only he would fully understand the significance of the move. For Twyla not to finish a slice of cake meant that in her opinion, the world just might be ending.

"Yes, I'm serious. Ask yourself whether if anyone else said the same thing, you'd have this kind of a reaction."

"That's not even funny. You're *not* anyone else." She

took a breath and whispered her next words. "You're Will's brother. You…you almost died out there, too."

"Now, Twyla…let the man finish." This from Twyla's grandmother, thankfully, the voice of reason.

She didn't let him finish.

"If this is my surprise, I don't like it." Twyla stood.

With that she walked right out of her grandmother's kitchen.

"Twyla!" her grandmother chided. "Oh, dear. Noah, I'm sorry. She's had a rough year. The bookstore isn't doing well, and—"

"Let me talk to her."

"Noah? Are you sure about this? If Twyla reacts this way, you can only imagine how your poor mother—"

"I know. *And* I'm sure."

He found Twyla outside on the wraparound porch's swing, bare feet dangling as she stared into the twinkling sky. Without a word, he plopped himself next to her and nudged her knee.

"Hey."

"Hey." She leaned into him, and he tamped down the rush of raw emotion that single move brought. "I'm sorry. I may have…overreacted."

She couldn't stay angry at him for long. Neither one of them could. Not since they'd been kids.

"You think? It's not that I don't understand the concern but everyone seems to forget I grew up boating. Will and I both did. I'm going to be careful and follow all relevant safety practices. Probably go overboard with them." He chuckled and elbowed her. "See what I did there?"

"Funny man."

"I just…can't pretend anymore."

Starting over had served its purpose. He'd lived in a city in which no one knew him as Will's younger brother. A new place where he'd excelled and never been second best. He'd tried to settle down into a stable relationship with Michelle. But he hadn't been happy even before the roof collapse.

"What are you pretending?"

"That I'm okay living someone else's life. I don't want to live in Austin. I want to live here. You do realize the ocean is not the only danger in life?"

"Sure, I'd prefer you do something normal like… I don't know, real estate? You'd make a killing. *Everybody* loves you."

Wind up the only surviving brother after a boating tragedy and you're bound to get a lot of sympathy. He was tired of that, too. Another reason he'd left town.

He grunted. "Real estate is not going to happen. Too much paperwork."

"Why now? Did something happen?"

While he could tell her, letting her realize that it wasn't only water that could kill a man, this didn't seem like the right time. Later, he'd tell her about the roof collapse. Later, he'd tell her about Michelle.

And everything else. Someday. Just…not now.

"I think Will would want this. And I want this. This was our dream when we were kids. We'd wake up every day and go fishing. Every day would be like a vacation."

"I know he would want you to be happy."

"*This* is going to make me happy. I'm tired of living for other people. You only get one life. This one is mine."

They both sat in silence for a beat. Will had been only eighteen when they'd lost him in the accident that nearly took Noah's life, too. Their family had never been the same. When Noah's parents divorced, his father left the state and now rarely spoke to Noah. His mother still lived in Charming and had never truly gotten over the loss of her oldest son. She'd laid her dreams at Will's feet, who had done everything she'd ever asked of him. He'd been the good son, the strong academic. Noah had been the classic bad boy, unable to live up to the impossible standard that Will set.

"Remember when you, me and Will would lie under the stars at night?" Twyla pushed her legs out to start swinging. "And Will renamed the Little Dipper 'Noah Dipper' after you, and the Big Dipper was Will Dipper?"

"Yeah, even if Bill Dipper would have sounded better."

Noah smiled at the memory. Will believed in the power behind words and used to play around with letters all the time. Mixing them up, creating new words. Like Twyla, he was a bit of a book nerd. The valedictorian in his graduating class of Charming High. He and Twyla had been so much alike that it was no wonder that though Noah met Twyla first, it was Will who wound up dating her. His courtship with her might have been short and sweet, but at least he'd had one.

"He used to like renaming stuff. Combining two words together, shifting letters. Word play."

"Mine was easy. Twilight was hereafter renamed Twyla for short." She chuckled. "Totally made sense."

It had been a long while since they talked about Will.

Remembered. He was that silent spot between them, keeping them apart but making Noah wish for nothing more than those good times.

"He had the biggest crush on you."

Of course, Noah had been the first to have the crush except *crush* might not have been the right word. He'd been astounded. He recalled literally gaping when he first laid eyes on Twyla helping her mother at the bookstore, dressed in a pink dress and matching shoes. Pushing her horn-rimmed glasses up her nose and giving him a shy smile. She looked like an angel to an eleven-year-old boy.

"We should do that again sometime," Twyla said. "Lie under the stars together."

He almost jerked his neck back in surprise. She'd never suggested anything like this before. It amounted to doing something together that they'd only ever done with Will.

It was like…reinventing it.

"Why?"

"Why?" she spoke just above a whisper. "Because they're still there. Still twinkling. Is it okay with you if I want to look at them again and see them in a different way?"

He reached to lighten the moment. "Rename them, you mean?"

"Anything. Of course, maybe Michelle wouldn't like it. You and I spending so much time together."

Ah, that's why she'd brought it up. She didn't know about his breakup with the woman he'd dated while in Austin. He'd brought her to Charming once, where she'd met Twyla and the family. She thought Michelle was still there between them, a safe buffer from getting too close to him. There was no point in telling her the truth. Let her relax in her false belief. Their guilt had kept them apart this long. What was another decade?

Noah would throw himself into work. His dream. He'd live his life the way he wanted to and reach for happiness wherever he could find it. Around every blind corner. Behind every rogue wave. Fake it till he made it. He was excited about the future for the first time since he could recall.

Life was too short and if Will hadn't taught him that, then certainly the roof collapse had.

"No, probably not. She wouldn't like it," he lied. "But I don't care."

Twyla took off her glasses and wiped the lenses on the edge of her shirt.

She didn't say anything to that—probably because they didn't usually talk about any of his girlfriends. It was better that way.

He changed the subject. "Is it true you're having problems with the bookstore?"

Twyla sighed. "Why do you think I want to lie under the stars like when I was ten? Yes, we're having trouble. What else is new?"

"I thought everything was better after the last holiday season. You always say December counts for ninety percent of your business."

"Welcome to the book world. A lot can change in a year. The ground is constantly shifting under my feet."

"Well, you can't close the bookstore."

"Everyone says that."

"We grew up in that museum. Reading dragon slayer

books in those cozy corner nooks filled with pillows. I'll help. Just put me to work."

She smiled. "You're going to be busy if you insist on this madness."

"I'll figure out a way."

"Hey, does this mean you'll be at the tree lighting ceremony tomorrow?"

"Wouldn't miss it."

"Wait until you see the little book shaped ornaments we have for the tree."

She sounded excited and like her old self for the first time tonight.

"Let me guess. Dragon slayer books?"

"Among some others, of course. We can't ignore *The Night Before Christmas* and the other classics."

Sometimes, Noah could still see himself and Will sitting among the shelves of dusty books. They'd read quietly every afternoon after school because Twyla's parents didn't mind being an unofficial after-school center. It wasn't until much later, when he and Twyla had been in the depths of their shared grief, that they'd found "the book." The one that had defined the years after Will. They'd take turns reading chapters. One week the book stayed with Noah and he'd read three chapters, and one week it was with Twyla. He'd write and post stickers in the margins of the book, which had technically belonged to Twyla.

Noah would comment: *That idiot deserved to be killed by the dragon.*

And Twyla would answer: *Sometimes the dragon chooses the right victim.*

They'd mark significant parts, but almost never the

same ones. Noah was far more impressed with dragon slayer tools while Twyla loved the mushy stuff about love and sacrifice. The book came to belong to them both, since they'd literally made it their own. Noah had never done this with any other book before or since and he'd venture she never had either. For reasons he didn't quite understand, they'd made this particular book, *A Dragon's Heart*, their own. They shared the words until the day Noah stole the book from Twyla. There was just no other way to put it.

He'd "borrowed" the book without returning it.

That, at least, was something he'd never tell her.

Chapter Three

The next day, having risen before dawn to drive to the docks, Noah watched the sunrise while he waited for Mr. Curry to arrive. The view was calming and soothing in the way a Gulf Coast native could appreciate. Gold mixed with shades of blue and painted the sky with morning. Noah found little more beautiful than a Gulf Coast sunrise other than a sunset accompanied by fireflies. Over the years, he'd been seeing less of them lighting up the coastal nights.

"You're early." Mr. Curry emerged from his brightly detailed pickup truck.

The truck itself was practically a Charming landmark. Granted, it had seen better days and could definitely use a paint job. But the etching of two dolphins meeting halfway, blending into sharp blue and purple hues still grabbed attention. The letters spelled *Nacho Boat Adventures* and the phone number. Boat tours, fishing charters, diving excursions, water skiing, rentals. Group rates available.

A walking advertisement. Not that Noah would need to take out an ad because the business, decades old, was practically the apex of Charming tourism.

And if Noah was early, it was because he couldn't wait to get started.

He handed Mr. Curry a coffee cup. "Will you throw in the truck, too?"

"Let's talk inside." Mr. Curry put his key in the door of the unimpressive A-line shack on the pier.

Weather-beaten and somewhat battered, the outside could also use a makeover. So could Mr. Curry, for that matter, who had grown his white beard down to his chest and looked older than his sixty-five years.

"Are you doing okay?" Noah asked, watching him hobble inside.

"Ah, it's the arthritis. Makes me a grump most days. Don't take it personal." He took a swig of coffee, then held it up. "Thanks for this."

"No problem." Drinking from his own cup, Noah took in the shop he hadn't been inside for years.

A handwritten schedule of boat tours hung on a whiteboard behind the register. Surf boards were propped against the rear walls, hung near boating equipment like ropes and clips. The smells of wood and salt were comforting. Noah inhaled and took it all in. It was his burden to have never had a healthy fear of the ocean. And even after all he'd been through, he still didn't shy away from the memories of long summer days boating. Their father had taught both of his boys everything he knew, and they'd manned the captain's wheel from the time they were thirteen and fourteen. Two boys, a year apart. Irish twins, his mother called them.

"You should know. I'm moving." Mr. Curry interrupted Noah's thoughts.

"I know. That's why you're selling."

"Me and the Mrs. We're headed west to Arizona."

"Landlocked?" Noah raised his brow. This he had not expected.

"Hell, yeah. They got lakes. Need the dry and hot weather for my stupid arthritis." He went behind the counter and seemed to be fiddling around back there. "That's all to say that while I want someone like you to take over, I also need someone who's going to stick around. Do I make myself clear? I can stay on awhile and take some of those boat tours we've already scheduled for the real die-hards, but there's no turning back. No second thoughts. Of course, you could sell, but you see how long it's taken me. This isn't the greatest moneymaker in the world."

"I figured." Noah had some ideas of his own to increase business but best not interrupt the man's flow of thoughts.

"You won't get rich owning this business, but you will also never be poor."

"I'm in this for the long haul. I picture myself a grandfather, like you, finally retiring someplace dry because I have arthritis." Noah reached for some other older person's ailment and came up with nothing. "Or something."

"That's what I want to see. You, growing old in this town. Safe. Giving tours. Teaching. Because, well, you know…"

Noah let the silence hang between them for only a

moment. He knew where this would be going. Knew it far too well.

"I know," Noah completed the sentence. "And the accident still doesn't define who I am. Never did."

"My wife is going to kill me twice when she finds out who I sold to. I told her I had an offer from a local. That I'd offered financing to help the young man out. She thinks the idea is great. But she doesn't know it's *you*."

Noah sighed. He'd felt the protectiveness of this town come over him like a chokehold. It no longer felt like protection. It felt controlling. Unreasonable.

"It's time for all of us to move on."

"*If* you're sure." Mr. Curry crossed his arms. "Then this…is a done deal."

"I'm absolutely one hundred percent sure. I'm never going back to firefighting again. One roof nearly falling on me is enough."

Mr. Curry gaped. "Hot damn, son. You might be the luckiest man I've ever met. All right. Welcome aboard."

He chuckled, then went on to give Noah the speed version of the business he'd managed for two decades. It was all written down, of course…somewhere. Though good help was hard to find, Noah would have two staff members staying on through the transition. They were both part-time workers—teens who loved boating and were willing to be paid a microscopic salary for the pleasure of working for the new boss.

Concern hit Noah like a hot spike, but he forced himself to shake it off. Teenagers near water did not *automatically* mean danger.

"What do they do around here?"

"As little or as much as you want. Diana answers the phone and takes the bookings. Sells the little equipment we have for sale and the surf boards." He waved his hand in the air. "Tee, that's the ridiculous nickname he goes by, is working on a boating license. You can fire them both as far as I'm concerned but they're good kids and for a while they'll know more than you will about how we run things."

He had a point.

"Be at the bank tomorrow morning and we'll sign the papers. Owner financing the first year. It's all in the contract." He then reached under the register and came up with a small box. "May as well take these with you since you're here."

Noah accepted the box. "What's all this?"

"Christmas."

Indeed, dozens of tree ornaments in the shape of boats announced "A Merry Christmas from Nacho Boat." They were for the tree lighting ceremony tonight. This meant a couple of things. After tonight, almost everyone in town would know Noah was the new owner of Nacho Boat Adventures.

He was on borrowed time before his mother heard about the contract he'd sign tomorrow morning.

But he told himself one more day wouldn't hurt anything.

Just before the tree lighting ceremony, Twyla closed up shop and drove her sedan the short drive to the boardwalk. She carried her basket full of ornaments for the lighting of the Christmas tree. This had always been the first Charming event at the start of the month, which kicked off the season festivities. This never failed to make her heart buzz with anticipation, even if the excitement was dulled tonight due to Noah's unexpected news. She didn't like the idea of him taking over Nacho Boat any more than his mother would. But, more than anyone else, she understood what it was like to live under the heavy weight of opinion.

Charming was a small town and its residents were similar to an extended family you loved to hate. Even if more than a decade had passed, she was still thought of as "Will's girl." Even though she and Will barely dated for a year before he broke up with her because he'd be going away to college. Of course, that never happened. He'd never made it to college. She was Will's *last* girlfriend and some people, Noah's mother included, saw her forever frozen in the tragic role. The reason, she understood, was that Will himself would remain forever eighteen.

Twyla, on the other hand, would be twenty-seven this year. Like Noah, who'd been trying to escape his role as town hero responsible for the biggest water rescue in Charming history, she'd been trying to move on from the role of grieving ex-girlfriend. She'd signed up for some of the dating apps and forced herself on the occasional date. She'd even expressed her interest in Adam Cruz when he'd arrived in town over a year ago. He'd been single for about two minutes, however, and then there went that opportunity.

Over the years, she'd dated men here and there that Noah interestingly always found fault with. Yet he'd never even tried to fix her up. Not even with his best friend, Finn. Noah would sing the guy's praises all the live long day but whenever he was single, Noah stopped talking about Finn. She and Noah had never been on dates together, keeping that part of each other's life separate. She never complained about guys to him, and he never complained about women. But as far as she could tell, Noah never had any issues with the female population, other than the fact he'd never seemed ready to settle down. Michelle, someone he'd met in Austin, was simply the latest and Twyla wondered how long they'd last long distance.

Walking toward the boardwalk along the seawall, Twyla took in the holiday scene. As usual, the decor on the boardwalk was already in full swing. Many of the vendors would stay open through their mild winter, their shops decorated to the hilt with snowflakes, trees and more lights. Sounds from the roller coaster on the amusement park end of the boardwalk were as loud as on any summer night, only with residents and not many tourists. Families were out having fun, creating memories. She strolled along accompanied by the sound of seagulls cawing and foraging for food in the sand. Aromatic and delicious scents of fresh coffee, hot cocoa and popcorn competed. She would need some hot cocoa sooner rather than later.

Despite the lower tourism rate, which tended to hit every business, winter in Charming was her favorite time of the year, when temperatures hovered in the low sixties and, on a good day, reached the high fifties. She loved sweater and boot weather. Finally, she could haul out her cowboy boots and wear them without anyone teasing her.

She waved as she passed the Lazy Maisy kettle corn

store, selling their classic peppermint-flavored, red-and-green popcorn as they did every December, each worker dressed like an elf for the entire month. Strands of white lights hung from every storefront. A plastic model of Santa and his sleigh guided by a reindeer were suspended across one side of the boardwalk, cheery signs everywhere announcing a "charming" Christmas. Yes, thank you. Twyla would have a charming Christmas indeed.

Noah was back. Christmas would be even better now.

She had to keep telling herself that. Nacho Boat had a great safety record. Noah was bright and intelligent. He'd take all necessary precautions because he'd never want his mother to hurt again. For so long, they'd all walked on eggshells around Katherine Cahill. Twyla included. The woman had suffered enough but Noah did have a point. His career as a firefighter wasn't exactly a desk job. At least here, they'd all be able to keep an eye on him. Keep him safe. Yes, she'd do that. For Will and for Katherine. But mostly, for herself.

"Hey, Twyla."

She turned to find herself face to face with Valerie Kinsella, a third-grade teacher and wife of one of the three former Navy SEALs who ran the Salty Dog Bar & Grill.

"Check these out. I think the ornaments are amazing this year. I found a specialty shop in Dallas with a great price." She handed the box to Valerie, who would mix it up with the others.

"You've outdone yourself as usual." Valerie smiled.

Baskets filled with all donated ornaments would be passed around to the residents, who each got to choose at least one to put on a branch. People were already gathering around the huge tree in the center. Ava Del Toro, president of the Chamber of Commerce, climbed up the temporary risers hauled over from the high school.

Meanwhile, this year's Santa walked through the crowd, handing candy canes out to kids as the ornament baskets made the rounds. Twyla glanced in the crowd for Noah, since he'd texted her that he'd be there early and she should come and find him. At first, she didn't see him at all, and then noticed him talking to Sabrina, one of his old girlfriends. Most of his life, Noah had never failed to get the attention of girls, and later, women. It was the whole bad boy thing. He'd surfed, driven fast cars and even had a motorcycle for a nanosecond. Twyla hated motorcycles but she loved those boots Noah got to wear when he rode one. Even teachers liked Noah. He wasn't a stellar student, but he was funny and kind.

When he'd been hospitalized after the accident, there had been so many flowers in his room that it resembled a botanical garden.

Twyla watched now as Sabrina leaned into Noah, touched his broad shoulder and tossed back her long red hair. The familiar and unwelcome pinch of jealousy, this time on Michelle's behalf, burned in Twyla's stomach. Then Noah turned, saw Twyla, and his smile brightened. He gave a little "see ya later" wave to Sabrina.

He walked over to Twyla, hands stuck in the pockets of his blue denim jeans. "Hey, Peaches."

She grinned, ready to tease him. "Um, I'd be careful. You're going to make Michelle jealous."

A flash of guilt crossed his eyes. "Yeah, about that—"

But he was interrupted by a loud Ava nearly yelling through the bullhorn in her hands.

"Welcome, everyone! It's time for the lighting of the tree! So! Fun! This year our tree is donated by Tree Growers of Bent, Oregon. Another Douglas fir. Before we hit the switch and light up the night sky, you'll each get to place an ornament on the tree. Just reach in the baskets we're all passing out. Find an ornament in there and put it on the tree! And don't forget next week's Snowflake Float Boat Parade, followed by the first annual literary costume event at Once Upon a Book. Come dressed as your favorite literary character and support the giving tree! One of you could win a gift card worth hundreds of dollars, which ought to help with all that holiday shopping."

Many turned to Twyla and smiled, giving her a thumbs-up. She'd love to claim the idea as her own, but it had been yet another one of Ava's creative brainstorms. The woman was a marketing genius when it came to town tourism and supporting local business. Before Noah's return, the costume event would have been the most excitement she'd have all year. She'd been planning for months, her own ideas swinging between Elizabeth Bennet and Hermione Granger. She hadn't yet decided, but she already had the long Jane Austen-style dress she'd found for a deep discount on eBay.

"Literary character." Noah winked and tipped back on his heels. "Does dragon slayer count?"

Her heart raced at the memory. Their favorite book. She'd misplaced *A Dragon's Heart* about a year ago, just before the move into a smaller rental to save money. Books tended to get swallowed whole in a bookstore and half the time she expected to come across it on a shelf. So far, she hadn't. Everyone, including Mr. Finch, was on the lookout. This particular copy was unlike any other, and even though the genre had grown out of popularity with most readers, Twyla liked to read the book once a year. She'd ordered another copy for that reason alone, but it could never take the place of the one she'd lost. Noah's handwriting was in the margins of that book, along with her own.

"You can come as anything you'd like. I'm just happy to have you."

She nearly corrected herself but then let it go. He knew what she meant. She didn't *have* him. Michelle had him. And though she wondered with every moment that passed what he'd meant when he said, "About that…" she refused to ask.

"I kind of look like a dragon slayer and I'm sure I can find a cool sword."

She chuckled. "You do *not* look like a dragon slayer and I'm fairly sure you already own a plastic toy sword."

"Are you calling me an overgrown child?" He narrowed his eyes, filled with humor and mischief.

"Maybe."

"Got to say, it's tough to hang out with someone who knows me so well." The basket came around to them and Noah dug for several long seconds, causing even Valerie to quirk a brow. "Ah, yeah. Here we go."

He held up the ornament depicting the cover of *Where the Wild Things Are*. "My favorite book. Still read it every night before bed."

"Bless your heart," Valerie said, and waited while Twyla dug through the basket.

She picked out an elf from the Lazy Maisy store and together she and Noah went forward and placed the ornaments. Side by side like they'd done for years. Just like old times.

A few minutes later, the lights slowly went up the giant tree, starting from the lower half and scrolling slowly to the top until bright lights beckoned.

Noah turned to Twyla. "Let the wild rumpus start."

Chapter Four

The night was clear and bright, not socked in with fog like the Gulf Coast could get on some nights. Twyla and Noah strolled along the seawall. She should go home soon and feed Bonkers, even if he was the most anti-social cat on earth. Also, she looked forward to changing into her favorite jammies and curling up under the covers with her book.

But she kept hoping Noah would restart the conversation from earlier without any prompting.

About that...

"I'm signing the contract tomorrow morning."

Noah went on to explain how he'd managed to get Mr. Curry to agree to owner financing and then cashed out all of his savings to invest. He'd now be the proud owner of a catamaran, rental equipment and big plans to grow the business. Twyla swallowed hard at the thought of how fully invested Noah was in this new venture.

Now she'd have no choice but to be his cheerleader or stand by as he lost…everything.

"I'm all in."

"Have you told your mother?"

Twyla could only imagine how that conversation would go over.

"Not yet."

She walked next to him as he ambled onto a pier and sat, his long legs swinging over the edge. It was on the tip of Twyla's tongue to ask how Michelle felt about him moving back to Charming and whether or not she'd be joining him. But she simply let Noah take the lead as he asked questions about the bookstore, and drilled her on the finances until she asked him to drop it.

"But I'm worried," he said.

"Don't be. If we have to, we'll sell. It was a nice run."

He snorted, understanding her words betrayed how difficult it would be for her to let go. "And what will you do then?"

"Ganny always promised me a trip to New York City to introduce me to some of the booksellers she'd met over the years. Last night, I thought that was going to be my surprise."

"Sorry to disappoint."

She playfully slugged his shoulder. "You never could, Noah. Stop it. You are always the best surprise."

He turned to her then, so close she could breathe in his delicious scent. The moonlight made his dark eyes shimmer and her heart tugged with the familiar warmth. *Noah.* She didn't think she'd ever love anyone quite the same way she loved her best friend.

"Yeah. Something you should know about me and Michelle. We're not together."

Poor Noah. Weren't they a pair? He had about as much luck as she did in the relationship department. "What happened?"

"I told her the life she wants to lead is not my life. Then she accused me of having commitment issues. Commitment-phobe, I think she called me." He whistled. "It was ugly. It wasn't great to admit to myself that she's probably right. But I wasn't going to ask her to come along with me on this new adventure. This is my thing, my dream, and I won't answer to anyone."

She linked her arm through his. "When you're ready, the Almost Dead Poets Society likes to play matchmaker."

"Um, no thanks."

Twyla chuckled. "Last month they set me up with Tony."

"That would never work. For obvious reasons."

"It was better than Zoey, who fixed me up with Gus."

Noah's neck jerked back. "*That* loser?"

"He's a bit handsy but I wouldn't call him a loser."

"Did he *try* something with you?" Noah narrowed his eyes.

Her cheeks flushed. "No, and never mind."

They sat quietly for another few minutes as the waves lapped against the wood piles of the pier.

"Do you think you'll leave town if the bookstore closes?"

"I don't know, but I might need to leave. At least for a while."

"Why? I just got back."

"Noah, you're not the only one that thinks it might

be nice to start over somewhere else." She swallowed hard. "Do you realize I still occasionally get referred to as Will's girlfriend?"

"You mean by someone other than my mother?" Noah shook his head. "If you want her to move on from your tragic love story, you need to give her something else to talk about. Give *everyone* something to talk about. Learn from my experience. Life is too short to please other people."

"You must really mean it this time. Breaking up with another girlfriend is going to make your mother pretty unhappy."

"Yeah, well, so is buying Nacho Boat."

"That one's going to worry a lot of people."

"Don't you be one of them. I'm going to stick around for a long while. Long enough to make sure you don't get fixed up on any lousy blind dates. Everyone is going through me from now on." He thumped his chest.

"Really? You're not going to find something wrong with every date I have? That's kind of your thing."

"It's only *been* my thing because of the men you've picked."

She bristled at the memories, because she had a truckload of them. "How was I supposed to know Jimmy Lee was engaged to be married?"

"You couldn't have known. That's why you have me."

But she also had him to stop her from dating some of the better-looking guys in town.

"Well…what about Finn?" she asked.

Noah blinked. *"Finn?"*

You would have thought she'd asked him to fix her up with Chris Hemsworth.

"Is that so crazy? Isn't he single again?"

"Finn is going to be busy. He's my partner and is helping me get this business off the ground. He won't have quality time to spend with you and that's what you deserve."

She hesitated from stating she wouldn't be that picky with the right man. For reasons she didn't quite understand, Noah did not want her dating his other best friend. To her, it was further confirmation that, in his mind, she'd never belong to anyone but Will.

"Fine." She stood, frustration spreading through her like a wildfire. "This lonely spinster is going home now."

"Hey." He followed her, coming within inches of her before he stopped and reached to slide a warm palm down her arm. "Don't be mad."

His touch, the warm timbre in his voice when he apologized, never failed to squeeze her heart with a powerful ache.

"I'm not *mad*. Just…tired of being lonely. I don't need forever but I refuse to spend another Christmas alone. This might be one of the few times when you're single at Christmas, but it's not new to me."

"Great. If that's really what you want, I'll ask Finn if he's interested in dating someone again." He grimaced, like the thought of the two of them together made him sick. "What's so great about Finn, anyway? I don't see it. He's tall, sure, but so am I."

She nearly rolled her eyes. *Tall* had never been on her list of qualities for the perfect man.

"What do you mean? He's a nice guy, and he's got one fantastic quality. He's available."

* * *

The next morning, Noah left the local bank as the proud owner of Nacho Boat Adventures. He drove the truck Mr. Curry had indeed thrown in as part of the deal straight to the docks. A few residents honked when they saw him driving down the road in the painted truck, giving him a thumbs-up.

Today, he'd called for a meeting of his staff to discuss the transition. Noah had a running list of things to do started on his phone app and he glanced at it now.

1. Staff meeting
2. Inventory
3. Boat inspection
4. Check the ledgers
5. Make plans for grand opening
6. Join the Chamber of Commerce
7. Talk to Finn about Twyla (maybe next week)
8. Call Mom

Nope, he hadn't called his mother yet. For all she knew, he was still on the job in Austin. No harm done. The fact he'd listed talking to her below talking to Finn said it all. The problem was that Noah was like many men in his generation. He hesitated to disappoint women until the last possible second.

It was the primary reason his relationship with Michelle had gone way past its natural expiration date. He'd tried to fall in love with Michelle with everything he had, agreeing it was time to settle down and have a family. He wanted that, too—children and a wife to grow old with. Someone who made him feel good about himself every day, someone who loved him uncondi-tionally. Someone he looked forward to *seeing* every day and not out of obligation. Someone who looked just as good without makeup and perfect hair.

Someone like Twyla, but…*not* Twyla.

Noah opened up shop, and as the morning progressed, he set up, pinning a scrolled red banner Ava had handed him this morning after his signing at the bank: *Under new ownership.*

The first staff member to arrive was Eddie Pierce. He had a Mohawk and wore board shorts, boat shoes and a black T-shirt that read: *I hate it when the voices inside my head go silent. I never know what they're planning.* According to Mr. Curry, he was the one working on his captain's license. Well, he'd be working on it for a while longer if Noah had anything to do with it. He intended to keep everyone on his staff safe.

"Call me Tee, Bossman." He fist bumped with Noah.

"Tee?"

"I like to wear T-shirts year-round. It's kinda my thing."

His other staff member, Diana, arrived just behind Tee, the girl who booked appointments and answered the phone.

When he greeted her and introduced himself, she barely looked at him.

"What do we call you?" Tee said. "Mr. Cahill? Can I call you Bossman? Head honcho? Captain? Nacho Man?"

"Nacho Man is my favorite of those, but just call me Noah."

"Chill. Dude, that's super easy. I had a lot of other great names but that one works, too."

The girl had still not looked at Noah, but she made an agreeable sound.

"I know Mr. Curry has given y'all a lot of freedom here, but I'm a stickler for rules. Regulations. Safety first and foremost. Got me?"

Jesus, he sounded like a drill sergeant. Tee's neck jerked back slightly, and Diana continued to study her shoes.

He pulled back some, clearing his throat. "Of course, we're going to have fun here, too. No doubt about that. This is a great part-time job and I appreciate your dedication. I'll be hiring some others as time passes and we grow the business like I plan. But first things first. Let's take a look at the inventory. Today, I want a list of everything we own in this shop and how many we have."

"Um, we did inventory," Tee offered.

"A year ago," Noah said. "I have to believe there might be some changes."

"He's right," Diana said, looking up for a second. She caught Noah's gaze and blushed a thousand shades of crimson.

"Yeah, I guess." Tee shrugged.

"Inventory is not fun, I know, but it's necessary to a solid business plan. I'll start ordering right away if we're short on anything." He offered Tee one of the laptops he'd invested in to bring the business into the new millennium. "Everything has to reconcile with what we have listed on the master spreadsheet."

Tee not so discreetly passed the laptop to Diana.

"Also, all boating excursions are on hold until I personally inspect every inch of the catamaran. I have to prep it for the Snowflake Float Boat Parade."

"But—" Diana began.

"Shouldn't take me long." He pointed to Diana. "You can reschedule. Blame it on the switch in ownership and the fact the new boss is a hard-ass."

She flushed an interesting shade of purple. "Um, yes."

Noah scrolled through his phone notes to see if he'd missed anything. "Any questions?"

"Can we have Pizza Party Saturdays?" Tee said, scratching the side of his Mohawk. "Mr. Curry said that'd be up to the new owners."

Far be it from him to ruin all the excitement around here. He remembered the fun of being a teenager far too well.

"Sure. Let's see how we do this week, and then we'll talk."

Don't miss
Once Upon a Charming Bookshop
by Heatherly Bell,

available December 2023
wherever Harlequin Special Edition
books and ebooks are sold.

www.Harlequin.com

#3025 A TEMPORARY TEXAS ARRANGEMENT
Lockharts Lost & Found • by Cathy Gillen Thacker

Noah Lockhart, a widowed father of three girls, has vowed never to be reckless in love again...until he meets Tess Gardner, the veterinarian caring for his pregnant miniature donkey. But will love still be a possibility when one of his daughters objects to the romance?

#3026 THE AIRMAN'S HOMECOMING
The Tuttle Sisters of Coho Cove • by Sabrina York

As a former ParaJumper for the elite air force paramedic rescue wing, loner Noah Crocker has overcome enormous odds in his life. But convincing no-nonsense bakery owner Amy Tuttle Tolliver that he's ready to settle down with her and her sons may be his toughest challenge yet!

#3027 WRANGLING A FAMILY
Aspen Creek Bachelors • by Kathy Douglass

Before meeting Alexandra Jamison, rancher Nathan Montgomery never had time for romance. Now he needs a girlfriend in order to keep his matchmaking mother off his back, and single mom Alexandra fits the bill. If only their romance ruse didn't lead to knee-weakening kisses...

#3028 SAY IT LIKE YOU MEAN IT
by Rochelle Alers

When former actress Shannon Younger comes face-to-face with handsome celebrity landscape architect Joaquin Williamson, she vows not to come under his spell. She starts to trust Joaquin, but she knows that falling for another high-profile man could cost her her career—and her heart.

#3029 THEIR ACCIDENTAL HONEYMOON
Once Upon a Wedding • by Mona Shroff

Rani Mistry and Param Sheth have been besties since elementary school. When Param's wedding plans come to a crashing halt, they both go on his honeymoon— as friends. But when friendship takes a sharp turn into a marriage of convenience, will they fake it till they make it?

#3030 AN UPTOWN GIRL'S COWBOY
by Sasha Summers

Savannah Barrett is practically Texas royalty—a good girl with a guarded heart. But one wild night with rebel cowboy Angus McCarrick has her wondering if the boy her daddy always warned her about might be the Prince Charming she's always yearned for.

Get 3 FREE REWARDS!

We'll send you 2 FREE Books plus a FREE Mystery Gift.

FREE
Value Over
$20

Both the **Harlequin® Special Edition** and **Harlequin® Heartwarming™** series feature compelling novels filled with stories of love and strength where the bonds of friendship, family and community unite.